STACKS

Truth Will Set You Free

Book 3

Kathy J. Forti

RINNOVO PRESS
StacksLibraryofTruth.com
StacksLibraryofTruth@gmail.com
Facebook: @stackslibraryoftruth

Copyright © 2023 by Kathy J. Forti

All rights reserved. No part of this book may be reproduced or transmitted in any form or by any means electronic, mechanical, photographic, audio, or by any other means, including information storage and retrieval system, or translated into another language, without permission in writing from Rinnovo Press and/or the author. Reviewers may quote brief passages.

ISBN: 978-1-7923-9809-4
Printed in the United States of America

Cover Photo: Sean Pierce
Cover Design: Chana Messer

Forward by the Author

STACKS is a work of fiction. Names, characters, businesses, events, and incidents are the product of the author's imagination. Any semblance to actual persons, living or dead, or actual events is purely coincidental.

Prologue

Overnight the little Valley Island of Maui, a slice of paradise in the middle of the Pacific Ocean, became ground zero for UFO researchers, tabloid journalists, and mainstream news reporters from around the world hoping to reap the financial benefits of what was quickly becoming the story of the century. Photos of the mammoth size alien space craft immediately went viral as those who had been clear-headed enough to film the event spread the word. By the end of day everyone connected to a news source knew the government had been lying for the past 75 plus years if they hadn't already come to that conclusion.

"We Are Not Alone" or "Aliens Invade Hawaii" headlines spanned the globe. It was a nightmare for the intelligence agencies who had been denying such a possibility since the Roswell, New Mexico crash in 1947. The proof was in the pudding. Photographs and videos of the large craft were tweeted and retweeted at lightning speed. No longer were people buying it was just another weather balloon. The photos from all angles spoke volumes.

The Grand Wailea Beach Resort, which now hosted the dubious distinction of being the new go-to alien vacation spot, was quickly overrun with UFO enthusiasts hoping for a return of the mysterious pyramid-shaped vehicle that had filled the daylight skies. Not since the event of the 1997 Phoenix Lights sighting had such a blatant display of other worldly presence been witnessed by so many.

Only a few realized something more sinister had happened over the hotel beachfront that day than merely witnessing an "Unexplained Aerial Phenomenon". A female journalist and a small seven-year-old girl had been covertly abducted in front of hundreds of terrified eyes. The two had been beamed up in a nanosecond. Most beach goers would never recall the blatant extraction, their memory of it virtually wiped clean. Some would have disturbing dreams about a moment of missing time that would forever knock at the door to their subconscious wanting to be let in. The truth stayed hidden at bay in the recesses of their minds, too frightening to examine or contemplate.

The abduction scenario signaled to Zach Eldridge the message Kaggen was sending to him as well as the world at large. There would be no more hiding. His kind were in control and that day would mark the beginning of a whole new world.

Table of Contents

Foreword by the author .... *iii*
Prologue .... *iv*
Chapter 1 .... *1*
Chapter 2 .... *19*
Chapter 3 .... *31*
Chapter 4 .... *41*
Chapter 5 .... *49*
Chapter 6 .... *63*
Chapter 7 .... *87*
Chapter 8 .... *101*
Chapter 9 .... *113*
Chapter 10 .... *129*
Chapter 11 .... *143*
Chapter 12 .... *157*
Chapter 13 .... *169*
Chapter 14 .... *177*
Chapter 15 .... *187*
Chapter 16 .... *199*
Chapter 17 .... *215*
Chapter 18 .... *227*
Chapter 19 .... *241*
Chapter 20 .... *257*
Chapter 21 .... *267*
Chapter 22 .... *277*
Chapter 23 .... *295*
Chapter 24 .... *303*
Chapter 25 .... *313*
A Note from the Author *318*

"The truth will set you free, but first it will make you miserable."
– James A. Garfield, Assassinated 20th U.S. President

Chapter 1

The new Governor of Minerva who was not averse to change. Everything in Zachary Eldridge's world took on new meaning as he assumed this global role. Some changes came naturally, others were like a domino effect that would cause the world to change around him. It was a harbinger of things to come where the life would never be the same again…

Those who had brokered their souls to Minerva within governments, within industry, within age-old religious institutions, and within the multiple criminal cabals that thrived on the pain of humanity, were desperately struggling to keep up the illusion that it was business as usual. Few would know the details, but it was spoken about in whispers, sometimes with disbelief or denial, that in the highest hierarchal realms of the shadow government, leadership had suddenly and inexplicitly changed, threatening them all. Those who were astute enough to read the signs took their money and ran--immediately declaring resignation or retirement. It was felt by many around the globe that some unknown force had their finger on the financial nuclear codes—bringing them all one degree closer to bankruptcy and annihilation.

Revenue streams, the very lifeblood that fed their enterprises, had slowed. It was the first indicator of trouble ahead. Routine intel used against their enemies, garnered from satellite feeds that functioned as their spies in the sky, were suspiciously malfunctioning frequently and without explanation. Those who controlled such operations found this situation unfathomable and beyond coincidence. Reliability and continuity of function had never been an issue in the past. Those at the top had seen to such matters. Whatever information managed to trickle through was like watching a drying up riverbed under severe drought conditions. For those who had been in the business of Minerva for a long time and had experienced first-hand the well-oiled wheels of the organization, the signs of a weakened support structure were becoming self-evident. Confusion abounded, as the truth behind what was occurring was unknown, creating anxiety everywhere.

Most were clueless that there was a new Governor in town. Zachary Eldridge had not planned to step into that role, but circumstances had pushed him into seizing the leadership of Minerva after both his father, the Counselor, and several other Minerva members had been vaporized right before his eyes during their last meeting. They were now gone without a trace, leaving a huge leadership vacuum. Zach was the only one still standing who had access to the Library of Truth—the very key to their secret knowledge base.

It was only a matter of time before a coup took place. It didn't take a rocket scientist to know this. Which meant Zach had to act fast before his tenuous position was usurped and he, as well as everyone else within his close circle, was exterminated.

With this new powerful position came a wealth of information that made his head spin. As the new puppet master, he had his finger on all the control buttons of a mammoth empire of information and corruption. However, he was acutely aware that circumstances had placed him between a rock and a hard place. His very survival depended upon his willingness to play the aliens' game. Anything less than that would neither be welcomed nor tolerated.

With Zach now having the master tools to follow the money trails which greased the tracks of Minerva's vast multi-tentacled network, time was of the essence to make haste and do something about it. Throwing caution to the wind, he went to action within their banking network--the very funding source for their evil. He drained political slush funds, froze unacknowledged, unaccountable, and bloated military intelligence budgets, fully conscious of the havoc it would create.

Playing the role of a modern-day Robin Hood filled him with immense satisfaction. He completely zeroed out numerous accounts of non-governmental organizations masquerading as nonprofits, whom he knew to be linked to human trafficking. Instead, he transferred their balances into trustworthy charities that existed to help mankind and the Earth, not destroy them.

With unfettered access to a consortium of banks, Zach orchestrated what would be perceived as a digital hack of mammoth proportions, causing an unforeseen glitch in the world monetary system. That it was completely selective, not affecting everyone, did not go unnoticed. Those who pretended to be in the know blamed it on Russia waging monetary warfare. Let them think what they wanted, he thought. From what he had learned from Minerva's data systems, every major power in the world was in on and part of this great deception.

Zach quickly discovered what his father, as past Governor of Minerva, had been ruling over and orchestrating for so many years. The depth and breadth of it was staggering, yet he was learning fast, without mentors. There was no choice. Fate had dealt him this unexpected hand. The more he learned about their mechanisms, the deeper the rabbit hole grew.

Minerva was a massive operation, like spiders that kept spinning bigger and more elaborate webs, ensnaring the whole of the Earth in their sticky steely strands. The intelligence agencies, the Mafia, the church, royalty, numerous other secret societies which protected the elite--they were all involved in some form. Their secrets, the puppet regimes they had put in place in other countries to stay in control, the elections they had bought or rigged, and even the large-scale killings and assassinations that had been carried out—it was all there in their records like a criminal library of truth. And the truth was staggering. There were a lot of surprises to be found in his father's meticulously kept records. It was a conspiracy theorist's treasure trove of proof—the ammunition to take down a lot of influential people if ever revealed. And much of this information had been used as blackmail material to ensure Minerva compliance.

The dominoes continued to fall. The eight remaining Minerva members, still distraught over the Library of Truth (LOT) visually displaying their heinous deeds for all to see, believed they would be allowed to go back through the jump-room portal to resume their old lives. They quickly discovered this was not the case and scrambled to protect themselves and their financial interests.

Zach learned that there was a drawback to seeing one's own future records in the LOT-- something his friend, Roone Sawyer, must have learned. The price one paid was that the future then became accelerated in time, coming into fruition sooner rather than later, both the good and the bad of it. His father and the Counselor had to have known this.

The remaining Minerva members would rapidly meet their fates head on. What they had seen of their future was now set into motion, rendering them hapless and defenseless to change it. Their sense of freedom would be short-lived as karmic retribution took hold. This rendered many of them temporarily inert before they scrambled to do personal and professional damage control. Zach counted on this distraction to play out before the remaining power collective attempted to stop him. It was inevitable that news would spread, alliances would be re-formed, and a new head of the dragon would rise again.

One of the first things Zach did was swap out the Antarctica Base's current DOLARIS Communication System for his own re-programmed software version with hidden backdoors. This would continue to put a virtual wrench into their global network operations, crippling them enough to allow him time for additional corrections and adjustments, as needed. His programs specifically targeted intelligence satellite systems and bank accounts used to fund criminal worldwide enterprises. In essence, he was temporarily putting a lot of criminals out of work while he maneuvered their elaborate operation network into a more permanent solution aimed at doing the least amount of harm.

Not surprisingly, the U.S. stock market immediately reacted to Zach's throwing a wrench into their securities system. It caused a snowball effect across global markets, abruptly curtailing trading in certain sectors and forcing many worldwide hubs to go into survival lockdown mode. A temporary trading holiday was called for as gold and silver rose in value. Those manipulating and suppressing these precious metal commodities for years were suddenly cut off from their trading funds. Helpless elites stood by watching as they lost billions.

His father had once told him that sudden change, even with the best of intentions, can cause serious infrastructure damage. Everything is so intricately connected that Zach's changes affected organized crime's involvement on Wall Street. The fraudsters, the scammers, the insider traders and manipulators, were being exposed for who they really were once covert funding began drying up. Those who had bought into such enterprises were demanding pay outs that were not forthcoming. Houses of cards, built on sand, were collapsing under the weight of those wanting to cash out.

There was no avoiding the damage resulting from the shake-up of Minerva's power network. The people were being awakened like a sleeping tiger. And they did not like what they saw once their eyes were opened. Outrage over pervasive corruption that had been allowed to flourish was exploding as people called for justice and accountability. Zach watched the situation slowly unravel as disgruntled people, far and wide, took to the streets demanding change. The rise of the masses was the greatest governmental fear of all. Once it started there was often no stopping it.

Zach had brought Meghan with him to Antarctica after Kaggen abducted Izzie and Cali to parts unknown. There was no place safe on Earth for her anymore but beside him, hidden deep within the icy bowels of the frozen continent. For now, it would be a temporary solution. He was not fool enough to believe that even the protection the Antarctica Base afforded them would last forever.

Izzie's whereabouts in the universe were presently unknown, causing them both untold anguish. Zach was doing all he could to find them utilizing all the advanced resources still operational throughout the Base. The aliens had wreaked a moderate amount of damage when they evacuated. Critical infrastructure had to first be repaired. As soon as they were back up and running, Zach ordered numerous Minerva interstellar probes to search the cosmos looking for Kaggen's SolarVector7 ship. They found no trace of the Mantis leader.

There were numerous obstacles to overcome in their search. Tracking on all alien space vehicles was being cloaked by the Mantises, while other races working in conjunction with them followed suit. These beings had the capability of winking out into other dimensional space realms and they were using it to cover Kaggen's tracks. Which meant the aliens had broken all their treatises and Zach was now in an undeclared space war with multiple alien races.

In a short period of time, he had made matters worse for the safety of Earth and its human inhabitants. An alien war was untenable. He wished his father were still alive to advise him on what to do about this cosmic mess, but not even his father could have foreseen Kaggen abducting Izzie and evacuating the Base for parts unknown. This only confirmed what his father had told him--the aliens were an unpredictable lot.

He was thankful for the presence of Meghan in his life. Everything he had revealed to her about the Library of Truth, the portals, Minerva, and the human-hybrid Mantis agenda meant they now had no secrets left between them. Not even the troubling question concerning the true blood lineage of their child, whom she now carried within her, was kept from her.

Zach was also grateful that Satya had finally told him the truth of his genetic lineage. He was not a human-hybrid like his father or his grandfather before him. He was a human angelic pureblood, and his son would be as well. At Zach's birth the Mantis DNA insertion had been blocked from intermingling with his human DNA. How that genetic anomaly had happened Zach wasn't privy to, but the knowledge of it filled him with tremendous relief. When he revealed the misconception he held about his lineage to Meghan, she finally understood his initial hesitancy at hearing the news of her pregnancy. They were both relieved.

While their little family unit was growing, it did nothing to dampen the fear of what might be happening to Izzie or whether they would ever see her again. Kaggen was extremely clever and powerful. He had yet to issue any demands for his two abductees. Instead, the Mantis leader was letting them sweat it out until he was good and ready to show his hand.

Meghan had pleaded with Zach to use the Library of Truth to learn where Izzie was and whether she was still alive. He didn't need to access the LOT to know Izzie was still of this world. The two had an energetic psychic connection that felt unbreakable. Just like she had once known he was lost in the portals and needed to be saved from the Bodleian Library, he also knew Izzie was alive right now. For how long, though, was anyone's guess.

Having not heard any news or even rumors of Kaggen's whereabouts, was more than unsettling. A lot of things could go wrong before they located him. He didn't want to tell Meghan that Izzie's and Cali's life files were both missing from the LOT. The implications of that felt quite ominous. There was no good reason to alarm her more, so he said nothing. It was clearly a lie of omission which he hated himself for doing.

Learning the machinations of Minerva, overseeing Base operations which was the heart of their organization, and continually searching the universe looking for that demon Kaggen, forced Zach to put all his other obligations on hold. He let the Library of Congress (LOC) know he was taking an immediate leave of absence due to personal family matters. The world knew his father had recently died, so no one questioned his decision to take time off from his library employee job.

They would never know he still had unlimited access to the LOC, any hour of the day or night, which was how he preferred it. Until he knew more of what he was up against at the Base, he opted to leave his portal artifacts behind in the LOC's stacks, safe from curious eyes. Deep down he knew that's Gizmo's cloaking would keep them protected.

So much had changed in such a short time. Meghan and he had become like two minds working in unison for a common goal. It was she who suggested he try remote viewing to locate Izzie. He had successfully used such a technique on Nordekka, the dwarf planet located beyond the Sun's interdimensional portal. Applying this skill, he had discovered the hidden *Minerva File* information buried deep in an underground lake. Truthfully, he didn't know if he could do it again without Ishannika's strange bio-chair, but it was worth a shot. He was willing to exhaust all options to rescue Izzie and Cali.

"Tell me how you do it," Meghan prompted. "Maybe with both of us working together, we might be more successful. I just need to know she's okay. I'm going mad not knowing."

Zach seriously worried for her. This pregnancy was turning out to be a difficult one under the emotional stress of Izzie's abduction. He didn't want to place any more strain on her. And he knew it could be difficult for him as well. The last time he had attempted the physical manifestation of remote viewing out in the depths of the universe, he had experienced a strong seizure reaction. He dreaded that happening again, leaving her to have to deal with it.

"It's not safe," he told her, continuing to pace the confines of his father's former quarters they now occupied. He couldn't afford to lose either her or the new baby if something bad or unexpected happened.

Meghan was surprisingly adamant, showing a defiant side to her he hadn't seen before. "Zachary Eldridge don't tell me what's safe and not safe when it comes to saving my daughter. We either do it together, or I'll find a way to do it myself."

Making joint decisions and living closely together was affecting them in ways he hadn't anticipated. He didn't dare point out that her newfound defiance might be a hormonal side effect from her pregnancy. However, it was evident to him that she was becoming more confident and assertive in expressing her needs. Zach had been observing the slow metamorphosis not knowing if it was a normal process or not. He had never cohabitated with a woman before. It was a unique experience for him, unlike all others, and yet strangely he liked it. They were now a team. He had never been a team with anyone in his life. It reminded him that he was no longer alone in this world.

This new emerging Meghan was shedding the roots from her past where she had existed in the shadow of a very powerful father, much as he had with his own influential parents. Such familial circumstances often caused doubt about one's capabilities. However, no one was holding Meghan back now and neither would he.

"Okay," he acquiesced, talking her through the relaxation process, preparing her to empty her thoughts, rise above her physical body and allow her inner eye to open and her mind to soar.

They laid down on the king-size bed together where she reached for his hand. He could sense she was nervous, wanting to please him, wanting to be successful yet fearful she might not be. He told her not to worry and allow him to do the work. Chances were he might have to go it alone anyway. He had been practicing altered states of consciousness for years through meditation and Qigong. Meghan hadn't.

So, he was pleasantly surprised when his mind lifted and flew out into the cosmos, only to discover Meghan was right there beside him. He released that moment of elation, striving to attain a neutral state, knowing that strong emotion could quickly ground one back into the physical body and their mission would be aborted before it got started. Maneuvering during lucid dream states had taught him as much.

Zach allowed his mind to lead the quest, functioning as a light beacon searching the furthest corners of space for Izzie's unique numerical frequency signature. To ensure that he wouldn't lose her, he instinctively tethered his mind to Meghan's, not even realizing he knew how to do this, or that such things were possible. This knowledge surprised him. His mind was expanding in consciousness and stretching the boundaries. He needed to stay focused on the simple truth that all things were possible if one abandoned one's human propensity towards limited thinking. He embraced that belief now as they moved forward.

It became clearly evident to him, within such heightened awareness, that Izzie was not to be found anywhere within the Milky Way Galaxy but somewhere beyond that. Together they continued searching, until Zach finally picked up a faint signature pulse coming from the Andromeda Galaxy, almost 2.5 million light years from Earth. Kaggen was hiding his prey well beyond the reach of any of Minerva's star space fleet.

In his mind's eye, Zach could see through the physical cloaking the Mantis employed to evade detection on their SolarVector7 space craft. The creature hadn't counted on remote viewing or psychic spying being employed to track and find them. But there was an inherent risk in pushing one's mind inside the SolarVector7. The aliens had a way of locking onto intrusive thoughtforms, which displayed a uniquely detectable frequency that was trackable. So, once they went in, he knew they couldn't stay long.

Zach also knew Kaggen's kind were also capable of "mind grab," rendering an intruding remote viewer virtually powerless. This astounding fact came from touching the organic skin of one of their Antarctica space craft. The mind of the craft had provided him with a download of unusual information. Pertinent memory now pushed its way to his conscious awareness. Zach allowed that information to be transmitted to Meghan via their mind tether. Her acknowledgement was instantaneous. Together they were like one mind, functioning in complete unison. It was the closest connection he might ever have with another human being.

Zach's mind retrieved another stray bit of information from the alien download—the nullification of a detectable frequency. It wasn't the same as scrambling a cell phone signal, causing it to be dropped, but the outcome was similar and just as effective. He flooded his thoughts with prime numbers, mimicking Kaggen's own frequency signature pattern which, if nothing else, would certainly confuse their detection technology. Being in a total mind state, one could do such things that could never be done encased in mere physical form. But this was war, and he would use whatever tricks he could.

Their consciousness pushed through the dense outer walls of the pyramid shaped SolarVector7 space craft. It was multi-leveled, dimly lit, as the Mantis preferred, and teeming with alien life. They wasted no time moving towards Izzie's unique frequency. They found her imprisoned in a tiny spartan cubicle on a lower-level deck. Curled up in a fetal position on a makeshift bed, her hair and clothes disheveled and her little body unmoving, she appeared to be asleep. A tray of food, untouched and inedible looking, sat on a metal table beside her.

Zach immediately warned Meghan to suppress any strong emotional response, which he knew would be extremely hard, seeing her daughter in such a state of neglect. He moved in closer, gently poking Izzie with his mind. She didn't stir. He did it again, this time with Meghan's help. Izzie's eyes immediately fluttered open. She sat up straight on the bed, staring out into the dimness of the empty room.

"Mommy?" she whispered. "Is that you?"

"Yes, honey, it is," Meghan mentally answered. "Mommy misses you so much. Zach's here, too."

Izzie's eyes brightened, but she kept silent. The child was quick to understand this game. "I hate this place," Izzie loudly thought. "The big bugs are creepy. I told Kaggen he's ugly and mean and now he won't even let me have any books. He said I was belligerent, and I can't even look up what that word means."

Her mind continued to babble. "I go to Pink Heaven all the time to play with Zariah the unicorn and see Satya. She tells me to be strong. She told me I would see you both very soon, but I can't see you at all. I can only hear you in my head, which I don't know if it's real or not. Are you real?"

"Yes, we're real," Zach silently told her. "And we're going to do whatever it takes to bring you back."

Izzie started to cry. "I just want to go home. Please take me home, now."

Zach could feel Meghan starting to fill with emotion. He was determined to make this fast. "Izzie, do you know where Cali is?"

"No," she shook her head. "But she totally freaked out when she saw the big bugs on the ship. The little one, they call Mapu, took her somewhere. I don't know where. This spaceship is filled with lots of strange creatures. Some even have tails and lizard skin. Oh, please get me out of here," she thought, a tear running down her pale cheek.

"We will, Izzie, very soon," Zach assured her.

"Mommy loves you," Meghan added. And with those words, she just lost it. Like a flood gate opening, waves of emotion spilled forth. Instantly they were sucked back to their physical bodies, their one-mind connection immediately severed.

"I'm so sorry," Meghan apologized, turning to him on the bed. "I just couldn't hold it in any longer. She looks thinner and so forlorn. She's scared and I don't think she's eating either. And now she's escaping into another reality. Oh God, Zach, we've got to do something before it's too late."

Zach remained silent. Satya hadn't told him she was entertaining Izzie in this other world she called "Pink Heaven" and that gave him an idea. However, he would have to wait until Meghan fell asleep to find out more. He didn't want to get her hopes up again, only to have them dashed. Things were stressful enough.

It was beyond incredible how easily she had joined with him on his mind quest. They had been like one person together, which was such a turn on in so many ways. The mere thought of being inside her head aroused him, which he found embarrassing under the current circumstances. What was wrong with him? Sensing his awkward predicament, Meghan touched him, cupping his hardness, setting him completely on fire, yet he hesitated to make a move.

"Just make me forget," she implored, shedding her clothes, offering her lush body into his care. "Make me feel like there's nothing else in the world that matters right now. Can you do that?"

The hell if he wouldn't die trying. "Yeah, I can do that," he said, quickly unzipping his pants and freeing his manhood, which was more than ready to oblige. He let her take the reins of control and she did. Zach sensed she was desperate to release all the anxiety, fear and powerlessness that had built up since her father's death. There was a warrior energy in her wanting to wage battle and fight.

She moved astride him and placed his hands on both her breasts, letting him feel their new fullness, which he did. Then, without saying another word, she rode him, harder than she ever had before, not stopping until she finally achieved the release she sought, coming again and again—a loud primal scream escaping her lips. It was a revelation to watch. She looked like a conquering goddess that had defeated her enemy through sheer force of will. He didn't mind being her vehicle to conquer the demons that invaded her world. He would gladly let her take out her sexual frustration out on him any day. He grabbed her to him, kissed her like he would possess her instead, then finally gave in to his own release. God, how he loved this woman!

Zach waited for Meghan to fall asleep before venturing back into the LOT to speak with Satya. She had been mysteriously missing a lot lately since he had been able to tune into the Mind of the LOT and was nowhere to be seen. Once again, he relied on the wherewithal of Gizmo.

"Take me to Satya," he instructed. In the blink of an eye, he found himself in another world, another reality, the stuff of children's storybooks and fantasy. It was a bold and brilliant world painted in a hundred different shades of pink.

Zach immediately picked up the energy signature of Izzie. Here it was unmistakable. Her imprint was everywhere in the fabric of this realm she had so obviously created. This had to be Izzie's "Pink Heaven" which she had mentally escaped to.

Everywhere he looked it was flowing with an abundance of number sevens, like Izzie, its creator. There were flocks of rainbow-colored unicorns running wild and free amidst the pink clouds and magenta mountain landscapes. Zach dodged out of their way, letting the pink animals pass as he moved through a thick garden maze filled with an overflow of sweet-smelling pink jasmine, poppies, and tulips.

Izzie had made quite a large, magical, and definitely colorful playground for herself. The garden maze opened onto a pink sandy beach with clear blue waters, filled with an assortment of watercraft and toys. He had to smile when he spotted a "free" pink bubblegum ice cream stand on the beachfront. What else had her little imagination created to make herself happy under the duress of her captivity?

"Satya?" he called out, for he sensed she was also near at hand. A second later she appeared, laughing delightedly like a child—a decidedly unusual site for a recordkeeper of her serious stature. Had she also drunk the pink Kool-Aid that flowed through the rosy landscape of what he now thought of as "Izzieland"?

"She is quite a joy," Satya remarked, glowing with praise. "The child is so adept for one of her years and her delight is purely infectious. Her curiosity is boundless—much like your own. She wants to know and learn everything."

Satya paused, returning once again to her serious almost regal bearing, for she knew Zach had come searching for truth about the child. "She says she wants to live here," she quietly informed him.

Zach experienced a deep foreboding. This was exactly what he feared. "She can't stay in this reality, Satya. You and I both know the longer she does, the more difficult it will be to return her to the real world she comes from. Her mind is already transitioning further away the longer she sleeps."

"I am monitoring her situation closely," Satya explained. "Rest assured. She will not lose her mind. Much is expected of her in the future of your world."

This was interesting news to Zach. "I can't find her life file. What future outcome can we expect?" he asked.

"Where you go, she goes," Satya revealed. "She came into form and matter during this time to aid you. Your destinies are linked, no matter what Kaggen does."

The words: 'No matter what Kaggen does' filled him with dread. "I need to find a way to extract her now--today. Tell me. What should I do?"

Satya's look was of an exasperated teacher dealing with a remiss student. "You have an entire library filled with answers. You don't need me to tell you what needs to be done. The answers are here and within you as well," she pointed out.

The ball was being thrown back into his court. Satya had a way of doing that. She seemed to think that he alone was able to find a solution to fix the ills of the world--either by destroying Minerva or saving humanity. It was an insane gig for any human being to take on.

"I know you came here to talk to Izzie," Satya said, changing the subject. She stepped aside as the sound of harmonic bells was heard throughout Izzieland, summoning the child. Zach wasn't surprised to see Izzie gallop in on the unicorn named Zariah. She came to a stop at his feet, the animal's hoofs prancing in anticipation of its child master's next command.

"Zach, it's you!" Izzie happily screamed, her face aglow with excitement. "I'm so glad you're here. I want to show you everything I've created!"

He just bet she did. The evidence was all around him. He checked himself. How could he be angry with her for finding a clever way to escape her captors?

"But where is Mommy? How come you didn't bring her with you?" Izzie asked. "She needs to see what a good rider I am. And I'm teaching Zariah tricks, too."

Izzie lovingly touched the unicorn's silky mane. "Dance, Zariah," she commanded. "Then lay down."

The rainbow-striped unicorn danced sideways, then backwards, it's pink hoofs doing intricate steps. It spun around and twirled before easing down on all fours, allowing Izzie to jump off.

"Isn't she just the cleverest thing you ever saw?" Izzie remarked, rubbing the unicorn's white horn. "I make a wish on her every day, and today my wish came true. You're here!! But I wanted Mommy to be here, too."

She looked so happy, he hated to dampen her enthusiasm and joy. "Next time, Izzie," he told her apologetically. "Your mother is sleeping right now."

Izzie vigorously rubbed the unicorn's horn again and again. "Wake her up, Zariah! Send me my Mommy!"

Zach stepped back as a wavering thoughtform immediately began to re-assemble. If he hadn't seen it with his own eyes, he wouldn't have believed it. The image of Meghan slowly morphed into solid matter until she appeared to be in the flesh in the here and now. Izzie had captured her mother right out of a deep dream state from the confused and disoriented look on Meghan's face. That is, until her eyes fell on Izzie and she ran to her, embraced her in her arms, not wanting to let go.

There was no doubt in his mind he would have a hell of a time extracting Meghan back to their world now that she had access to her child in Izzieland.

Chapter 2

Cali Cavaleri was certain God hated her. I mean really hated her. And now he/she/it/they/them was punishing her for all her numerous past transgressions. There was no other way to explain this frightening new nightmare she found herself in. Who would ever believe she had been abducted by aliens, in no less than a pyramid-shaped UFO, then thrust into a sci-fi world of giant bugs, who walked, talked, and seemed to have some nefarious human agenda? It was nonsense stuff, like a bad horror film, until one finds oneself living in such a reality. A rag magazine would scoop up the story and sell millions to bored Moms waiting in grocery lines everywhere, but certainly no legitimate news operation would ever touch such sensational garbage. If she ever lived to write about this day, she would be accused of hitting the booze again, big time. Which was sounding like a very good idea right now. AA would certainly not fault her for falling off the wagon under such terror-filled circumstances.

She could kick herself for being so gullible. Delusions of having been miraculously delivered to a Maui paradise, and into the arms of a sexy, smart screenwriter (who loved her ass, no less) and who would change her life, was simply a cosmic joke of universal proportion. Maui had been nothing more than a brief interlude to lull her into thinking life could be normal, even good again, before the gates of hell opened to her.

There was no denying that she was the victim of being in the wrong place at the wrong time. If only she had gone straight to the AA meeting as planned that day and not stopped to look up at the sky like all the other tourists on the beach. The powers that be had to be having a good laugh at her expense. She had escaped the life and death threats being thrown at her in Washington, D.C., only to be thrust into an even worse case scenario.

So here she was, imprisoned in her little cell, waiting for what to happen next, she could not say. The Mantis beings were not telling her their plans. They had separated her from Izzie soon after being sucked up by a vacuum force into the heart of the space craft, where she started screaming her head off at first sight of the giant bugs. It was the stuff of her worst nightmare, her deepest insectoid fears, especially hearing their high pitched clicking and hissing sounds and their tentacles reaching out to her—pushing and probing.

Cali couldn't help it; she became utterly hysterical. It was not something she was proud of but, unlike Izzie who was stoically silent once she saw the bugs, this scared the bejesus out of her. God knew she had seen some nasty things in her journalistic career, but nothing like this. An intense beam of green light was pulsed at her, drugging her into immediate submission with its anesthetizing rays, like some cosmic Valium. She was incapable of thought, let alone words. After that she had no idea what happened to Izzie. The rest was a complete blur until she came back to reality sometime later to find herself locked in spartan quarters.

Cali couldn't explain why, but she suspected they didn't really want *her*. These beings were more interested in Little Betsy Ross. She seemed to be the real prize. Which meant Zach hadn't told her a shitload of information. Before being put out of commission, she vaguely remembered hearing Izzie bravely tell the beings: "Zach is going to get you, you big bad bugs!"

The kid certainly had *cajones*. Cali needed to put her big girl pants on and grow a pair as well, instead of sitting in her cell like a victim waiting to be rescued by some white knight. Swallowing one's fears is not an easy thing to do, but she would do whatever it took to get the hell out of there and back to Eric.

A small hairless being with a big black eyes and grey skin, the kind you see in alien movies, always brought her food. He identified himself as "Mapu" and smelled somewhat like rotten eggs. But then again, she wasn't sure if it was him or from the food which he brought her. The offerings were unrecognizable and didn't look at all appetizing. They were predominantly green in appearance, with a strange lumpy texture--a far cry from the real veggies she was used to. She hesitantly attempted a small bite, but it was basically tasteless, perhaps even synthetic in nature, and she spat it back out. They seriously might be trying to starve her to death with such crap.

Since they had yet to torture her, outside of a bad meal plan, her curiosity kicked in and she craved information about her captors. The three-foot-tall being with the big head could hear her, despite having no noticeable ears. Whether Mapu was male or female was unknown, as it appeared sexless. There was no noticeable little dick lump under its clothes either. But at least this creature was less frightening than the giant Mantis beings. She questioned Mapu, but it gave her short robotic-sounding answers back, making her question if it was a living thing or a machine.

"Who is your leader?" she asked.

"Kaggen is our Supreme Leader," Mapu replied.

Cali figured this must be the more frighteningly large Mantis being. "What does he want?"

"He wants what is best for all races--to be as One," the creature answered, retrieving her uneaten food tray.

Cali was not at all sure what that meant. It might sound like a good thing, but if that were the case, why was she being treated like a prisoner of war? "Where are you taking me?" she asked.

Mapu turned to leave. "We go where Kaggen tells us to go."

Could this being get any more obtuse in its responses? It was maddening. "Why are you holding me here?" she shot back, now having covered the journalistic who, what, where and why of the situation, but still lacking any real answers. "I demand that you take me to Kaggen. It's imperative we speak without further delay. Tell him I have valuable information to share."

What her 'valuable' information might be for such an audience she had yet to come up with. Her real goal was to get out of that room so she could figure out what the real story was. If they had wanted her dead, she would have already been history. If they had planned to anal probe her, they would have already gone to town. Her butt felt just fine, thank you very much. The only viable premise left was that she was a hostage. If so, the big question was why and for what?

Mapu appeared immune to her pleas and gave no indication of any intent to do her bidding. The creature exited the room, dismissing her without another word, emotionless to her plight. Cali cursed as the door locked behind the little alien. Nothing more had been learned than the name of the being running the show. She could be annoying as hell when she wanted to be, and this would have to be one of those times. However long it took, she would continue needling Mapu, drive it nuts or short circuit it, if possible, until she was granted an appearance with the big bug named Kaggen.

~~*~~

Kaggen could have cared less about the screaming human woman who had identified herself as Cali Cavaleri. The child was the real and only prize, but something was terribly wrong which didn't fit with his plan. Izzie was not eating. She slept too much, at times being impossible to wake, her tiny body slowly wasting away without continued nourishment. It was if she was unexplainably slipping into a comatose state and it had happened so rapidly. Very few things alarmed him, but this did. Without the child, he would have very little to bargain with.

He had a ship medical technician run a mind scan, which showed she was no longer functioning in this realm. The kid had mentally checked out and was beyond his grasp--just like the SolarVector7's escape to the Andromeda Galaxy was well beyond Zachary Eldridge's technology reach. Either way, things could change for the worse. He would need to act fast before his prize captor died and the humans became retaliative.

Kaggen had an emissary deliver the Mantises' exchange terms to Zachary Eldridge, who he learned from his spies was the new Governor. While his trusted Oracle cube was failing to tell him the specifics he needed to know about young Zachary, he would operate from the belief that he could be a rogue Minerva leader, one who threatened to disrupt Mantis plans.

Kaggen knew what must be done regarding the human child, Izzie. It would require him thinking and acting like a human, which he detested, but some things were a necessary sacrifice for the preservation of his race, his genetic creations, and his continued Mantis leadership.

~~*~~

Izzie hated to say goodbye to her mother and Zach when they departed her Pink Heaven. She wanted them to stay there with her forever. This world contained everything she ever needed or desired except, of course, them. But Zach had promised he would come for her, and they would all be together again very soon—like a family.

In this magical pink world, one only had to ask for what one desired to know or have and it was provided. When her mother left, Izzie declared aloud that she wanted to meet her new little brother, and there he was, already grown to her own age and wanting to play. Unlike her, he had dark hair like Zach, and blue eyes like her Mommy. He told her his name was "Caleb" and that he was a soul waiting to be born but was currently in the 'in-between" until the right time he could join her family. She held out her arms to her little brother and embraced him.

"I will love you forever," she declared, feeling deliriously happy. She knew deep in her heart she would never be alone again from this day forward. Caleb was her Pink Heaven gift.

Without warning, Izzie's little body began to shake causing her to release Caleb and take a step back. There was a strange swirling in her head she couldn't stop, but in some ways didn't want to as she followed a familiar voice drawing her back to her physical body in that other world. It was Zach! The doorway to her little prison was wide open and he was sitting beside her on the bed, trying to rouse her from her deep sleep.

"Wake, up, Izzie. I'm here to take you home," he told her, smiling, as his hand soothed her forehead before moving to the top of her head where she felt a slight, uncomfortable pinch. She flinched and her body suddenly twitched in response.

"You have to stay awake, Izzie, if you want to see your Mommy," he told her, shaking her a little harder.

Izzie was suddenly wide awake, her mind cleared of the lofty clouds of her Pink Heaven. It became just a memory left behind in the far away past, along with her little brother Caleb. She sat up and stared hard at the being in front of her who looked and sounded like Zach and knew instantly it was not. She eyed him warily.

"What number am I, Zach?' she finally asked him.

The trickster continued to smile. "Why, you're my number one girl, Izzie. Have you forgotten?"

Of course, she hadn't forgotten. "No, I mean what number do you see when you look at me?"

The pretender being hesitated, suspecting that he was being tested. "The number I see isn't important. We can talk about all that later. Right now, there's more important things we need to do."

She smiled back ever so innocently, never letting on what she was now certain of. Zach would have known she was a seven, like he was an eight, and Mommy was also an eight. This was NOT her Zach. Her instincts told her this was a big old bug in disguise.

Izzie tried to close her eyes and return to Pink Heaven, but for some reason she could no longer do so. When she attempted to slide back to that reality there was an insistent pressure at the top of her head. Her hand reached up and found a small, raised bump where she had felt the trickster's pinch. That protrusion had not been there before.

"Did I fall?" she asked tentatively touching the smooth bump.

"Yes, you did," the trickster hurriedly replied. "But don't you worry. You'll be just fine in no time. Now, please stand up and come with me."

"Why? Where are we going?" Izzie cautiously asked.

The trickster helped her from the bed, which was not as easy as it had been in the past. Her limbs felt weak and did not want to work, causing her to be unsteady on her feet and a little dizzy. Her clothes had not been changed since her abduction and her shorts and pink top now hung loosely on her body. She didn't know why or how this had happened.

The trickster Zach gently escorted her from the confines of her cabin. "I've seized control of this ship and all your 'big bugs' are now gone, Izzie. I'm going to take you home to your Mommy," he replied, as his hand rested on her back. "And I've arranged a wonderful treat for you before we arrive home."

Izzie said nothing. When she entered the space craft's main flight deck, all she saw were humans at work. But underneath their facade, she knew they were really bugs and other creatures in disguise. They weren't fooling her one bit, but she decided not to let them know that she knew.

She watched two human-looking bugs wheel in a cart with the biggest pepperoni pizza she had ever seen. The trickster's "treat" looked real and smelled so delicious, too. But was it? She suspected she might be in a fake world as well.

"I don't like pizza anymore," she lied. "What else do you have?"

"Anything you want," the trickster told her.

Izzie thought about it for a moment. Mantis were meat and insect eaters, avoiding all garden green plants according to the internet. She had looked it up when she started having nightmare dreams about the big bugs harming Zach.

"A veggie burrito would be perfect with hot sauce mixed in," she told the trickster.

When it arrived a few minutes later, looking picture perfect like it had been lifted off a Mexican restaurant menu, she had one last request.

"Zach, will you see if it's just the way I like it? You know I can't eat it if it's too spicy. You don't want me to get sick..."

Izzie could tell she was pushing the patience of the trickster Zach.

"It's perfect. Just as you like it," he said, moving away from the food, which told her all she needed to know. "Trust me, Izzie. Just eat it," he added a bit more gruffly, seeing her hesitancy.

If there was any lingering doubt it was now gone. Her Zach loved Mexican food and would gladly have taste-tested it for her when asked. She took a small tentative bite. Despite its appetizing appearance, it was tasteless. The cheese and meat were rubbery. She could barely swallow a tiny morsel.

"I'm full," she declared, pushing the perfect-looking food away. The trickster Zach seemed none too happy with her rejection of the prepared meal.

Izzie was determined to be brave and not let Kaggen and his Mantis people see how scared she was. That bump on her head was pulsing. At first it had made her unable to sleep or return to her Pink Heaven, but now it was telling her to do things she did not want to do. Like eat and enjoy their awful food. When she tried to fight the impulse, it caused an uncomfortable pressure to build up on both sides of her head which would not ease until she obeyed. She heard her own voice in her head giving these orders, but Izzie knew the voice was not real either. This, too, was a trick, but there was no escaping it. Izzie ate their crappy tasteless food, practically gagging with each bite. She feared what else they would make her do before the real Zach rescued her.

~~*~~

Zach and Meghan knew immediately that something had changed for the worse. Izzie was nowhere to be found in Izzieland, and Satya had informed them that the child was no longer accessible through a dream state. When Zach demanded to see her life file, Satya finally produced a section of it. From what he could see, Kaggen had employed some kind of mind insertion to control Izzie. She was not being allowed to escape into another reality and away from the creature's grasp. But she was alive and Kaggen wanted her to stay that way until he no longer needed her for his purposes.

"She will be free soon," was all Satya would tell him. "She is very clever and will find a way."

Unable to take immediate action that would miraculously return her to them was something he and Meghan were both having difficulty dealing with. The Base's ships were doing reconnaissance of the universe, but the SolarVector7 continued to remain elusive as long as it stayed hidden within the Andromeda Galaxy.

Satya had finally allowed Zach to access just the here and now of Izzie's life, denying him knowledge of the child's future because his future was enmeshed and entangled with hers. Viewing one's own life file meant that the timeline would accelerate, both the good and the bad in it, she reminded him. Zach feared that what Satya was intentionally keeping hidden from him was that he too would meet a similar fate as his friend, Roone Sawyer. He tried desperately to bury such thoughts.

Once again Satya impressed upon him the need to take stock of the information he already possessed and gathered. But before he could, he finally received word from Kaggen, addressed specifically to him. The creature's terms were concrete and clear. Izzie and the woman, Cali, would be returned only upon the signing of a new treaty which guaranteed unlimited powers to the Mantis, the Zeta Greys, the Dracos and the Reptilian alien races.

Zach worked his way through their demands: All transhumanistic DNA hybridization programs would be openly acknowledged, sanctioned, and supported by all governing bodies and world leaders. All those opposing this, in any sector of government power would be replaced with their own human-hybrids, easily controllable. The Mantis wanted unlimited access and control over all planetary entry points into Earth's realm. Now that they perceived Minerva's human leadership to be inherently weakened, Kaggen and his kind saw their golden opportunity. This time they were asking for it all.

Kaggen had employed the same work-around to Earth's being a free choice non-interference zone as had been utilized countless times in the past. Once humans agreed to their terms, having little choice to do otherwise, particularly those holding the reins of power, he and his kind would have unfettered freedom to act. They would subject Earth to the ultimate bio-invasion takeover of their species on all levels—changing the planet forever. It would be theirs, despite its inhabitants looking very much human in all respects. And if the new Governor of Minerva refused any of their terms, it meant annihilation of the remaining pure bloodline human species. They could easily wipe them out via plague, advanced space weaponry, or total weather and geological manipulation of the planet until they agreed. Free choice be damned. Their kind would survive regardless of what they inflicted on the humans.

Zach realized all this. None of the terms were acceptable. It was an impossible choice between saving Izzie and saving Earth and humanity. The outcome of either decision would be catastrophic no matter what he decided. Which indicated only one thing. It meant total war.

~~*~~

Cali was finally brought before Kaggen. She trembled inside, trying not to scream when his long antennae reached out towards her and wrapped loosely around her neck. She felt the threat of death and couldn't have found words, even if her life depended upon it.

"You will not speak, only listen," the Mantis commander warned her, tightening his hold around her throat. "I do not like your silly screams. There will be no more of that. Do you understand?"

Cali barely nodded her head. Hell, yes, she understood. Any bug that big was not someone you entertained having a debate with. Kaggen released his grip, his antennae retreating, yet she could not take her eyes off them fearing they would return and strangle the life out of her.

"Your life will be spared if you watch over the child Izzie. You will make sure she eats and remains healthy and strong. Do not allow her to escape into other realities. And you will report back to me all her thoughts and actions. Do I make myself clear?" Kaggen demanded.

Once again Cali nodded. Her intuition was correct. They could care less about her welfare. Izzie was the real prize. The only thing she didn't know was why. But she dared not press the issue. She wanted very much to survive. As of this day forward she would become Little Betsy Ross' devoted nursemaid, no questions asked. This she could do and would do it well.

Chapter 3

Despite strict eligibility requirements, Arlington National Cemetery honored the Eldridge family's request for burial when they were informed of Martin Eldridge's sudden demise. They knew who they were dealing with. The man had been considered an unofficial veteran of all service branches of the United States military, whether he had actively served or not. He was a leader of many of the covert and unofficially acknowledged space forces. Therefore, he would be given a proper send-off for a man of his rank who was not only dedicated to his country but had protected the homeland from unseen forces far and wide.

Like his burial arrangements, the funeral services for Martin Eldridge were carried out with the same degree of patriotic acknowledgement. His death managed to fill all the church pews of the Washington National Cathedral, a venue primarily reserved for presidential funerals, inaugurations, and high-ranking service leaders. Few there knew Martin Eldridge had hand-picked most of the presidents during his time, as well as thrown out of power a few of them when they did not play by his or Minerva's rules. His true power would be known only by an elite few, yet his influence was widely acknowledged throughout Washington and Capitol Hill.

A procession of dark cars slowly wove their way to his final resting place, followed by the media covering Camille Eldridge's presidential campaign. They knew a good sad interest story when they saw it. As the chaplain conducted the memorial services, Camille Eldridge stood stoically at the gravesite, playing the perfect grieving widow for all the politicians and media to see, allowing an occasional tear to roll down her cheek, letting everyone know the extent and depth of her loss.

At her side, her son, Zachary, stood tall in a dark suit and even darker sunglasses. It was the first time many had seen the Minerva Governor's prodigy in public. A few strained to get a better look, despite the dark shades that obscured closer identification. The Minerva members present at the last devastating meeting of their Council, where Martin Eldridge had been vaporized, knew full well who the son was.

While others scrutinized him, having heard the whispered rumors, the remaining Minerva members avoided all eye contact. They were now dealing with the repercussions of their own deeds which had been shockingly viewed by the other board members. No one would forget the truth of what they had witnessed. Outrage consumed them.

Zach was not oblivious to the silent drama playing out around him. He knew he was surrounded in an orchard of bad apples who were attempting to regroup, seize the power back and salvage what they believed was theirs to rightfully claim.

But in the public's eye, center stage was reserved for the Eldridge widow. Camille was not about to let a little thing like her husband's sudden and unexpected heart attack get in the way of her political aspirations. She was determined to become the first female President of the United States, no matter what it took. And it would take a lot now that Martin was no longer alive to help fund her campaign and steal the vote.

Camille watched them lower her husband into the ground. She knew there was no body in the coffin. It was empty when it arrived from Antarctica. Zach was cognizant of the fact as well, as he had made the funeral arrangements. But if her son knew where his father's remains were, he wasn't saying. There was no discussing the matter, either. *Close-lipped just like his father*, she thought!

The empty coffin situation required the undertaker being sworn to secrecy and paid off handsomely when the casket was finally sealed. It was a rather expensive burial for just rocks. Camille was certain someone in Minerva had killed Martin, just like they killed James Talbot. There were hundreds, if not thousands who might have wanted him dead. The actual killer might be here right now amongst them.

Camille looked around hoping to spot Elisabeth Vandam who had been avoiding her since Martin died. Vandam was a Minerva member who had her pulse on the mainstream media and would probably know the real story behind Martin's demise. There she was, extracting herself from the throng of mourners, making her escape to a long black limo waiting to whisk her away. Damn! Had she not been the grieving widow, Camille would have immediately waylaid her. Curiously, she felt her son rest his hand on her shoulder, restraining her impulses, as if he knew exactly what she was thinking.

Zach did. His mother was so transparent. Always calculating who was still usable to meet her needs, even now as she buried her husband of 30 plus years. He knew many people were in attendance out of duty and curiosity, not so much for Martin Eldridge, whose power dissipated the moment he died, but for Zach as the newly self-ordained Minerva Governor. It's not that he ever wanted the job, but life circumstances had thrust it upon him. He would make the best of it until he no longer could.

Like his father and his father before him, Zach now had his own security detail. He had not wanted Meghan at the memorial services, not only because she was pregnant, but he didn't want to place her under undue scrutiny by his mother or anyone else. He wanted to keep their personal life private as best he could. She was back at her Bethesda home, under strict protection, awaiting his return. His mother, thank God, was still clueless of who he now was and the orchestrated changes he was slowly attempting to put in place. He hadn't decided yet if he would or would not let his mother continue her charade of running for President. However, it was one way to keep her busy and out of his hair, like his father had done before him.

Zach knew she knew that the coffin they were now paying their respects to was empty. It wouldn't be the only questionable coffin contents at Arlington National Cemetery. Minerva records spanning decades revealed former President Jay Fitzgerald's memorial crypt didn't contain his remains either. There had been a body switch to cover up a barrage of bullet wounds from eight different snipers—throat, right temple, the occipital lobe. And not one of those snipers was the accused patsy that took the blame. It was a historical massive cover-up by some of the most powerful men in the world. The names of the perpetrators were all there from the CIA operatives, FBI bosses, the Mafia heads of five different crime families, and three former complicit presidents. When Minerva wanted someone eliminated for coming up against them, it meant deadly business.

As the new Governor there were people he needed to meet and attempt to put their doubts to rest—important and dangerous men who didn't like anyone messing with their business operations. From the information he had initially exposed from the LOT about the human trafficking component of Minerva, it was now evident that their network had longer reaching tentacles than even he could have imagined. They were everywhere and into everything, controlling borders worldwide with cartels comprised of their own foot soldiers.

The day-to-day operations of Minerva, along with the daily logs of Base operations, were hidden within the DOLARIS system. They provided a wealth of information on who ran what, which banks and wire services were involved in the daily activity of money laundering, and the whereabouts of numerous offshore accounts belonging to the power cartels.

Zach studied it all—from the above ground networks to those functioning below the surface. He now knew that there were deep underground bases everywhere in the U.S. as well as throughout Europe and Asia. It came as a shock to learn that there was an underground military base right under Capitol Hill, the tunnels going down even deeper than the LOC's personnel access tunnels. Some were still being used for human trafficking, others for covert military operations. Somehow, they would all have to be destroyed in order to bring things out in the open.

Zach knew about the underground military tunnels because his meeting after the funeral services was taking place right now in a large conference room many levels underneath the Capitol Building. There was a jump-room gate from this installation to other jump-room gates across the globe. Air travel was obsolete to these people. Natural Earth portals had been opened using alien technology. While none of these jump-room gates led to the Library of Truth, or the other 12-dimensional portals, they did provide protection to all Minerva operatives and operations.

Calvin Benjamin, one of the eight remaining Minerva board members who possessed space exploration and military ties, had been instrumental in arranging this meeting of minds. Zach didn't trust him at all. But right now, everyone was playing a fake game of cooperation. Their key obstacle was that Zach was the only person who knew how to access the Library of Truth. They desperately wanted entry to this information portal now that the Counselor no longer existed. So many of their scientists had tried to break the complex code into the LOT but had been unsuccessful. Some had never returned, which deeply concerned them. They couldn't afford to lose valuable minds to unknown factors. They realized they needed Zach whether they liked it or not. Eventually they would extract the sequence code from him when the time was right. Until then, they believed they could make him work for them.

Zach realized this, which meant he would have to work faster to accomplish his goals, or not live to survive this transition. The conference room was filled with 50 or more high ranking military and intelligence agency personnel. Some had come directly from his father's gravesite burial to see what they were up against. He noted that Gizmo had been clever to eliminate General Parnell Tanaka from the Minerva board, or Tanaka would have been conducting this meeting right now, plotting ways to quickly dispose of Zach.

The men and women before him wanted assurances that little would change and what was now amiss would be promptly fixed. They wanted it to be business as usual, as their livelihoods depended upon it. These individuals didn't care who was running the show, just so long as that person didn't get in their way.

Martin Eldridge's death had caused disruption to the flow of their vast networks and the monies that sprang forth from such lucrative enterprises. A Minerva Governor had more power than any country's leader. Therefore, their strategy was to listen first, address enemy obstacles second, then take final corrective or lethal action—whatever was necessary. They were there for guarantees that all they had built would be righted and the coffers would continue to flow again. They would give the new Governor's son a one-time chance to prove himself.

Instead of leading with their expected agenda, they were stunned to learn that Zachary Eldridge was determined to move forward with his own grandiose plans. He intended to open the cosmic ray collector satellites and start transitioning the world to an unlimited energy society. There were exchanged looks of shock, suppressed laughter, and grimness seen around the room. Nothing the new Governor said sat well with any of them. Such outlandish ideas were out of the question. It meant immense loss of profits and control.

Zach had anticipated their resistance. He started detailing the ways they could still profit from providing the vast amount of technology and equipment that already ran the large Antarctica Base efficiently. The profits were in the hardware. The electrical grid was antiquated and could no longer sustain the requirements needed if they completely moved away from gas and oil, despite what the green activists claimed. Rebuilding the infrastructure with such advanced technology would and could prove profitable.

He assured them the cosmic energy collector satellites in space were far superior to existing solar panels now used on houses and buildings. These deep space collectors could store unlimited cheap and clean energy. This energy, generated from the Sun, was a limitless source no matter what the time of day or the season. By adapting, the electrical grid would never go down and the environment would not be negatively impacted. To any logical mind, it sounded like the perfect solution.

Zach knew most of them could care less about the environment, but they did care how much money they could make off a new technology, so he tried to steer it in that direction. It was one way to skin a cat.

"It's time we stopped operating in the dark ages," he told the skeptical assembly. "Too many useless wars are fought over gas and oil and the control of energy. I know that war is profitable to many of you, but it's not the only solution to prosperity. My father knew this transition to an unlimited energy source would take time, but the time is now. Instead of stifling such innovation, as has been done for more than a century, we should openly embrace it and move forward."

Zach hoped he was getting through to them. Could he appeal to their sense of humanity? He knew he was threatening their world, but he also knew that if they didn't move forward and make concerted progress, then the Mantises would completely overrun them.

"We are sitting on advanced technologies of all sorts that the aliens have given us that could make this a better world for you and your families," he said. "We need to take back our world, so we are the masters of our own race and are no longer controlled by outside alien forces."

There were nervous looks exchanged all around. Many of them knew exactly what he was referring to and were uncomfortable with such talk. The alien treaties were not openly discussed. It was the dirty little secret that they had been keeping for decades during their time, and for the ancestors which had preceded them.

Zach was not foolish enough to think there wasn't a human-hybrid alien amongst them. Their hive mind would report back to Kaggen every detail of his plan. His ideas were a declaration of war, along with all its accompanying radical changes.

There were some good questions, which Zach did the best he could to answer. With humans it always circled back around to power, weaponry, and profit. He gauged the temperature of the group to be tepid to his suggestions at best. He did not expect wide scale enthusiasm, hoping for openness instead. His intention was to leave them thinking. To that end, he had prepared a briefing report, anonymously authored, detailing how to implement his suggestions in stages, as well as a profitability analysis, which was distributed to each of them.

Cell phones were not allowed in the Sensitive Compartmented Information Facility (SCIF) room to avoid all information transmission to outside sources. The attendees who had come to hear Zach were instructed to read the report in its entirety and return their copy at the door prior to leaving. He didn't want copies of it floating around, even though he was sure there would be eventual leaks. It was the nature of the beast.

His hope for a better future for his world might seem naïve to these men, but someone had to try, or all would eventually be lost. When he was finished and everyone had vacated the meeting room, Calvin Benjamin congratulated him on a brilliant speech. All around the man he saw twisted and distorted numbers emerge signifying he was lying through his teeth. Zach had come to recognize this tell-tale sign early in life as his built-in lie-detector. Benjamin and his kind could not be trusted. He wondered if there was anyone in Minerva who could be.

Chapter 4

Cali hated her new job as Kaggen's appointed snitch to Little Betsy Ross. There wasn't much of anything to report. Granted she got Izzie to eat a little more, but she couldn't blame the kid for avoiding the unpalatable stuff. Whatever it was made up of was unearthly in origin.

Izzie was only too happy to have company in her little prison cell and asked non-stop questions between wanting to play word games to pass the time. Children were like energy vampires. They exhausted you. If it was like this with all children, Cali vowed to tie her tubes the first chance she got. That is if she even survived this ordeal.

Izzie also liked to talk about the portals. She was fascinated with where they all led and who might have made them and how to get back there. This is how Cali learned about the Library of Truth, Satya, and dreams that led into Pink Heaven where her new little brother, Caleb, lived until he was born. Little Betsy Ross continued to be a truth font of strange and bizarre information. Cali listened in fascination, now understanding why Izzie had been sleeping so much, necessitating Kaggen's intercession. The kid had found a temporary escape route to deal with her captivity. How absolutely clever of her.

Izzie was a sponge for information. She now wanted to know everything about Cali's experiences with Zach as ZLOT, starting from the very beginning. "Don't leave anything out," she instructed Cali, sitting cross-legged on the floor, all ears. "Zach is an angel, you know. He's not from here," she added matter-of-factly.

Okay, so the kid did have some pretty crazy notions. "Where's he from then?" Cali wanted to know.

"Satya told me he comes from a different dimension, beyond ours. That's why he's so smart and thinks so differently." She sighed wistfully. "I wish he was my daddy. Caleb says he also comes from this other place, like Zach."

The conversation was turning more bizarre by the moment, but certainly no less fascinating. Cali kept probing. "Did this Satya person tell you why Zach is here?"

"Oh, yes. His job is to stop Kaggen and all the other big bugs," she said before adding, "There's one more thing he came here to do, which my Mommy is helping him with."

Cali's ears perked up. "Oh, yeah. What's that?"

Izzie smiled. "He came here to find love."

Cali started laughing, practically rolling on the floor with mirth. "Oh, man. Yeah, him and everyone else. Good luck to him on that one!"

Izzie frowned. Cali was good at getting people to talk and maybe, just maybe, Izzie had told her too much. She would have to work on that. Her mother had always taught her to be truthful, but she was quickly learning that sometimes it was okay to not divulge everything one knew--like the big bugs could change shape and trick you. Or how Kaggen had tried to pretend he was Zach, but she had seen right through the masquerade. Instinctively, she knew not to tell anyone about how she knew this, not even Cali. Her intention had been to get the reporter to tell her all about herself. She wanted to know how Cali had become a reporter (just in case she decided to become one herself someday when she grew up). But more importantly, she wanted to know how Cali had come through the portal without Zach's help. Did Cali know the same portal entry sequence Zach used? This still puzzled her, so she asked.

"I knew this guy named Bond. We had a thing…" Cali began, shaking her head. "Anyway. Long story. But big mistake, that one. He had to have known about the portals. He drugged me, dumped me on Haleakala, then ran, leaving me there. I had no idea what had happened. Which is one big lesson you should learn now, missy. Don't ever trust men. Especially ones who work for the government!"

Izzie frowned. "I can see your Bond," she said closing her eyes. "Oh, my. Yes. He's the same man who became our security person when bad men broke into my grandpa's house. I told Zach this man had black and red colors all around him. I warned him he was bad and not to trust him."

Cali's mouth dropped open in surprise. The kid had better instincts than she did. Izzie opened her eyes and just shrugged. "But he's gone now. Don't worry. He won't ever come back."

"What do you mean 'gone'?" Cali prompted.

"He was killed by the red light and then he was gone. I can see it in my head," Izzie replied. "Zach was there when it happened. Your Bond won't ever be coming back."

The shock of such unexpected news hit her harder than she would have thought. Cali closed her eyes, searching for words. In barely a whisper, she asked, "He's really dead?"

"Yes. He's dead," Izzie confirmed.

~~*~~

Kaggen knew the Cali woman was not telling him everything she had learned. She was holding something back. But what? It was all well and good that the child was eating again and not looking so waifish. Having companionship served its purpose to keep her from escaping into her sleep world, but there had to be more. He could sense it.

Kaggen probed deeper into Cali's mind to extract what she was failing to reveal and saw the face of a man she was mourning, a man he recognized as belonging to Minerva. The Old Governor's security man. Izzie had told the woman this man had died, and she was still coming to terms with the sudden knowledge of her loss. How interesting, he thought, immediately seizing on an opportunity.

Kaggen preferred not to shapeshift in front of his prey. Instead, he retreated from the room to his lair and moments later returned in the physical form of the agent known as "Bond". He watched the Cali woman sink to her knees upon instant recognition.

"I'm not really dead, sweetheart," he said, flashing her a brilliant, almost sexy, smile. "I've made a deal with the Mantises for your release."

The shock of seeing Bond again made Cali tremble, her knees turning weak. Her savior, her white knight in the flesh. She wasn't a fainting woman but felt damn close to it right now as she stared at him wide-eyed, unable to speak. Her hand reached out to touch him, feel his warm skin, and confirm what her eyes saw.

"You're real," she whispered in awe.

"Very real," he replied extending both arms out to her. She ran into those welcoming arms, wrapped hers around his neck and held on. She felt his body pressed against hers invitingly, and she responded by kissing the hell out of him. There was something slightly different about his kisses, but she pushed the thought away. She was just too happy that he was still alive and here with her now. Thoughts of sexy Eric on Maui flooded in—

her Eric—loving, trusting, and reliable. Suddenly, she felt ashamed to have succumbed to Bond again so easily.

She took a step back and slapped him hard across the face. "That's for drugging me, taking my computer, and stranding me on a cold deserted mountain top!" Was it her imagination or did Bond's face seem to momentarily waiver? Prolonged captivity must be making her eyes play tricks on her.

"Sorry about that, Cali," he said. "But we don't have a lot of time. Kaggen thinks Izzie told you something important. I've got to know what you know, or I can't get you safely out of here."

"And what about Izzie?" she whispered.

"Her, too," he quickly added.

Cali shrugged. "I can't think of anything that sounded important. It was all just jabber."

"Think harder," he prompted, again.

She did. "I don't know. It was mostly weird, nonsense stuff," she began. "She talked about accessing the portals you took me through. Then she tried to tell me that Zach is an angel from another dimension—imagine that? Oh, and about her going to some Library of Truth where she viewed people's life records, and someone named Satya told her about Zach being some sort of savior."

Bond's eyes lit up. "She's accessed records in the Library of Truth," he said, more a statement than a question. Cali nodded. "Yes, that's what she said."

Kaggen could barely contain the shapeshift form of the human called Bond at hearing such news. "Well done, sweetheart," he said kissing her hard on the lips, before pushing her aside.

This time Cali felt instant revulsion at the touch of his lips. Bond seemed to be dismissing her, tossing her aside. His body movements now appeared almost jerky, his limbs moving at an odd angle. His eyes momentarily glowed. Was she hallucinating?

"Go back to Izzie and find out how she accesses the Library of Truth," he ordered her.

Cali stood there transfixed.

"Now," he shouted. "Get moving. In the meantime, we will be turning this ship around and returning to Earth."

Cali felt unable to move as doubt flooded in. Something felt terribly wrong. There was no denying it. The next words out of her mouth came from somewhere deep inside her which craved answers.

"Who are you?" she demanded to know.

Kaggen laughed in what sounded like a roar of locusts. He dropped the veils of illusion and the vision of Bond waivered then dissolved in front of her eyes, replacing it with who he really was. Kaggen morphed into his full frightening form, towering over her, hissing his disdain for the woman as he did. Stupid human.

Cali could not stop screaming.

~~*~~

Certain high-pitched frequencies felt like a thousand daggers attacking Kaggen's Mantis body all at once. Because of this, he almost killed the screaming woman with his claws that could crush and eviscerate any prey on the spot. Instead, he knocked her out with one quick swipe to her head and had her unconscious body removed to her lair. There was always the chance he might still need her if she survived the blow. If so, he would tear out her vocal cords, so he and no other being, Mantis or human, would ever have to hear her incessant screaming again. He devilishly smiled, knowing he would be doing the universe a big favor.

As far as he was concerned, the woman had served her purpose. Her life was no longer of any value. Under the guise of Bond, she had revealed to him a way to get around Ishannika's banishing him from the Library of Truth. That's all he cared about.

Izzie, on the other hand, was now even more valuable to him. She could access the LOT and extract information for him. It was the answer to his problem. Through the child he would learn how Ishannika and the Universal Council of Higher Planetary Guardians (UCHPG) were using Zach to undermine his genetic re-population agenda.

Kaggen's plan immediately took form. It would require him creating an artificial byway into one of the LOT's 12 universal portal access points for which to send the child. While he himself couldn't get into the LOT, he knew just how to ensure that Izzie came back with the information he desired. She couldn't escape him, now or ever. The mind insert would take care of that.

Kaggen immediately called for his trusted portal engineers.

Chapter 5

Back in Antarctica, Zach waited until Meghan fell into a deep exhausted sleep. He quietly removed himself from their bed, careful not to wake her, and grabbed Gizmo. His intention had been to go directly to the LOT to see Satya, but fate had other plans for him.

This time the portal took him to an arid desert location, filled with enormous ancient ruins that looked like they had weathered the test of time and had been built for giants walking the Earth. Tall Corinthian columns, which had to have once been quite majestic in their day, were now tumbled over and scattered into broken pieces everywhere in the rubble of land. Many were riddled with bullet holes and were missing sizeable stone chunks, telling him the site had been a battleground over the centuries by numerous groups, including Muslims and Christians.

Ancient sites, especially UNESCO reconstruction projects, had always intrigued Zach, so identifying where he was not difficult. Portal 9 was linked to the Ruins of Baalbek in Lebanon, which had been sacked by the Byzantine Army in 748 C.E. Every invading army for centuries had tried to conquer this site. Was it because they knew it sat on a portal into another world, which they wanted access to? The same had happened to the ancient ruins of Palmyra in Syria which the terrorist group ISIS had partially destroyed in August of 2015. Through back channels he had heard that the invading infidels had been trying to locate a lost antiquity--a statue. Could they have been searching for a Golden Minerva?

"Is this a double-terminated site portal?" he asked Gizmo, getting a quick flash of heat in the affirmative. Okay, so Palmyra and Baalbek were linked. But why?

Zach employed his direct Einstein-Rosen bridge mind connection to the LOT for more information. He was standing inside the remaining ruins of the Temple of Baal, erected by an earlier Roman Minerva group to worship the sky gods Jupiter, Venus, and Bacchus.

From what Zach understood, there were elements which did not make sense. The god Jupiter was referred to as Baal in ancient time, but the LOT records were pointing towards Bacchus being the real Baal, which was interesting. Half goat, half human, a hybrid being, Bacchus' powers were of pleasure, madness, and manipulation. He was the last deity to join the 12 Olympian Roman gods. Linked to Baal and Beelzebub, pagan demon gods, some believed this temple was erected to glorify Satan's work on Earth. In this case, Satan through Minerva. Thousands had come here over the centuries drawing forth the energy of its magic and power. No wonder there had been so many attempts to destroy it.

The Baalbek ruins were mysteriously quiet and dark, not a living soul in sight anywhere. Whatever the hour, it had to be the middle of the night when tourists had no access. There were no security guards on duty either, which was rather odd for a partially restored UNESCO site.

There was a feeling of heaviness in the air, left behind by energetic imprints this area had experienced over the centuries. It was the energy of warring factions and death. Many had lost their lives here. Yet, this evening as Zach walked between the fallen columns, there was also a faint feeling of expectation, like something was coming to culmination.

Unlike the Sakya Monastery in Tibet, there was no library here for him to discover. But his instincts told him at one time this site contained a treasure trove of information which was now gone, scattered to the four corners of the world.

The Mind of the LOT showed him that this portal site was where the 12 tablets, *The Universal Covenant* of man, had originated from before being seized during an earlier invasion. This invaluable antiquity had exchanged many hands over the centuries before finally being sealed up in a hidden room of the Vatican's Secret Archives, never to be seen again until Zach unlocked it.

Information streamed into Zach, as the energetics of the site activated knowledge inside him. He saw that Baalbek was once the primary settlement site of the Anunnaki race—the "Sky Gods" as they were known back then. It was here in their "space center" that the Anunnaki seeded their DNA to create the human race. Even today, they still referred to this ancient site in Mesopotamia as the "cradle of civilization" where man's true origins began. And a Golden Minerva statue had been placed here in the past to mark this significant ancient space center portal. But had the statue also been stolen by infidels like the 12 tablets?

Zach knew there was something here that had yet to be found. His senses were attuned to it. If it was embedded in the stone crevices, it would probably have been discovered during restoration attempts a long time ago.

"Show me where to look," he instructed Gizmo.

And like before, Zach felt a tremor ripple through the Earth beneath his feet. This site *did,* however, sit on an active fault zone, the most sizeable earthquake dating back to 1759. He followed the seismic energy it radiated, finding his steps bringing him up and along a nearby hill leading to the Temple's quarry. There the energy line went straight to three monolithic stones of massive size and weight. The stones lay on their sides partially buried in the earth. Zach immediately moved to the largest of the three monoliths which was shaking in place. Called the "Forgotten Stone", it had to weigh well over 1500 tons. His mathematical mind calculated that it was almost 64 feet long, 19 feet high and perhaps 18 feet wide. It had to be the largest quarried stone outside of Egypt. And it was now shifting in place like a weightless rock, before rolling on its side about 10 feet away.

Zach moved closer to the shallow pit that the massive stone had once covered. He squatted down and spied a partially exposed metal box buried amidst the debris. Dusting aside the dirt, he recognized it was made of the same meta-terrestrial properties of Gizmo, but looked as good as new, showing no signs of wear or age.

He paused to quickly glance around, confirming he was alone and not being observed, before reaching for it and breaking open the clasp. Inside was a statue-size bundle, bound in an unknown black fibrous material with thin metal strappings holding it together. The bindings melted off like rivulets of liquid mercury the second Zach touched it. He immediately dropped the bundle and stepped back as it released a voluminous black vapor. It had a foul odor, like Sulphur, and all around him the air was saturated with the scent of sea salt.

Zach watched the eerie cloud evaporate and disappear into the ethers, leaving behind a perfectly preserved Golden Minerva statue. It tingled in his hands when he retrieved it from the ground. For a brief second it pulsed with light, feeling momentarily alive, before its glow was extinguished and it turned eerily silent.

Zach couldn't explain how he knew it, but he just did. A binding seal had been placed on the statue and his unearthing of it had somehow broken its spell. Sulphur, salt, and mercury were the three elements of ancient alchemy. They were the sorcerer's tools for magic. He searched the Mind of the LOT looking for who had put the seal on the statue and what it might mean now that he had broken through. His mind brought up three faceless individuals, like the three who had buried the Golden Minerva in the underground tunnels of Oxford's Bodleian Library centuries ago. Who were these people? And why was a protection seal placed on this statue and not the others?

The simple answer came to him. This Minerva statue was never meant to be unearthed by any archeologist or treasure hunter. And to guarantee it remained buried, both a spell and an unmovable stone had been placed over it. No wonder the statue had never been found by centuries of invaders. It had been entombed under tons of marble.

The Mind of the LOT spoke to him again, informing him that his actions had also released a secondary binding spell on the statue, freeing all 12 golden statues from the life and death status of Minerva. Which meant he could now freely gather the rest of them. He wasn't sure what to make of this last revelation. Free it from what?

Zach already possessed the Bodleian Library and Sakya Monastery statues. Baalbek would make three. He knew he could easily secure the Library of Congress one in the Members of Congress Reading Room balcony, as well the Antarctica one, which was probably hidden deep under miles of frozen earth and ice. No one had ever tried stopping him.

It occurred to him that he might make his world a whole lot easier if he just had Gizmo fetch all the remaining statues to him at once. But when he tried employing this tactic, Gizmo wouldn't budge. It was now apparent he would have to go back and retrieve each of them himself. The universe was not going to make this process any easier for him.

Zach tossed the statue's metal receptacle back into the pit. No sooner had he done this, than he had to quickly jump out of the way as the earth rumbled and swallowed it back up. Within seconds he witnessed the Forgotten Stone roll back and shimmy itself over the hole as if it had never been disturbed. There was feeling of emptiness in the ancient site. Baalbeck had given forth its last hidden treasure, having no more left to give or reveal. Zach felt it.

He turned to leave, troubled by the realization that although he had successfully retrieved this statue, he was getting nowhere fast. Even if he brought all 12 Golden Minerva statues together, it might not be enough to close the portals in time to rescue Izzie and Cali. Coming to terms with his mounting feelings of frustration and powerlessness was becoming more difficult as more challenges presented themselves.

With the advanced alien technology exchange spanning back hundreds of years, humans should have had space craft by now capable of reaching other solar systems like the Andromeda Galaxy where Kaggen and his kind were currently hanging out.

While in Washington, D.C., Zach had asked surviving Minerva member, Calvin Benjamin of NASA, to find out if there was a workable solution to sending a ship to the Andromeda Nebula. Benjamin had a pat, evasive answer. "The Andromeda Galaxy is 2.5 million light years away from our Milky Way Galaxy. It would take more than 10 billion years to reach it with our existing technology, and maybe half that with what the aliens gave us," he replied. "Obviously, they did not give us everything they knew. They made sure they could out distance us in the universe under all circumstances. There was only so much we could gleam from reverse engineering, but unfortunately not nearly enough."

That fact was abundantly clear. However, Zach was not willing to accept such limited thinking. It was questionable if Benjamin was even telling him the truth about the extent of what they knew about the exchange shared between the space agencies. For years mainstream scientists had stuck to the theory that there was nothing faster than the speed of light. Even travelling 186,282 miles per second, under those circumstances it would still take countless years to reach Kaggen. But was that true?

"How do you think they do it?" he asked Benjamin, curious to hear his thoughts.

The NASA Minerva member shook his head. "They were very sketchy about revealing secrets to intergalactic travel, preferring to keep us corralled in the Milky Way. You've got to remember that they've been doing this for hundreds of thousands of years and we're just beginning."

Benjamin shrugged, but Zach could still see distorted 2's and 5's coming out of him. He wasn't being totally honest. "But if you're asking my opinion," the man continued, "I suspect they've either found a way to stop, or at least warp, space time travel to move beyond the speed of light. There's the possibility they might use wormhole technology to get to other galactic realms, but it's hard to say. Only your father would have known, had he gotten that much out of them. However, we do know they use some type of renewable self-harnessing 'star energy' to fuel their ships."

Zach hadn't heard anything he didn't already know except the part about the 'star energy' fuel. His brain was suddenly on fire. A stream of information spilled forth into conscious thought from the hidden recesses of his memory, filling in missing gaps within his understanding.

The download he received from their space craft was linked to the Mantis hive mind--the keeper of their secrets. It now revealed that the aliens were way beyond the fundamental laws of physics governing his world. The Mantis had perfected a mathematical construct which moved pure information faster than the speed of light, then coupled it with quantum entanglement.

It sent a chill down his spine as he tried to make sense of it. Linked or entangled particles remain the same no matter what the distance, lasting indefinitely. It sounded so simple but was not so easy to accomplish. Yet the Mantis and other alien species had found a way to use this applied science. They could teleport their large ships into smaller compressed drives of information and send them to any distant place they desired, before reversing the process to reassemble them. That was how and why they immediately disappeared upon high-speed acceleration.

The copious notes he had scribbled down in the Duke Humfrey Reading Room of the Bodleian Library were the blueprint and mathematical equations Kaggen's kind used to affect such quick long-distance travel. Despite having been operating at the time under a diminished memory state, Zach knew the numbers didn't look the least bit familiar to him. Yet, to his credit, his brain was still trying to make sense of something it had just learned and was assimilating. This information was invaluable and not something he wished to share with Benjamin or any other remaining Minerva member. The less they knew, the better.

Back in Antarctica, Zach retrieved all his Bodleian Library notes. They now made a hell of a lot more sense. While teleportation, as he knew it, could be achieved by using the LOT's 12 portals to relocate an intact person from one place to another—the act of disassembling molecules, beaming them to a distant place, then reassembling them at the new location was something entirely different. Science simply had not been able to do that yet with people and large objects, the likes of which Kaggen had accomplished. It was still in the realms of *Star Trek* fantasy, not here and now reality.

The Laws of Physics proclaimed that anything that moved faster than the speed of light had to first overcome growing larger and larger in mass, which slowed a vehicle down making fast intergalactic speed and distance impossible. The Mantis had figured out how to effect mass inertia cancellation and shield their craft to overcome this physical limitation. As a result, their space vehicles remained super light and incomprehensibly fast as they drew "star energy" from the environmental vacuum of space and time. They could go anywhere in the solar system in less time—like the Andromeda Galaxy, by sizing down upon accelerated travel.

Zach's memory was retrieving their mathematical equations. He had never taken an advanced physics course, yet he was now deciphering their secret. Math was the key. Math never lied. This he understood.

Their unique space craft design now made more sense as well. He could see how they copper-wired their craft, lacing and layering its strands through the bottom plates as a propulsion component. It was both simple and brilliant.

His mind brought up moving images of how they utilized liquid mercury as their fuel source. They used two separate counter-rotating cylindrical chambers, run through compacitors placed under their craft, which gave their saucer-shaped bottom a practical reason. As the liquid mercury spun in a closed upward loop in opposite directions around the central core and circumference of the craft, it emitted a high voltage electrical charge the equivalent of an alien souped-up turbine engine. It was self-perpetuating for long distance travel making it the most efficient source of unlimited fuel. The electromagnetic field propulsion it generated, upwards of several million volts, cancelled out the effects of gravity, giving it immediate lift and super-luminal speed.

Zach's comprehension for what they had accomplished over hundreds of thousands of years of their species' civilization, left him with a sense of awe. He couldn't help but smile to himself that the mercury propulsion solution had been evident for centuries. Some of the Ancient Egyptian tombs were found to have spontaneous combustion Mercury lamps still brilliantly lit in them after being sealed up for thousands of years. When opened to air, their light died out emitting toxic and deadly Mercury vapors to those who had disturbed the dead's resting place. It became known as the "Curse of the Pharaohs". As in the Egyptian tombs, rivulets of liquid Mercury were also found under some of the major pyramids of the world where few, if any, understood their true purpose. The aliens had left traces of their propulsion secrets behind, in plain sight, and no one was any the wiser.

The impossible now became the possible as Zach understood how they effected long-distance travel. Had his father known this secret? Or had he known it only as a theory, not a reversed reproduction vehicle fact?

Zach immediately called a meeting of the Base's best engineers, physicists, mathematicians, and scientists, where he shared his findings and encouraged them to make implementation a priority. Intergalactic travel was not something they would accomplish overnight, but he felt compelled to set it in motion to prepare for the future. Somewhere down the line it would be key to man's survival.

~~*~~

Izzie leapt off her bed when several Mantis beings, disguised as humans, stormed into her cabin. Without a word, they unceremoniously dumped Cali Cavaleri's unconsciousness body on the floor at her feet. They then turned and departed, locking the door behind them.

A dark bruise was already forming on Cali's left temple. Izzie saw it and frantically kneeled down beside her, trying to shake her awake. The child panicked when her fellow abductee's lifeless body failed to stir.

"Don't you dare die on me!" she cried out repeatedly, her ear pressed against Cali's chest, trying to listen for a heartbeat, like she had seen them do in movies. Izzie was only slightly relieved to hear a faint beat. It gave her hope.

If only she were a grown-up, she would know what else to do. She looked around the room, thinking, and ran to get a pillow from the thin foam mattress, which functioned as her bed. She put it under Cali's head, where she saw a trickle of blood oozing from an open wound. Izzie searched for something in the barren little cell to stem the blood, but their captors always brought things in for them to use and then took them away when they left. There were no towels, no bedsheets, no nothing. She dabbed at the cut with the edge of her pink tee shirt, getting blood all over her as Cali continued to bleed. Izzie banged on their prison cell door, screaming for someone to help, but no one came.

Cali's skin felt cold to the touch. Izzie instinctively knew this wasn't a good sign. There were no blankets in the cell to cover her either. Izzie wrapped her little arms and body around Cali trying to give her some of her own body warmth and vital energy.

"I need you, Cali," she implored, hugging tighter. "Don't leave me here all alone. Please, oh please, don't die!"

Izzie, who sensed minute energy shifts, suddenly became silent and still. She looked up and glanced around the cell, searching for its source. There, in the corner, she detected a faint hint of swirling energy forming. It felt strange and unreal. She didn't understand where it came from or what had caused it, only that it was becoming stronger.

The door to their cabin was suddenly thrust open and Kaggen, still masquerading as Zach, entered the room. He barely glanced at Cali bleeding on the floor, only Izzie, her tee shirt wet with smeared blood. She sat up, frightened, wondering if her life, too, was now in danger.

"Calm down," Kaggen reassured, sensing her fear. "I have a way to get you out of here."

Izzie continued to play Kaggen's stupid pretend Zach game. She pointed to Cali. "But she needs help. She's not waking up. What did they do to her?"

"They did nothing," Kaggen replied. "She fell, Izzie. Don't worry, she'll wake up soon."

"I want to go home, now, Zach!" she demanded, placing her hands on her hips. She could see the color emanating around him was colored yellow with lies and getting stronger.

Kaggen suspected the child was no longer falling for his ruse. First the screaming woman, now the petulant, defiant child. It was sorely trying his patience. "I promise you will. We're going to bring Cali home and make her well today. But first, I'm going to need your help to make this all possible."

"My help?" she asked cautiously.

Kaggen laid it out. "Yes. Satya has opened a new portal in this very room, so you can find your way out if here to the Library of Truth. It's very important you go there now and quickly. She needs you."

"Oh," Izzie uttered, somewhat confused. "What does Satya need me for?"

There was no reason the child should know what Kaggen wanted from her. The mind insertion implant buried under the skin atop her head, would compel her to do his bidding once she got there.

"She's going to take you home. Do you think you can get back to the LOT without me?" Kaggen asked, trying not to sound too hopeful.

Izzie wasn't exactly sure what Kaggen was up to, but she played along. "I think so but aren't you and Cali coming with me?" she asked.

"You must go first. Now before it's too late," Kaggen urged her. "Do you remember how?"

"I think so," she murmured.

Izzie had a very good memory. She remembered the exact number sequence she had heard Zach repeat in his head when he had taken her through the portals in the past. Whether it would also work for her, she was scared to find out. Explorers are brave and fearless, she reminded herself. She needed to be courageous and find a way to outsmart this stupid bug.

"Do it now, child!" Kaggen demanded, no longer sounding like Zach.

Izzie was determined not to leave Cali behind with this awful being. For all she knew, Cali might die if she did. She had to save her, but surely Kaggen would try to stop her. In her mind she replayed what she needed to do, hoping to make it a reality. She moved closer to Cali who lay prone on the floor, still not moving.

"Step away from her," the Mantis firmly instructed, sensing her intentions.

"But the portal energy is shifting," Izzie tried to explain. "It's not strong like the other portals. It's jumping around the room, and I need to catch it to step into it. It's very difficult."

"Try harder!" the Mantis ordered.

Under the pretense of having to pinpoint the portal's exact opening, Izzie continued to move around the room, allowing the swirling vortex energy of this new portal to surround her. Slowly she began Zach's re-entry algorithm in her head, hoping it would lead her from this artificial portal towards a primary portal into the LOT. Nothing was certain and she silently prayed to anyone who might hear her, especially Satya, to *please help me out of here*.

At the very last second, she pretended to lose her balance, falling onto Cali's body where she held on tight as they were both swept into the portal. Behind her she heard Kaggen's loud and angry curse as he lunged for them both.

Chapter 6

Meghan and he were now a team—two minds working in unison for a shared common goal. Racing against time to save her daughter, they knew it was imperative to step up their efforts. It was time to extract information from the four remaining portal locations, then attempt to pull it all together. Satya had told them as much.

Contrary to his original belief, their recent travel through the portals served to produce a positive effect on Meghan's pregnancy not a negative one. She was no longer feeling the pains and lethargy of morning sickness, but instead felt boundless new energy. During their evenings alone, Zach was teaching her Qigong postures he had been practicing for years, which she claimed was sharpening her mind and memory, something that had failed her during Izzie's pregnancy.

While he knew she did not relish living in the underground denizens of the Antarctica Base, a virtual city within a city containing all the creature comforts one would expect from a massive military operation, she accepted it. There were parks, swimming pools, gyms, procurement stores and stations, and even eateries. Security came with them everywhere, which was unavoidable in his new position. The only time they were allowed to be alone was in the late evening and early morning hours when they retired to their personal quarters. This time was used to privately explore the remaining portals, without anyone becoming any the wiser. There was information to be extracted which they hoped would provide answers to bringing Izzie safely home again.

Zach had written into the DOLARIS communication system a feedback loop he could activate which blocked their being detected on portal monitoring screens in the central communication center. It was better if no one knew they were searching portal locations for answers. Zach was sure there were spies in their midst. They would always need to take some precautionary measure. They resided on a Base that virtually never slept. Minerva powers of resistance could break out at any time of day as power always looks to usurp other power.

One early dawn morning, from within the confines of their private quarters, the two of them had their first unexplored portal experience together. Zach could tell Meghan was apprehensive. She would often chew on her bottom lip when she was plagued with uncertainty and anxiety. But as they held onto each other through portal re-entry, he felt something he hadn't expected to feel so soon—the baby quickening inside her.

His son, for he knew it would be a son, responded to the energy transfer of not only his parents but the dimensional energy change of the portal. He moved, or rather jumped, something improbable at such an early stage of fetal development. It wasn't an outright kick, but a zinging acknowledgement of his presence through Meghan and directly to his father. They both felt it. The surprised look on their faces as they landed in Portal 10 was one of disbelief.

Meghan put her hand to her stomach and affectionately patted it. "He must be a little space traveler. I think he actually liked going through the portal."

Zach knew she was right about that. "Something tells me he will be a highly unusual child," he ventured to comment. "There will be a lot of 8's in this family. Do you think Izzie will be able to keep up?"

Amusement was written in their eyes. "Oh, yeah," they laughed in unison.

This time the portal had taken them to an older library, which Meghan immediately recognized from her art history studies. They were now in the National Library of Russia in St. Petersburg, known during the reign of Catherine the Great in the 1700s as the Imperial Public Library.

"Oh, Zach, it's so beautiful," Meghan said doing a complete about circle, taking in every aspect of the medieval looking Gothic room which the portal had brought them to. The red, gold and cerulean blue painted cross vaults of the ceiling were exquisite in color and architecture.

She spoke in a hushed whisper, for fear someone might hear them. "We're standing in Faust's Study, which is part of their Rare Books Collection Room. I've seen pictures of this place. Which I would have to say don't do it justice. The design details are even more stunning in person."

Zach agreed, but while he knew Meghan would have hunkered down, wanting to explore and catalogue every nook and cranny of the room's artistic design, he had to take matters in hand. "Gizmo wants us to go this way," he pointed out, feeling an urgency to move on. Gizmo was getting hotter and that meant they were nearing the mark.

Meghan nodded. She followed his lead into an entirely different room, oval in size and nothing like the one they had just left. Their eyes were drawn to the center of the room where a bronze statue of a seated Voltaire graced a squat polished wooden pedestal.

Zach stopped, scanning the room's interior. "What we want is here somewhere. Gizmo is pulsing like mad. It's like a patterned beat."

The room was roped off with metal stanchions. A gold plaque informed them in Russian, that they were in "Voltaire's Library" and that it was closed to the general public. Zach paid no attention and moved around the barricades.

Meghan stood her ground, not sure about going forward. There was something about the restricted space that was disquieting, almost spellbound. "The other room felt like a pretty distraction meant to overlook this room," she observed.

"Exactly," Zach agreed as he slowly circled the room.

"I wonder why?" she mused aloud.

Zach moved towards bookshelves that were heavily stocked with all manner of reference books. He suspected he knew why the area was off limits. Francois Voltaire was more than just an 18th Century philosopher. He studied obscure science and mathematical works, including those of Isaac Newton and penned what were known as the "Enlightenment Writings". This was a valuable and rare collection that contained over 6800 volumes Voltaire acquired during his lifetime, contributing to some very controversial beliefs for his time. Not generally known was the fact that the man was known to write personal notations in the margins of his books, giving one an insight into his thought processes. There must be something Voltaire had written which they needed to find, or they wouldn't be here right now.

"It's somewhere," Zach said running his hand along the spines of many of the leather-bound books, hoping to get a hit on which book it was.

"What do you think it is?" Meghan asked.

Zach shrugged. "Many people don't know this, but Voltaire is considered the first sci-fi writer of all time. He wrote a short story called *Micromegas*, a philosophical tale between two celestials, or I should say alien visitors. One from Sirius, the other from Saturn, discussing how Earth was created solely for man, implying aliens were man's creators. It was referred to as 'Voltaire's Astronauts' and was not well received, to say the least."

Meghan pulled out a thin book and started paging through it. "Wasn't there a woman in the picture?"

Zach softly laughed. "There's always a woman in the picture. But this one didn't stay in the background as many women did during that time."

"Who was she?" Meghan asked.

"She was a 27-year-old mathematical prodigy by the name of Emilie, Marquisse du Chatelat, and was married to someone with peer titleage. If I recall correctly, Voltaire was a lot older when they met in 1733, but he fell madly in love with her, and they spent several years together as lovers and collaborators. He called it the most productive years of his life. The two were virtually inseparable."

Meghan came over to him and kissed him on the lips. "That's a very romantic story. Did she leave the Marquis for Voltaire?"

He shook his head. "No, she stayed with her husband. But she and Voltaire remained good friends until his death. It's believed that she may be the one who interested him in worlds beyond this world. She was well versed in Newtonian physics, which for a woman at that time was unheard of."

Meghan glanced around. "So what do you think we're looking for here? Something of hers or something of his?"

Maybe both. He didn't know. He would have to rely on Gizmo pointing him in the right direction. "Show us what we need to know," he instructed the AI device.

Gizmo instantly shot a red beam right past the top of Meghan's head, to a section of book shelving that contained a small empty gap between the books.

"But there's nothing there," Meghan pointed out.

Zach stared at it, frowning. "I think there is. We just can't see it. There's a number '11' floating around between the books." Zach set Gizmo down and reached up. Carefully he moved his hand around the entire open space. "I can't feel it Meghan, but I know it's here." He picked Gizmo back up and pointed it at the empty spot. "Disengage object cloaking," he instructed.

A slim red bound book suddenly emerged, bearing no title. They both saw it as it fell over onto the shelf that held it. Meghan reached for it immediately and opened it. It contained only blank pages.

"There's nothing written inside," she said, clearly disappointed.

Zach's eyes lit up. "I see numbers spewing out of it, which means there are thoughts and ideas on those supposedly empty pages."

Zach ran Gizmo over the blank pages. Handwritten script lettering slowly bled through each page he opened. Meghan gasped in surprise, watching the inked words reveal themselves.

"Is it a diary?" she asked, breathlessly.

It was written in French, one of six languages Zach knew. "Not quite," he said, riffling through the pages. "It appears to be a scientific journal. There're two distinct handwriting styles throughout the pages. One has to be Voltaire's. The other one feels more feminine. It might be Emilie's."

Meghan, who had learned French in school, began translating. They both slid down to the inlaid wooden floor, huddled next to each other, while they began reading. Instantly they realized this was not a scientific journal at all, but a woman's personal diary.

"Oh, my God," Meghan said, repeating a particular phrase aloud. "She admits it right here. I can't believe what I'm reading. Can this be true?"

Zach was already ahead of her. Truth would always be stranger than fiction. Emilie, Marquisse du Chatelat, had admitted a disturbing little detail in her diary, one which she had only shared with Voltaire and was never meant to be divulged. Her bizarre secret was that at the age of eight Emilie had met an unusual creature who she claimed came from the stars. Her description of the being, who resembled "a giant praying mantis," would become her mentor. It was this being that turned her towards the study of physics and the universe. This was the knowledge that she would eventually share with Voltaire, allowing him to take scientific credit for what she had been told by the being about the world beyond.

Zach scanned ahead. "This diary also details her findings of the Mantis beings and other races that were revealed to her."

Meghan's eyes grew wide. "So it was Emilie who inspired Voltaire to write his *Micromegas* story about aliens from another world. I wonder if Voltaire ever met this Mantis being as well?" Meghan's thoughts were racing. "Oh, my God, Zach. This all makes crazy sense."

Zach wasn't seeing it the same way. He thrived on definitive facts and data. "It's interesting, but I'm not sure how this is supposed to help us?" he mumbled aloud. "It definitely tells *a* story. But is it *the* story we came here to find? If it is, what facts are we missing?"

Meghan liked that Zach had used the "we" word. They felt like a "we" now. Never in a million years would she have thought meeting Zach Eldridge would propel her into a strange new world, the likes of the one she now found herself in. She rather liked it. Together they would find a way to bring Izzie back. Perhaps the diary was the key.

Lights from an overhead crystal chandelier turned on, taking them by complete surprise. It had to be close to opening time and employees would soon be filtering through to their departmental posts. There wasn't much time left.

"We've got to take this with us," Zach whispered, quickly closing the book. He scrambled to his feet, extending a hand to help her up.

"C'mon. Let's get out of here!" he said, clutching the diary to his chest.

"But what about the Golden Minerva?" Meghan reminded him. "Zach, we need to find it and bring it back."

Damn it. He had forgotten about the statue and knew she was right. They might not get another opportunity again like this one. Perhaps there was still time. He would have to bypass Gizmo this time. He couldn't take the chance of an earthquake striking this library or the City of St. Petersburg, possibly causing massive damage, if he left retrieval up to Gizmo. There had to be another way.

He would see if he could tap into the Mind of the Library of Truth and ask for help. When he did, he visually saw a three-dimensional holographic layout of the library building, along with all its many levels. The schematic radiated numbers detailing the sizing of each room and gallery along with its cubic space. Numbers floated around every book that resided in the Russian archive. Zach's eyes scanned each nook on every floor until he spotted two side-by-side glowing number eights telling him where he and Meghan were in what he knew to be Voltaire's Library room.

Two floors below them was a glowing number 10, marking the Golden Minerva's designated portal number. Zach got his bearings and looked around. "This way," he instructed, grabbing Meghan's hand and turning them to their right.

Zach led her through various reading rooms, down narrow iron-railed spiral stairwells, until his holographic directions told him to stop. He pushed through a closed door into the Russian library's closed stacks. He and Meghan stopped dead in their tracks. This stacks was the exact mirror image of the closed stacks in the Library of Congress where Zach worked.

"It can't be, can it?" Meghan breathed, clearly as dumbfounded as he. "Are we back in the Library of Congress?"

"I don't know," he said, walking down the long aisles of bookshelves, taking stock of everything he saw. It looked the same, even felt the same. He continued forward, rounding a sharp corner and headed towards the back of the stacks where he knew his desk would be tucked away in his Library back home. That's when things turned stranger.

Beside him, Meghan gasped. Sitting at a similar workstation was another Zach, a real in-the-flesh copy, quite possibly a clone, who was professionally dressed in a dark suit and tie working away on a desk computer. He immediately looked up upon hearing their approach. This Zach didn't seem the least bit surprised to see his twin self, in all his uncertainty and puzzlement, standing in front of him. In fact, he smiled enthusiastically, rose from his chair, displaying a similar height, and came forward to welcome Zach in Russian.

"Oh my God. Is this a parallel reality?" Meghan whispered under her breath. These were his thoughts precisely.

Zach found himself staring at the person who looked too much like him to be mere coincidence. Scanning his countenance, he desperately searched for physical differences, subtle variations, that would differentiate them from each other but found none that were obvious. His mathematical mind couldn't help but calculate the astronomical odds of this being a long-lost biological twin he didn't know about. It didn't make sense. He knew he wasn't adopted. Nor would his parents have allowed an Eldridge heir, especially a second son, to be given away.

Zach struggled with how to react to this new development which defied his sense of logic. He reminded himself that Gizmo had led him to this spot to retrieve the statue, not stand there and gawk at his doppelganger. Right. He gathered his wits and told the man in Russian that he was here to retrieve the library's Golden Minerva statue.

Without question, his twin simply nodded then did something even more bizarre. He bent his head over slightly and parted his hair to reveal an "8" infinity birthmark imprinted on his scalp. Standing beside him, he heard Meghan's barely audible gasp, yet she remained silent waiting to see what Zach would do next.

The birthmark was exactly like his own. He knew it; she knew it. But he gave no visible indication of its significance, despite his curiosity. His twin watched his non-reaction before gesturing for Zach to show his own. The simple request caught him off guard. How did his twin know he was also identically marked? He hesitated then finally shrugged. If it meant getting answers, then so be it. Zach hung his head and displayed his own birthmark located in the exact same spot. His twin smiled and nodded his approval, not the least bit surprised. It felt like they were exchanging some secret club handshake.

"What's your name?" Zach wanted to know.

"Endre Zegorov," his twin replied. "We were not given the same name, Zachary Eldridge. Does that surprise you?" he added.

Nothing surprised Zach anymore. Not even the fact that Endre knew his name. It did not escape his notice that his twin had the same initials he had, only reversed. His mind returned to the question of 'not given the same name'. By whom? Before he could voice this inquiry, Endre turned quickly and motioned for them to follow him.

Together, the three of them moved deeper into the stacks. It became a déjà vu experience for Zach. It was exactly like being back in the LOC stacks in Washington, D.C., not St. Petersburg. It all felt so familiar, yet he had never been to the Russian library. How could both places be such exact replicas? The laws of coincidence made it an improbability.

Endre's steps came to an abrupt stop in front of a tall metal bookshelf filled with storage inventory boxes. There was an empty space on the very top shelf. Seconds later a box appeared on that same shelf. His eyes darted back to Endre to see how he had accomplished this fete. Zach had not given Gizmo the command to uncloak anything, yet in Endre's world it seemed to happen without AI assistance.

He patiently observed Endre bring down a file box slightly larger than the one Zach had hidden in the LOC containing his own artifacts. Endre motioned them again to follow him. Silently, they returned to his workstation where he opened the box and proudly invited them to examine the contents. What they saw astounded them. Inside were five Golden Minerva statues, all lined up neatly in a row.

Meghan immediately turned over each statue to identify its markings. "He has Minerva 2, 4, 6, 7, and 10," she reported. "This is incredible!"

This other Zach had clearly been a lot busier. He, himself, had only retrieved three thus far. Zach knew he had statues "5" from the Bodleian, "8" from the Sakya Monastery, and "9" from the Ruins of Baalbek and, of course the ones still in place at the LOC and Antarctica. Two were still missing, despite having visited 10 portal locations so far.

He asked Endre where his five statues had come from and learned "2" was from the Great Pyramid of Giza; "4" from the Vatican Secret Archives; "6" from Haleakala; "7" from Lake Titicaca; and "10" from his own National Library of Russia. These Minerva's were all from portals Zach had visited but failed to retrieve.

Zach didn't know what to make of having a double in some parallel reality working with him, or in this case working even harder than him. Yet, upon questioning he was able to verify that they were both striving towards the same common goal—to obtain all the Minerva statues in order to close the 12 portals.

Endre revealed this was a job he had always known he was supposed to do. No one had told him so. Zach also found this extremely strange. If this was the case, it appeared as if the universe had hedged its bets. Could Endre be someone he had unconsciously created, or had someone else inserted Endre into the mix to guarantee his own success? And if so, whom?

Upon closing the box, Endre hugged him enthusiastically like a long-lost brother. When he finished, he proudly handed the box of Minerva's over to Zach. "These are yours," Endre told him. "You should go now. They will know you have these new statues in your possession."

Zach stayed his ground. "Who will know?" he questioned. "Endre, I need to know everything you know."

"You are close, my brother," he replied, before adding in Russian. "You will discover this with time. Everything is as it should be. Now go with God."

It was not the definitive answer he was seeking. Endre's words clearly implied he knew more than he was willing to say. How would he know he was close? Close to what? Despite his frustration with his twin, he felt an unusual kinship. Zach nodded and thanked him profusely in his native tongue. "I'll be back," he informed him, putting aside the box to return a final departing hug.

Meghan, who had been incredulously watching this exchange between the two Zachs and trying to wrap her head around the unexpected sight at the same time, now came over and hugged Endre as well. "Thank you," she murmured with a smile of gratitude, before planting a quick kiss on his lips. "For everything."

Zach looked on feeling a twinge of jealousy at her open demonstration of affection. It was an odd feeling for him to experience--one he had never felt before about any woman. The thought of sharing Meghan even with a twin self, was somewhat unsettling. It was a crazy thought. He chastised himself for this sudden feeling of possessiveness. He said nothing, but Meghan saw the look on his face and threw her arms around his neck, kissing him passionately. Unlike Endre, he returned it in in kind so there was no doubt in her mind, that she was his.

"Don't worry, love," she murmured, for his ears only. "You're a much better kisser." She turned, picked up their box and started walking towards the re-entry point. "C'mon. Let's take these statues home."

He silently followed, knowing he would follow her anywhere.

~~*~~

Izzie felt a strong force trying to pull Cali back to their prison cell. Her mind felt muddled, like someone or something was inside her head trying to tell her to what to think and do. And they wanted, no demanded, she let go of Cali, NOW. It hurt like hell to go against the voice, but Izzie fought it, trying to push it out of her thoughts. She clung to Cali as if her life depended upon it.

"NO, NO, NO," she screamed hysterically. "You can't have her! Get out of my head!"

For the briefest second, she felt its hold over her weaken, and knew it was a battle of wills. Hers against theirs. Over and over, like a mantra, she repeated, "I won't let you."

Izzie was smart enough to realize Kaggen was somehow inside her head trying to control her. She managed to wall off mental access to Zach's Library of Truth algorithm, fearing the big bug would learn that secret and follow her. The sheer energy it took for her to do that only served to weaken her battle against the mind control grip placed on her. It moved right back in with a vengeance, trying to paralyze her arms. Yet she never let go of Cali, determined to fight no matter what. She pleaded for help from anyone who could hear her. When that didn't happen, anger overtook her, sending adrenaline coursing through her veins. She began cursing like her dead grandfather had taught her, not caring who heard such bad words.

Satya heard her desperate pleas. Izzie was stuck somewhere in a portal in a push and pull death grip. Satya immediately acted. Like a beacon of light Satya zeroed in, putting up a black wall of protection behind them, allowing Izzie and an unconscious Cali to move quickly into the Library of Truth.

"Get this thing out of my head!" Izzie shouted, holding both hands over the top of her skull. "It hurts!"

Not knowing how she did it, Satya reached into Izzie's head and extracted something the size of a small grain of rice. It was like plucking out a baby's tooth. Izzie felt a small prick of pain and then it was gone, along with the bump on her head, leaving her exhausted and tired beyond belief.

"Thank you," was all she could mutter, before slipping to the floor next to Cali and falling into the deep sleep that Kaggen had denied her.

~~*~~

The portal return from the National Russian Library was noticeably different. It was considerably slower than on previous occasions, as if there was some unknown obstruction in its path affecting its regular swift flow. Meghan and Zach realized it immediately. And now the portal spun them around in reverse. Instead of taking them back to Antarctica it took them straight to the LOT where the first thing they saw was Izzie lying on the floor, not moving, with blood stains on her clothes, alongside an even more bloodied Cali Cavaleri.

Satya was kneeling between them, her hands placed on both their heads, her eyes closed. Meghan screamed, running over to her daughter to take her into her arms—checking for a pulse. Zach's heart skipped a beat at the unsettling sight before them and looked to Satya for an explanation.

"Both are alive and will be fine," Satya immediately informed. "They should wake shortly but will need plenty of healing rest." She addressed her next words to Meghan. "Izzie was a very brave little warrior. She found a way to escape Kaggen. He cannot reach her here."

Meghan heard her words, but nevertheless continued moving her hands all over Izzie looking for the source of the blood.

"She used her shirt to stop Cali's head wound," Satya explained. "She's tired more than anything else. It was an ordeal for her and showed her true level of strength. I've done my best to ease her memories."

"And Cali?" Zach asked, kneeling over her inert body.

Satya's mind continued to scan for additional damage. "Kaggen struck her head. The cut was rather deep. When Izzie brought her here, she was already unconscious, and her brain had swelled." She placed her hand back on Cali's head. "Any internal damage should now be gone. I've seen to that."

Satya stood, signaling an unusual impatience for one so stoic. "Kaggen has over-stepped his reach. It's best that you take them both back with you, now, and let me deal with the rest."

Zach handed over the box of Minerva statues to her. "I'll be back for these." And with that he gently scooped up Cali in his arms, cradling her head, while Meghan tightly clutched Izzie to her breast. Together the four returned to Antarctica not knowing what to expect next.

Eric Kline had gone from writing Hollywood who-done-its, to living one. He would never have thought himself a superstitious man, but something had happened out there in the ocean that fateful day signaling to him that his idyllic time with Cali was coming to an end. Call it a sign, or an omen, but something had badly spooked the pod of sea turtles he had been snorkeling with that was difficult to explain. They went from graceful, playful antics to erratic behavior where they were crashing into each other, swimming upside down—just bizarre maneuvers he had never witnessed before—nor had anyone else in attendance. He emerged from the water only to catch snippets of beachgoers recounting a sighting of a large UFO over the Wailea shoreline. Some were even calling it an "alien mother ship".

Eric suddenly had this weighty premonition that he needed to get to Cali immediately. Just throw your things in the car and hurry back to the hotel before it's too late, he told himself. Too late for what, his cognitive brain questioned? There was no answer to this irrational fear he was profoundly experiencing. An inner struggle between his conscious and unconscious mind took hold. His unconscious self was telling him someone or something was closing in on Cali. He knew she had some extremely shady characters who wanted her eliminated for the truthful reporting she had done exposing global human trafficking, but a part of him was still fantasizing that he could protect and keep her safe.

He checked his cell phone before pulling out of beach parking and saw she had left a message saying she was going to an AA support meeting at Kamaole 3 in Kihei. Good, he thought. She would be around lots of people, maybe even some big Tongan/Samoan guys who would deter any potential trouble. But she had still not returned by the time he arrived back at the Grand Wailea Resort. Impatient, he went looking for her but could find no trace of her anywhere.

It was too early to call in the police regarding a missing person. They would blow him off anyway. Eric knew something was wrong, but to report it to the authorities might tip off and alert those very elements who wanted Cali dead. He was torn as to what to do. They might have already gotten to her, and he would never know her fate. Sweat dripped down his brow as fear crept in.

After only two weeks of living together, Eric had found himself growing attached to Cali Cavaleri—both personally and professionally. She was gutsy and mouthy, but she inspired something in him that wanted to write outside the box. The script they had been collaborating on about ZLOT being her deep throat Washington, D.C., connection was pure dynamite. The political mayhem and murder that had ensued from her reporting information was writer's gold. Eric had no doubt it would sell bigtime in Hollywood. But more importantly, Cali made him feel alive again and he didn't want to lose that feeling or her. He had to find her.

It dawned on him to check on the whereabouts of her rental car. When he realized it was still in hotel parking and she had probably never left for her AA meeting, he really began to panic. He made the rounds of the hotel, showing everyone the last picture he had taken of her. The one of her smiling in her sexy little yellow string bikini. There were some employees who remembered seeing her near the beach. It didn't give him much to go with. There were no reports of shark attacks or drownings, or even a paddling accident. He had checked with hospitals and found there were no females or Jane Does matching her description. Instead, all he heard was talk about that strange UFO that appeared in the sky over the beach that day. People could talk of nothing else. Already the place was filling with media hoping for a return sighting.

Eric became frantic, not knowing if the UFO had any connection at all to Cali's disappearance, strange as that sounded. All her new clothes were still in their hotel room, but her purse and phone were missing. When he tried to call her, it continued to go straight to voicemail then stopped working altogether. The telltale sign that something bad must have happened was that she had left behind her computer, all her notes—and even her secret "I hide it in my bra" USB drive. That didn't bode well. As a hardcore reporter, preserving information was everything to Cali. That, he knew for certain. The only thing left to consider was she had met up with foul play.

As the days passed, with still no word, he checked to see if she had booked any flights, commercial or private. Nothing. That's when he finally called in the Maui Police, who were adept at giving speeding tickets on Piilani Highway to lead-footed tourists, but not highly skilled in investigating possible abduction and/or murder cases.

Eric knew he was on his own when it came to solving Cali's disappearance. He was running out of time. Soon his month vacation stay in Hawaii would come to an end and he would have to return home to Santa Monica. He had work obligations awaiting him there as well as several pitch meetings his agent had arranged for him and Cali's in-progress spec script.

The vacation that had become a fairytale dream come true had quickly turned into a never-ending nightmare of uncertainty and unanswered questions. His muse, his inspiration, his hotter than hot lover who he really liked and cared about, was gone. Eric didn't even want to entertain the possibility it might be forever.

~~*~~

Cali crawled her way back up to consciousness. A small hand was gently stroking her temple, smoothing her hair back, while little whispers could be heard in her ear telling her the bugs were gone and she could come out now. Cali opened her eyes to see Izzie kneeling on the floor next to the bed she was lying on. Izzie's eyes lit up as Cali's fluttered open. The child called excitedly for her mother, who came running.

Cali quickly glanced around. She noted she was no longer in her cabin prison. "Where am I?" she asked, nervously.

Meghan came to stand beside Izzie. "You're somewhere safe. Away from Kaggen."

Cali panicked, scrambling up against the wall. "It's a trick, isn't it? You're gaslighting me again! You're Kaggen, aren't you?!" She felt herself trembling. Who could she believe? She had been fooled once before and so effectively.

Izzie spoke up. "It's really me, Cali! We escaped through the portal into the Library of Truth where Satya healed your head."

Meghan nodded in confirmation. "That's true. Izzie really did save you."

Cali reached up to probe her head. The pain was no longer there. The last thing she remembered was being struck to the side of her head, then blacking out. Kaggen had done that after playing verbal judo with her. And now there was no sign of injury.

"And this Satya healed me?" she asked, wanting clarification.

Izzie smiled. "Oh yes. Satya can do anything. She took that thing out of my head, too. It was no bigger than a pea in a pod, just like the princess in the fairytale."

Meghan sat down on the bed next to her. "We understand that both of you have been through a lot. Izzie will stay here with Zach and me where she will be protected. You are welcome to stay here as well or return to Maui at any time through the Haleakala portal. It's your choice, of course."

Cali stifled a terrifying thought. "Won't that creature come back and try to get me there again?!"

Meghan reached for Cali's left hand, where a strange grey metal band, devoid of markings, now encircled her wrist. "Satya has instructed you wear this," she told Cali, showing a duplicate one being worn on Izzie's wrist.

"Just like Gizmo," Izzie chimed in.

Cali had no idea who or what this "Gizmo" was Izzie was referring to.

"It's Mantis technology," Meghan explained. "Wear it and it will thwart any future extraction attempts by one of their space crafts. However, right now Kaggen is in another galaxy, and highly unlikely to be coming for you from there."

Well, that was a relief. Cali sighed, trying to figure out her next move. Eric must be out of his freaking mind wondering what happened to her. But the reporter in her craved more information. Her memory recall was still fuzzy.

"Where am I really?" she asked Meghan, reaching for her hand.

Meghan took it and patted it reassuringly. She glanced towards Izzie, exchanging a knowing look. "I can't tell you, which is for your own good. It's an unknown place, not easily accessible, and for a very good reason. Just know that you're safe here."

Cali wasn't ready to accept Meghan's non-answer. Would the kid spill the beans? She looked to Izzie, who leaned into her mother, who then put her arm around her daughter and drew her close. Izzie remained tight-lipped. Apparently, she had already been warned not to say a word.

"And where is Zach?" Cali finally asked, breaking the silence.

"He's waiting to take you back, if you're ready," Meghan replied.

Not so fast, Cali thought. While she had a ton of questions about how Little Betsy Ross had managed to carry out their incredible escape, it really annoyed her that she had been passed out and had never seen this Satya woman who had healed her, or the Library of Truth she supposedly ruled over. And damn it—

she had been through the portals twice now in an unconscious state. If nothing else, she wanted to be wide awake and alert the next time through.

Cali finally nodded. "I need to get word to someone first."

~~*~~

Eric Kline nervously waited at the summit of Haleakala, where he had first met Cali Cavaleri only a few short weeks ago. But in that time, she had managed to change his life in unanticipated ways. There was never a dull moment with this woman. Her mind was like a sponge. Her curiosity intense, and her passion—well, that was another matter altogether.

Then less than 12 hours ago he had finally gotten word that Cali was still alive and coming for him. The instructions had been rather cryptic. He needed to collect everything at the hotel, leaving nothing of theirs behind and meet her on this cold desolate mountaintop at a designated time. She told him to trust her, not to ask questions, and that she would see him very soon. That was good enough for him. He could barely contain his relief and excitement at hearing her voice again.

Call him crazy, but while everyone else was coming down the mountain after watching a spectacular purple red Haleakala sunset, Eric's car service was dropping him off. He tipped his driver generously, telling him he was meeting friends who would be along shortly and that it was alright to leave him there.

It was freezing cold up on the summit and the parking area was nearly deserted except for a few stray tourists. Eric shoved his hands deeper into the pockets of his jacket hoping to stay warm as he continued to scan the area. His anticipation mounted. All Cali had said was that he would suddenly see her, as if coming out of nowhere. He wasn't sure what to make of that. It sounded strange, but still he waited and watched.

Finally, he observed the last car depart, leaving him totally alone on top of the world, not a soul in sight. Above him he could see every star in the cold nighttime sky. The beginnings of a new moon overhead, devoid of light, made the summit seem even darker. It was downright eerie. His breath came out in little wisps of steam. He walked around to keep the blood moving to his extremities. And then he saw her, just like she had said, coming out of the veiled darkness of the night and walking right towards him. There was a man behind her, who stopped and let her go on ahead towards him.

"Miss me?" she said, wrapping her arms around his neck and kissing him.

"Fuck, yes!" he said, kissing her right back. She threw back her head and laughed in only the way she could laugh. Totally full of life, like her.

"Get ready," she warned with a sly grin. "I'm going to take you for a wild ride you'll never forget."

Chapter 7

Kaggen had underestimated the child. He had not thought Izzie strong enough to thwart him, which made him even more suspicious of her intended role in his plans. If she had access into the LOT, then she had an advantage over him and this he could not and would not tolerate. Letting the screaming woman and the child slip through his hands, thereby losing his hostage bargaining power, now meant he would have to take more drastic measures.

The Mantis commander still had human-hybrid spies operating on the Base reporting back to him that security safeguards had been stepped up around the new Minerva Governor, as well as the child and her mother. The DOLARIS system that controlled all Base operations, had been quickly altered by Zachary and over-riding it was now a more challenging task to penetrate. However, Kaggen saw this as a minor obstacle. He and his kind were technologically superior and didn't have to work around such roadblocks but were quite capable of blasting right through them whenever they chose.

Zachary Eldridge had clearly conveyed through intermediary channels that the Mantis demands would not be met and that all underground Mantis laboratories had been burned. He warned them off from ever returning.

Kaggen found the lad's silly demands rather amusing. Prior to departure his people had made sure that nothing of true value had been left behind revealing thousands of years of research and experimentation. The hybridization secrets would stay with them so that no human ever truly understood their invasive methods.

But rumors abounded--some disturbing in nature. Young Zachary had stepped up his efforts to close the Library of Truth's 12 universal portals, as well as the Sun portal. Did he not realize this would have serious and vast cosmic repercussions? The Sun portal was the superhighway for all space vehicle connections and personnel coming and going throughout the multiverse. A reliable, stable, and non-flux conduit for high-energy particles, this portal was the lifeblood to alien intergalactic space travel. There were, of course, the fluctuating local-based wormholes and portals scattered throughout space which opened and closed without warning every eight minutes. But using them required exact calculations to avoid becoming swallowed up in the cosmos. They were nothing in comparison to the all-powerful Sun portal.

Last night the Oracle had confirmed Zachary's destructive intent. In the quiet denizens of his quarters, Kaggen had brought forth the glowing cube and let the euphoric violet rays of information flood through his eyes into conscious awareness. He did not like what he saw at all. The new Governor was quickly amassing Minerva statues that had been well hidden for tens of thousands of years. Kaggen knew exactly what this meant. The binding spell on the gatekeeper statue had somehow been broken.

The lad was still under the misguided assumption that the 12 portals only accessed Earth locations and the Library of Truth. But they were so much more. They influenced the universal timelines as well. Kaggen realized he was now in a race against time, or his world and others would cease to exist.

~~*~~

Zach made an evening portal run from the LOT to the LOC to hide the five Golden Minerva statues Endre had gifted him. They weren't safe at the Base where eyes and ears watched his every move, hoping to trip him up. He suspected that there were new covert factions already forming to dispose of him after he had slowed down the trickle of money being illegally funneled to their worldwide cartel operations. His plan had been to choke them off, stall until he had a better plan, but their tentacles were vast and insidious and easily replaceable. It appeared to be a losing battle with time. Which was one more reason to keep the Minerva statues cloaked in the closed stacks of the LOC, away from spying eyes at the Base, who would be only too happy to destroy them.

As for the Minerva statue displayed in the upper balcony of the Members of Congress Reading Room, he would leave where it was until needed. When he retrieved it, its absence was sure to cause a firestorm of scrutiny. It was the last thing he needed.

He had reservations about leaving Meghan and Izzie in Antarctica, despite the fact that they were heavily guarded. Their quarters were swept several times a day for surveillance bugs and initially they had located two. Which meant he was not being paranoid about there being eyes and ears everywhere. There was no place safe to go anymore, except the LOT, but it would mean leaving this world behind, perhaps forever.

Last night he and Meghan had taken a hot steaming bath, just for some much-needed privacy time away from prying eyes. Izzie was being understandably clingier after escaping her ordeal on the SolarVector7. She couldn't stop talking about how Kaggen had tried to trick her by shapeshifting into someone who looked and sounded exactly like Zach. While he knew of the

Mantis' adept ability to shapeshift, he hadn't foreseen that his likeness might be used as a weapon to trick her.

The kid was so proud that the ploy hadn't fooled her one little bit. Zach had to admit he was somewhat in awe that she had managed to escape by not only using her wits but by mentally recalling his exact LOT portal sequence. It was unsettling that he hadn't even known she had memorized the algorithm from tapping into and listening to his thoughts. He couldn't help worrying for her. There was always the possibility she might try to use the sequence again and find herself in deeper trouble. Sometimes there was just no stopping her once her mind was made up--kind of like her mother.

Meghan had checked on Izzie about an hour ago and she was still all wound up like a clock spring. It took her daughter a while to verbally process her abduction before eventually settling down. They knew it would be the first of many retellings, despite Satya having eased Izzie's memories of the painful implant struggle. They waited it out, letting her talk, until she drifted off to sleep, finally leaving them alone. Wasting no time, they escaped to the bathroom, shed their clothes, and eased into the soothing waters of a jetted hot tub.

Meghan sat back, nestling against his chest, feeling his arms wrap around her. She rested her head in the crook of his neck. They both slid down deeper into the hot water and sighed. He lived for these stolen moments with her. What would their lives have been like if they had met under different circumstances? If only they could have dated like normal couples did.

"We can't stay here forever," Meghan finally said. He knew what she meant. "Is there any place we can go that's safe for all of us?"

Zach had already given it some thought. Antarctica felt like an underground prison despite it hiding a massive city serving the needs of thousands of personnel. How his father had endured here for so long was a mystery to him. While Base personnel were provided underground leisure space, with colorful foliaged parks, simulated domed sunlight and vented air to feel the wind on their face, it was still not the same. It was all an illusion, like the world at large. Outside was a cold, harsh reality. They existed in a frozen land at the very bottom of a frozen continent where no man wanted to dwell for long.

"I don't know where we *can* go," he truthfully admitted. "I was hoping to talk with Satya about finding a viable solution."

Meghan lightly ran her fingers down his arms, lost in thought. "Izzie asked me again if we could all go live in Pink Heaven with someone named Caleb," she said. "I didn't want to disappoint her and tell her 'No' after all she's been through, so instead I said I would think about it and ask you."

They both knew Izzie's wish was an impossible one. She desperately wanted a playmate and to have fun like any normal kid, even though she wasn't the least bit normal by anyone's standards.

They silently remained locked in thought. The bath water was now cooling down and he felt a slight shiver run through her. She was the first to stand up, giving him a full display of her naked beauty. He reluctantly rose to his feet, grabbed a nearby towel and wrapped her snugly in it, before toweling himself down.

"I was looking through Emilie's diary today," she said, taking his hand. "Come, let me show you what I found."

She led him over to their bed, where she extracted from under her pillow the diary they had brought back from Voltaire's Library. Together they crawled into bed and burrowed under the covers. Meghan opened the diary to a page she had bookmarked and began translating.

"Emilie says here that she met a strange Mantis-like creature when she was only eight years old who would appear from time to time outside her bedroom window. At first it scared her, and she had nightmares, but then the creature started to leave her little gifts on her windowsill. Unusual rock specimens of incredible colors, some which even glowed in the dark. It entranced and captivated her. These visitations went on for many years into adulthood and no sooner did she see the creature than she would fall into a deep dream-filled sleep."

Meghan continued reading. "She says that in these dreams she would sometimes find herself onboard a 'ship that flew through the Sun' to the deepest corners of space.

Zach had a bad feeling where this was going. "Does it say how long these visitations lasted?"

Meghan scanned the page. "Yes. She says here that they stopped after she miscarried and married 'Claude'."

Zach frowned. "What came first, losing the child or marrying the Marquis?"

Meghan didn't answer at first, then groaned. "Oh, wow. She says she had never 'lain with a man before' but suddenly found herself with child at the age of 19. Her parents immediately married her off in 1725 to the Marquis Florent-Claude de Chatelet-Lomont, a naval officer. She miscarried shortly after the arranged marriage and her new husband was none the wiser."

Meghan stopped reading and turned to Zach. "Do you think the Mantis being impregnated her with a human-hybrid?"

"If he did, it was just as well that it didn't survive," he replied. "If I recall correctly, Emilie was very intelligent. She didn't want to marry but instead devote her life to the study of science. This was not something women were encouraged to do at that time in history. I'm not surprised with her intellect that she showed up on Mantis radar as being a viable host for their kind."

Zach took the French diary and paged ahead, translating as he went. "She says here that there were many times where she learned scientific concepts overnight and would awake the next morning filled with new and sometimes 'outlandish' sounding understandings of the mathematics of the universe."

He paused, thinking. "Now that's pretty cool. However, without her we wouldn't know that energy equals mass times velocity squared or that light travels as a wave. Apparently, she knew these advanced concepts at a much earlier age than when she shared them later in life with the rest of the world. I'm sure this is what attracted the older Voltaire to her. She was brilliant and shared with him all she knew and understood. If I recall correctly, she died at the age of 42 in childbirth, still married to the Marquis, so Voltaire had plenty of time to reveal some of her ideas long after she died. He lived to the ripe old age of 83."

"But he took credit for some of her knowledge about other worlds and alien races. Even beings from Saturn," Meghan pointed out.

Zach shook his head. "Women's ideas were not taken seriously during that time. She would have been laughed at and called a fool."

He continued reading. "When Emilie realized all this incredible science was coming through to her from the Mantis being she allowed it to continue, actually thrived on it. She admits she came to look forward to it for answers to all things. Then it changed."

"How?" Meghan asked.

Zach paused scanning ahead. "She talks here about there being a special connection between her and the Mantis being of student to mentor," he explained. "But then she relates an incident at the age of 19 when an unusual exchange of 'charged energy' shot from him to her right before he departed. It rocked her body and felt like a force was consuming her. She must have blacked out, because she found herself back in her bed as if nothing had happened. But she knew something had because her body was still shaking from the incident. It was immediately after this occurred that she mysteriously came to be with child yet was still a virgin."

Meghan's eyes grew wide. "Oh my gosh. How awful that must have been for her."

Zach sighed. "Wait. It gets weirder. Emilie didn't believe it was intentional, but when this energy exchange happened some of the creature's memory was also transmitted to her. She learned that the being was once human and then somehow became Mantis, which he never explained. She called him…"

Zach stopped, now understanding why he was meant to find and read this diary. "She called the Mantis being, 'Nehemiah'."

"Like the Minerva File's 'Nehemiah'?" Meghan whispered in astonishment. "The same one who disappeared into the multiverse, never to be found?"

Zach wasn't sure. It was merely speculation that they might be one and the same, but the synchronicity of coming into contact with this hidden diary and revealing these truths, had to be more than just coincidence. His silence spoke volumes to her.

"What are you thinking?" she finally prompted.

He turned to her and kissed her. "I think it's time we got some sleep. Tomorrow we can start looking at all the information we've gathered and try to work out a more detailed plan."

But no sooner did Meghan fall asleep then Zach was back at the diary devouring the entirety of its contents. Emilie's shared memory with Nehemiah had helped her to understand the

Mantis' vulnerabilities as well. Intense light was like a death ray to them. Certain sound frequencies were unbearable for them to hear and experience. Sensitivities to specific spectrums of light and sound plagued them, which is why they preferred living in dark quiet underground places, away from the intense rays of Earth's Sun. The more he read, the more Zach understood.

Had his father even known that the Mantis wore protective black lenses to hide their laser like red eyes? Or that they could shapeshift into any form? The most astounding realization was that they had some type of biological circuitry under their left shoulder, almost Bluetooth in nature, which they were born with which enabled them to silently communicate with others of their kind. Zach recalled observing Kaggen resting his hand on another Mantis' left shoulder, saying nothing, but exchanging a knowing look. It had appeared strange at the time. Now he understood. Disabling this biological circuitry could be one way to cut them off from their hive mind communication.

All this information Emilie had documented in her diary and entrusted to Voltaire upon her death. Just to him, no one else, which is how it came to be a part of Voltaire's Library collection in Russia. How it had become cloaked and inaccessible was still a mystery.

Zach searched through the pages Emilie had penned hoping to learn what had happened to the strange creature she called "Nehemiah". Had he died after disappearing? Or was he still alive somewhere, working behind the scenes? He had never thought to ask Ishannika what had become of Nehemiah after escaping through the Sun portal and secreting *The Minerva Files* deep underground in the hidden lake on the desolate dwarf planet of Nordekka. He had been too energetically spent after connecting the strands of numerical information that protected the secrets hidden within the nucleus of the cache to do what he did best—connect the dots.

Zach glanced over to where Meghan was fast asleep, the look of serene repose on her face made him pause to drink in her beauty. He still couldn't believe his good fortune that she had chosen him above all the others she could have so easily had. And she would be the mother of his child, a son. The thought filled him with wonder and trepidation.

He quietly got up from the corner desk in their bedroom and went to check on Izzie in the next room. It was the middle of the night and he was surprised to see that she was up and wide awake, dressed in jeans and her signature pink top. She sat on the edge of her bed, a large sketch pad propped up on her lap, using a red magic marker and making large broad strokes across the page.

"I've been waiting for you," she said looking up from her drawing. "Grandpa says you've got to stop..." she hesitated, not sure if she should say it. "He says to stop 'fucking around and get moving.' I'm sorry I used that "F" word, but Grandpa insisted 'I say it like it is.' And please don't tell Mommy I said that bad word."

Nothing surprised him anymore. Senator James Talbot was back again to sending messages from his grave to his psychic granddaughter. Zach felt like he was being pulled in every which direction with people alive and dead telling him what to do and what still needed to be done. "Okay, Izzie. I won't tell your Mom. Anything else Grandpa told you?"

She held up her sketch pad, displaying what looked like a large vial of blood, her red marker having filled it to the top, showing it spilling over. Seeing it unnerved him. It was scary stuff for a seven-year-old to be drawing. This was no place for a kid to be. He didn't know what to say. There were three twisted black ribbons in the vial, almost like intertwined snakes. Zach sat down on the edge of the bed next to her. "What are those?" he asked pointing to the black strands, hoping it wasn't as sinister as it looked.

Izzie examined them more closely. "I don't know. Grandpa showed me this picture in his head so I drew it."

"Is your grandpa still here with you now?" he cautiously asked.

"Ah huh," Izzie softly replied. "He says someone is hiding blood so you can't find it."

"Blood? Where?" he inquired.

It was if Izzie was listening closely to someone standing right in front of her. She nodded several times before whispering. "It's somewhere close and somewhere far." She shook her head, no longer sure. "Maybe Grandpa is confused. How can it be close and yet far at the same time?"

She finally sighed. "Grandpa says 'some blood got left behind by mistake and they don't want you or anyone else to find it. He says: 'it goes deep'."

"Hidden deep?" he tried to clarify. There were all those gruesome labs the Mantis had left behind in the deeper levels of Antarctica, hidden away from human eyes. It was experimentation that was the stuff of nightmares. Upon seeing it he had immediately told Bruno DiMaglia, the Base Commander, to destroy and burn it all. He had assumed it had been taken care of, but had it? He immediately rang up the Base Commander to confirm the truth for himself.

"Sir, those levels have all been destroyed," DiMaglia informed him. "Before we did, I was told that you wanted to preserve any viable samples that could be salvaged from the remains of the lab."

"Who told you I ordered this be done?" Zach questioned.

"The medical team came in and retrieved the samples..." the Commander told him.

"Where are they now? Those samples," Zach prompted.

"Sir, they were put in our lab freezers to avoid degradation."

"I want to see them—now." It was not quite a demand, but Zach knew something was amiss.

Izzie refused to be left out. "I want to go see them, too!" she declared.

He didn't have time to worry about her as well. "No, Izzie. You stay here. It's safer. I'll be right back. I promise."

~~*~~

It took longer than he thought. The head officer of the medical team was roused from a deep sleep only to confirm his suspicions. There were no marked blood or tissue samples from the Mantis laboratories to be found anywhere in the Base's deep military freezers. It was the first time Zach had seen what Minerva had been storing or hiding there. The sealed canisters of specimens were tagged with numbers, being of unknown origin, perhaps even multiple strains of deadly viruses and bioweapons. Standard security protocol required a hazmat suit-up just to enter the freezers. Zach couldn't get out of there fast enough.

The whereabouts of the remaining Mantis blood samples were unknown. The team's highest-ranking medical officer was unaware of any such procurement order ever being given. DiMaglia immediately had every person on the medical team summoned, while their private quarters were thoroughly searched. All 35 of them from biologists to lab assistants were put under a microscope, but nothing was found.

DiMaglia didn't recognize any of them to be the one informing him of the order to preserve Mantis lab samples.

Which left Zach to believe it might have been a Mantis being left behind who had employed a shape-shifting disguise. How many of them were still here, hiding their true identities?

All security records and footage for anyone entering and/or leaving the Base, under any circumstances, was closely examined. There was only one anomaly. A jump-room had been energetically accessed shortly before the Mantis labs had been completely destroyed, but footage showed no presence of a human or alien having used it.

Zach knew it was possible to evade Base detection using the Mantis cloaking technology Gizmo was capable of. He had done it himself not too long ago and then again with Meghan to explore the other remaining portal locations. A slight energetic signature of a being might be detected, but then it could also go unnoticed, like it had for him, unless someone was monitoring every security frame in real time. He was sure the shapeshifting being who escaped with the salvaged blood samples of the Mantis had his very own AI cloaking device. They might have been coming and going at will, cloaked and undetected, and carrying important intel to those who still had influence and control.

It was in that moment Zach realized being at the Base afforded him, Meghan, and Izzie no real protection at all. He had been deluding himself all along thinking he could rule Minerva and change it for the good. What a naïve fool he was. They were like sitting ducks, waiting for the ultimate shoe to drop. The Base was filled with spies, shapeshifting Mantis and otherwise, which from day one had been keeping a close eye on him, plotting their every move and countermove. They would terminate him when the time was right. They were just lolling him into believing he was in charge. Even the underground Washington meeting had been a total sham. They must all be laughing at him behind his back. Just paying him lip service. They were masters at it and had been doing it for centuries.

Fear took hold. They had to get out of there. Tonight couldn't be soon enough. The news would quickly spread that he was searching for blood. Which meant it must hold some secret they didn't want anyone to learn about.

Zach excused himself from the chaos he had caused in the middle of the night for the Base Commander and all the medical team personnel. He calmly instructed him that they would take up the matter again in the morning. But Zach had other ideas.

He returned to their living quarters where Izzie, now joined by Meghan, were anxiously awaiting him. When he stepped into the room, the first words out of Meghan's mouth expressed her deep concern: "We're in danger. Aren't we?"

Zach nodded. "We won't be coming back. Gather whatever's important, nothing else. Hurry."

Chapter 8

Camille Eldridge had just received the wake-up call of all wake-up calls--like being roused in the middle of the night to receive the totally devastating news that someone or something near and dear to you is forever gone. And truth be told, this had nothing at all to do with Martin's recent death. For Camille it was the loss of financial standing—her precious money reserves. While she had come to expect her fortune was secure and would always be there for her, it was a rude awakening to find out differently.

It wasn't her imagination. Everything around her was changing all too rapidly. Political contributions to her presidential campaign were barely trickling in. Then, to her shock and total horror, she found her own bank accounts, foreign and domestic, had been mysteriously frozen and no one seemed able to explain or fix it. A banking epidemic was spreading, seizing random control of accounts. She knew she was not the only one to have experienced this strange phenomenon. Something was terribly wrong.

After calling her banker and getting nowhere, as he too was in the dark, Camille had called on the Chairman of the Senate's Committee on Banking and received the same run-around treatment. It was a temporary glitch in the system she had been told. They were working on it, so they said. "Just be patient." Camille knew gaslighting when she heard it. It felt like certain parties were being singled out for financial extinction. No one wanted to talk about it for fear it would start a panic, causing bank runs, insolvency, and a catastrophic financial crash. They were all very real possibilities.

She called on Daphne Goldberg, head of the World Central Bank, who she knew to be a Minerva member and, for God sakes, ought to know what was going on in the banking world. She had been put on hold for an unacceptable amount of time, only to be finally told, "Ms. Goldberg is not available."

Not available? WTF? Camille Eldridge had been married for years to the most powerful man in the world--the Governor of Minerva--and now people were "unavailable" to her? Did they not know who she was? She was becoming more pissed off with each passing moment.

"Have you seen the news?" her campaign manager asked, entering her office and tossing a *Wall Street Journal* down on her desk. There it was--front page news. Daphne Goldberg was being investigated for "aiding and abetting" massive bank loan frauds involving money laundering, embezzlement and identity theft totaling in the trillions. Camille felt a cold chill run down her body. It was now apparent that the World Central Bank president no longer had the protection of Martin or Minerva.

Everywhere she looked, bad news was going off like a never-ending fireworks display. Sex scandals were surfacing, honey traps were being exposed, Ponzi money schemes were crashing like a house of cards. Both the famous, the infamous, and the those who remained nameless working behind the scenes to gain power were experiencing chaotic change. Even Elizabeth Vandam, CEO of one of the largest family-owned media empire, was under an FCC investigation for taking large monetary bribes for airing and promoting what some were calling "fake news". Had the world gone insane?

Throwing caution to the wind, because she still believed she was untouchable, it was Guiseppe Cullotta who Camille contacted next. Few knew that Cardinal Cullotta had been and still was an influential Minerva member representing the likes of the Holy See and the Patriarch of Rome himself. He controlled Vatican banking monies and had his hand in everything financial that happened throughout the Church. It was no secret the Church had been recently rocked with scandals of money laundering for the Italian Mafia. Being a State unto themselves, they were criminally untouchable, and they knew it.

Camille had no qualms whatsoever of calling the Cardinal and using Martin's past Minerva affiliation. Being a good Catholic, Cullotta had arranged a private audience for Martin and her with the papacy thirty years ago shortly after they married. They had received the Pope's blessing to their union and that had to count for something.

Cullotta would know what was going on and if Minerva would correct this sudden and inexplicable international blockage of monies. Camille pushed aside her knowledge of the growing rumors of his being a devout pedophile and satanist. Everyone had something in their closet to be accused of and as long as it didn't interfere with business as usual, who cared?

If the rumors were indeed true about the satanic pedophilia and he was destined to go down in a hellfire of flames, she was sure poor Guiseppe would eventually meet a similar fate to James Talbot. Perhaps sooner rather than later, which was why it was probably best to contact him now and ferret out the details before it was too late.

But at this moment in time there was one more important fact Camille was determined to learn. "Tell me who replaced Martin," she asked the Cardinal after finally getting him on the phone late one night. She could tell he had been drinking—

perhaps too much communion wine. In an unguarded moment, his words came out slightly slurred in a torrent of unintelligible Italian before cryptically telling her: "Beware. The devil resides in your own house."

There was an uneasy, yet accusatory edge to his voice. Was he scared to be talking to her, she wondered? "What do you mean?" Camille demanded to know.

Guiseppe Cullotta continued like a raving mad man, his words even more inflamed. "You will see. The sins of the father have been laid down upon your child… the Anti-Christ is hiding in your very midst."

Her brain was silently screaming at him to stop talking in nonsensical parables. Was he insinuating that her son had something to do with what was happening with the banks? Was he insane?

"Zachary?" she scoffed not believing for a second that the Cardinal could possibly be serious. "That's preposterous. You must be mistaken."

"Yes, your son!" he spat out, like she had spawned the devil himself. "He killed your husband and others, then took over. He has control over all truth. God help you and God help us all!"

She heard what sounded like a maniacal laugh and then a click as the phone connection went dead. The holy and esteemed second Patriarch of Rome had hung up on her.

Camille was shocked speechless. She slowly put down her phone and for several minutes just stared at her vanity wall of Senatorial accolades, trying to make sense of what she had just heard. It was unfathomable. She had to laugh at such an idiotic idea. Her hermit librarian son, who couldn't get his nose out of a book, had killed his father? Zach now "controlled the truth"? No. It was a totally insane accusation.

But despite struggling to make sense of what the Cardinal had revealed, crazy thoughts continued to bombard her with rapid lightning speed like a pinball machine on fire. Did his quiet demeanor and loner personality mask the makings of a latent serial killer? And what had he done with Martin's body after he killed him? They both knew they had buried an empty coffin at Arlington National Cemetery. For the first time in a long time, Camille had to admit she knew next to nothing about her own son or his life. No wonder he had been the first to call with the news that she was now a widow. Her Zachary was now in charge of Minerva!

Once that earth shattering bit of news sank in, along with all its ramifications, Camille wasn't sure if she should celebrate that the family was still running the show or down a stiff tumbler of scotch along with a bottle of sleeping pills to escape what would surely be a coming shit storm. She was positive Zach detested her for being a terrible absent mother and cutting off her funds confirmed it. He would wreak revenge on her. Right now, he was probably sabotaging her run for president as well.

With a trembling hand and a deep breath, she picked up the phone and tried to call him. Not to her surprise, it went immediately to voicemail. She tried to put on her best mea culpa voice.

"I've been thinking about you a lot, honey," she began almost tearfully. "It's just you and me now and I don't want us to be strangers. You know I love you, Zach. Daddy and I have always been so proud of you, and I know you'll miss him as much as I do. But we're still family and family sticks together no matter what. So, honey, please call me."

Camille didn't know what else to say without sounding completely phony. Zach had left so abruptly after the memorial services and burial they hadn't had time to talk. There seemed to be no interest at all in meeting with the estate lawyers to hear the terms of the will and trusts his father had left behind for both of them. It was sizable. And now, even those funds were probably frozen.

At the services she had noted a difference in her son's demeanor. He seemed so grownup, so cold, and even stoic--like he bore the weight of the world on his shoulders. At the time, she had put it down to the circumstances of the moment—his father's death. Now she knew more than she cared to know, but she still didn't know where in the world he was.

~~*~~

Cali Cavaleri was also in the dark in Santa Monica, California—literally and figuratively. The frequent rolling brownouts to conserve energy were driving her crazy. And the traffic and congestion were worse than Washington. But she couldn't complain. Eric's Spanish-style home on San Vicente Boulevard was her newest hideout, within walking distance of the Pacific Ocean and the Third Street Promenade. It wasn't the paradise of Maui, but here she could blend in and retain anonymity until she figured out what came next. Wearing a baseball cap, exercise garb and dark sunglasses she looked like everyone else that walked the affluent neighborhood streets.

Eric was still reeling from his mind-blowing trip from Haleakala to the Los Angeles jump-room portal located inside an empty aeronautical warehouse near the LAX Airport. Zach had taken them through the portal instead of flying commercial and risk being tracked. She felt conflicted about leaving Zach, Meghan, and Izzie in the unknown location they had taken her to after rescuing her from Kaggen and his God-awful bugs. She still didn't know where they were hiding out. Not even loose lips, Little Betsy Ross, had told her a thing. A part of her felt as if the story was there, wherever *there* was, and she should have stayed rather than cowardly trading that life for the normalcy of life with Eric.

But life would never really be normal again. This she knew and was certain of. Cali was loath to admit it, but she still felt somewhat traumatized by her alien ordeal. There were the occasional nightmares to deal with. And she practically flipped out when saw a praying mantis, a small one mind you, land on her leg while sunning beside Eric's backyard pool. It just stared at her. She momentarily froze before breaking through the spell in a state of terror. She leapt up and ran inside wondering if it was an omen of bigger insects to come. Her eyes remained glued to the sky for hours afterward, searching for the spaceship's return.

Cali found the term for her traumatic condition spelled out on the internet in black and white, in all its pathology. It was another diagnosis she could now claim to possess. The shrinks of the world had given her fear a name: *Entomophobia* or in layman's terms *Insectophobi*a. Her fear of bugs would be considered unrealistic by conventional standards, but then who had known there existed giant bugs the size of the alien Mantis? And that fear was also coupled with a fear of insect abduction. You just couldn't make this shit up. For God's sake, who would believe it?

Cali vowed never to take off the metal wrist band Meghan had given her which contained some type of technology which would supposedly thwart off any further abduction. Not a religious person, she fervently prayed now that it worked, but doubt still plagued her.

If nothing else, she was now living in the best place to be if she needed help. In Los Angeles everyone seemed to have some kind of trauma or affliction they were dealing with. There were more therapists per capita here than anywhere else in the world to help people deal with their fears and Cali had to admit she was having a hard time letting go of hers. She half-heartedly mused about finding a 12-step support group for Alien Abductees and was shocked to actually find one listed. Call it curiosity or something stranger, she was pulled one evening to attend the group to learn what others had experienced. She soon found herself in a meeting room of about 25 people, all looking very normal and composed. This surprised her, too. She half expected them to look like ComicCon attendees dressed up as Star Trekkies, but instead they came from all ranks of professionals—teachers, film people, engineers, health care workers, mothers and even an orthodox rabbi.

Cali listened, preferably to test the waters to see if any of them had undergone ordeals with the Mantis like she had. But so far, she heard nothing but detailed encounters dealing with little grey aliens, like that Mapu being. Every one of them believed the aliens' negative agenda was to create hybrid beings.

Cali tried to convince herself she was just there on a research mission for her and Eric's screenplay. Not a science-fiction fan by any means, alien abductions quickly became her obsession. A need to make sense of it all through the writings of others, whether true or fictional, seized her. After a group session she would talk one-on-one with a few of them, getting their story and comparing where hers fit in. A few remembered a Mantis creature standing silently in the far corner of the room observing while those little Mapu creatures probed and conducted their experiments. They had thought such an insect creature was only their imagination, as sometimes the Mantis being wavered in appearance.

"And the little Greys smelled, too," one woman abductee volunteered. "Really bad."

"Like farts?" Cali chirped in, unable to remain silent.

The woman turned to her and nodded. "Yea. Like really bad Sulphur farts! It was the first thing I smelled when they got up close to me. I was strapped down on their table and couldn't avoid the stink." The vivid memory of the event made her look away and shudder.

Cali didn't remember any experiments being conducted on her inside the space craft, but it left her wondering if anything had happened during the time she was knocked out and unconscious. Had those little fuckers taken her DNA then? Had they probed her as well?

Without exception, every last one in the abductee support group participants believed governments were complicit in this weird alien/human exchange program. For what, she always asked? Advanced technology exchange was always the reason they gave. "We're just livestock maintenance," one man said, who had been dealing with abductions since a child, only to later learn his mother had experienced it as well as a young girl.

Had Cali known all this before Zach took her and Eric through the Los Angeles jump-room, she would have bombarded him with questions demanding to know more. She was certain he knew a hell of a lot more than he was telling. Could the child trafficking info he had exposed been a part of some alien/human procurement network? And now that she was privy to the existence of some other-worldly Library of Truth, even though she had been too passed out to take advantage of this strange depository of knowledge at the time, this had to be Zach's true source of information. She desperately wanted in.

Despite her life being forever changed by her insane curiosity to always know more than most people wanted to know, they would never be able to take the investigative reporter out of her. It was hard-wired into her DNA. She craved answers like a junkie, or more precisely like the recovering alcoholic addict she was.

It occurred to her that there might be a way to go back to that empty aeronautical building near the airport and access that jump-room portal once again. If so, she would find the Library of Truth and get to some real answers for herself. She wasn't sure if such a thing was even possible, but it was worth a shot. If she didn't, she would spend a lifetime always wondering what if and why not. But could she disappear for a while and do this to Eric all over again?

~~*~~

Eric saw the deep questioning look in her eyes the moment it formed. He was a fast reader of human intent, as he had been creating believable characters most of his adult screen writing career and knew when a look spelled trouble. Cali was looking at him that way right now with a slightly raised eyebrow and an almost imperceptible tilt of her chin. It was her subtle sign, like a poker player giving away his tell. And she didn't even know it.

Their short relationship had shown him one of many things about her--Cali was an adrenaline freak. She took risks and often threw caution aside, which managed to get her in a heap of sticky circumstances. Even now he could see the wheels in her brain working overtime, calculating the risk factor for some new plan—and he knew he was part of that risk. That they were in the middle of having sex on the living room couch, his fingers deep inside her trying to give her an orgasmic release when he spotted that look, made a part of him want to laugh and cry at the same time.

"Stop thinking and just relax," he told her, inserting yet another finger and going right for her G-spot with deeper determination. The only thing that could distract his little minx was frequent and great sex and that he was willing to give her. He watched her eyes flutter and roll back as she came loud and strong, knowing the trouble she was plotting would be placed on hold for now. It was the least he could do.

Chapter 9

Without the fanfare it deserved, Kaggen gave the order for the first rollout event to commence. He had known the evolutionary timeline might necessitate long-range plans being stepped up and that time was now. His first indication had not come from the death of the Minerva Governor, or the usurping of that position by his son, Zachary, or even by being thwarted by the escape of the child hostage Izzie, but by a more subtle and foreboding sign.

The Earth's planetary grid was showing signs of tampering by some unknown source. There were new pools of energy beginning to swirl and grow where multiple-dimensional gridlines intersected. Which meant the frequency fence that had been erected throughout the Earth's ley lines by their own kind to prevent evolutionary ascension to higher dimensions, was weakening with this new influx of energy. This indicated that there could be a bifurcation of timelines occurring where they would suddenly be spun off into a new and unknown timeline where they would no longer be in control. This would nullify all they had done and prepared for tens of thousands of years. It would spell disaster for all those who had been working to conquer this dimension.

Kaggen gave the command with the full knowledge and consent of all members of the Inter-Planetary Consortium of One Mind (IPCOM) comprised of the fallen renegades, the cleverest leaders who had split off from other Federation Alliances, the innovative scientists and teachers for a One Mind World, and a host of other of like-minded thinkers that comprised his loyal hive.

If they could unleash enough "loosh" energy, they might be able to reverse course of whatever was now in set in motion in order to re-stabilize the gridwork intersections to their liking—the very fabric that kept this dimension intact for them.

The Aethien Mantis race had been harvesting hyperdimensional loosh energy for many millennia to fortify their planetary fence and the power they held over it. They were masters at it. Long ago they had learned that every human soul gives off loosh energy when traumatized, making it a very powerful energetic binding force when employed and directed for IPCOM's many purposes. It was the ultimate weapon, virtually undetectable in intent. A weapon of mass destruction when used against humans who resisted or attempted to push back.

Even Minerva had never figured out that loosh harvesting was one of the aliens' primary goals and intents, along with human hybridization. DNA experimentation was just a convenient ruse. It was a viable one, but only a small part of their bigger picture.

So human trauma would have to be increased by ten-fold to harvest enough loosh energy to stop whatever was happening in Earth's planetary grid. They had accomplished this throughout thousands of years by perpetrating wars, torture practices, child sacrifices, abductions, and a myriad of other horror-inducing methods that produced this desired effect in humans. Man could be easily prodded to hate, to kill, to burn with anger as well as other strong and destructive emotions, while their kind mined and harvested the loosh from the ethers like energetic gold.

Loosh energy could power the multiverse and somehow only human souls had been made the recipient of this potent energetic fuel the rest of the cosmos wanted. A peaceful earth was something they would and could never allow to happen. Their source of loosh gold would then forever be dried up and gone.

It was time to step up production, something Kaggen loved. It was such a fun little human procurement game.

~~*~~

The only place in the world that still felt safe was the Library of Truth. There Zach knew he could find answers. There Meghan and Izzie would be out of danger, and he could begin to tie all the loose threads together towards a solution. Whether Satya would agree or not to having unexpected company was uncertain. He had no idea how she lived, where exactly she spent her time, or what her life was like when he was not there. In fact, he didn't even know if she was a real flesh-and-blood recordkeeper or an informational hologram like the LOT itself. There was so much he didn't know—like how long she had carried out her job or how she had come to be picked for such an undertaking in the first place. In the past, she had never spoken about her life, always steering away from such probing private questions.

Not surprisingly, since she knew all human events, past, present, future, and probable, Satya was there waiting for them, expecting their arrival when they came through the portal. And she was smiling in a way he had never come to see or expect of her. As if she knew something he didn't and was personally pleased to welcome him and his little entourage to her world. He should have been immediately suspicious, but he was so relieved that her look was not one of disapproval for coming here to, in essence, hide out, that he overlooked what might have otherwise been a red flag. Satya looked too damn happy.

"Yes. I will take them to a safe place to rest," she said before he even asked. "Portal 11 is awaiting you and this you must do alone. Stay within the protection of the hologram and beware of the Dragon bloodlines, as they too have their power and purpose in this timeline conflict. Avoid them at all costs."

"What?! Did you say dragons?" Meghan remarked, anxiety written all over her. She turned to Zach, grabbing his arm. "Zach don't go. It sounds too dangerous. Stay here with us," she pleaded. "We need you."

Izzie was of a different mind. "He has to go, Mommy. It's his job. Angels have to fight bad people or they can't get their wings."

Zach hid a smile. Izzie was still of the belief that he was an angel sent down to save Earth. It was hard to fathom the child standing in front of him, sounding so grown up at times, was only seven years old. On a simple level, Izzie seemed to grasp what others could not. We all had our work to do, whether we wanted to or not.

Right now, he needed to find an answer to the Mantis blood experiments and stop "fucking around and get moving" as the dead Senator Talbot had channeled through to his granddaughter. It was time to get serious. Meghan had to believe in him. He could see the uncertainty in her eyes. She was afraid of losing him as much as he was of losing her. Therefore, he could make no mistakes.

"I won't be long," he promised, embracing them both—savoring their loving support. It reminded him that they were now a real family unit. This feeling was something he had waited his whole life to find. Of course, he would return.

He kissed Meghan again and ruffled Izzie's hair. "I'll be back soon. I promise."

~~*~~

Zach followed Satya's advice and allowed his physical body to stay in the LOT and initially view Portal 11 through a 360-degree hologram. He found by standing at its center he could manipulate it, from all sides and angles, much like Ishannika had on their trek to Nordekka. If he needed to physically step into the here and now of the hologram, as he had done in the Vatican Secret Archives to talk with Father Baldassare to retrieve the tablets, then he knew he could do it.

Portal 11 was a labyrinth maze of underground tunnels for miles in every direction. Zach was acutely aware that he was not alone. Inside the catacomb walls there were shadow watchers everywhere—unseen protectors of their labyrinth domain, many giant and shadowy chimera-like creatures. It elicited an uneasy feeling deep inside him. He was the intruder, the outside voyeur who had gained entrance through unsolicited means. The hologram viewer was quick to reveal them in all their dysmorphic shapes. He could see them but was fairly certain they could not see him. But, quite possibly, they were sensing his presence as parts of the walls began to quicken and undulate with the dark breath of life as his hologram moved past.

Some of the creatures felt almost demonic in nature—an army of shadow beings, keeping at bay all those who sought the underground tunnel's secrets. All around him, it felt like a Holocaust death camp. Blood sacrifices, both child and adult, had been carried out in this place. He could not only sense but smell it. It felt like a spiritual warfare battle had been going on here for centuries and was still being played out. It resembled the depths of Hell.

Zach questioned where he was. The records telepathically informed him he was on the Island of Malta, far underground in one of the most ancient of sites. Here many of the portal and gateway technology timelines intersected, creating an opportunity for amplified power harvesting through blood and sacrifice.

Like the Vatican, Malta was also a sovereign state unto itself without outside interference or rulership. It was supervised by an ancient order of knights whose sole purpose was to maintain and shield the planetary grid in order to manipulate the dimensional timelines. These protector knights were all human-hybrid beings that had been placed in key positions for when they would be called to planetary service as was their intended mission from the moment of their creation. They came from all walks of society and standing, pledged to service, some totally unaware of what they were really being asked to do, which was not to question, but to follow orders. They were of a hive mind and one of many corresponding secret societies within the ranks of Minerva.

This information was coming to Zach in a download. The world was inhabited by creatures whose sole intent was one of bio-invasion and control. Some were oblivious to the greater drama being played out on multiple dimensional levels around them. But somewhere in the midst of all this were the answers to the bloodline mystery and what was being perpetrated. Zach commanded the hologram to take him to its source.

The hologram penetrated the tunnel floor, going straight down like a sonic elevator, for miles and miles into what the LOT informed him was a capsule locked within "Inner Earth". It was a place he hadn't known existed, except for strange reports found in Admiral Richard E. Byrd's 1926 flight diary from the North Pole. They had been highly controversial reports and not well received by his governmental superiors.

Men of science accused Byrd of fabricating preposterous stories of discovering an idyllic paradise within the Earth itself. They dismissed Byrd's claims of locating an opening at the North Pole where compass magnets went haywire—where frigid salty ocean waters turned to warm fresh water which flowed into a verdant and flourishing Earth interior. Since discovering the LOT, Zach was of the mind that what man did know was miniscule to what he didn't know—which was practically everything. Man existed in a world of lies and cover-ups. The only thing more frightening to those invested in these lies was the inevitable emergence of the truth.

Penetrating deep beneath the surface of Malta, Zach could see he was not in some hidden "paradise" but inside a massive football-field-size bunker that functioned as a freezer. This was a very strange and unusual cold storage locker. Large clear glass vats, some as high as three stories in height and containing a bright red liquid substance, tightly lined the walls like a winery row. Zach was certain the substance inside was blood. Industrial-size magnets, resembling dark solar panels, were suspended above and below the blood vats in a grid-like pattern. Aside from the cold temperatures that permeated this place, which could be felt even from within the hologram, he sensed a distinct electromagnetic pull.

They were magnetizing and spinning the blood. Zach found this curious. What were they trying to attract or repel in the blood through inducing a highly super-magnetic field effect? He maneuvered the hologram to zoom in on the blood in the vats through the magnified lens of a darkfield microscope. Barely visible were the presence of the black strands seen in Izzie's blood drawing. They seemed to be alive, with an intelligence that prompted them to move away from the hologram scope, attempting to avoid detection. Not being a microbiologist, Zach was pretty sure this wasn't a normal thing to observe in human blood, if indeed this was "human" blood.

Zach called on the LOT records to identify all factors present in the blood. Streams of information ran across his field of vision as live blood analysis was performed. This was not Zach's field or expertise, but one thing was certain. This might have started out as pure human blood at some point in time, but what these tanks now stored was human-hybrid blood—a big world of difference. This place was an alien hybrid blood bank.

To verify this, he called forth past data images. They showed him pictures of humans being blood transfused, while others were being injected with something that fed into their blood—changing it in abnormal ways. Some of the patients were conscious during this blood change process. Others appeared to be suspended in a trance-like or deep sleep state. Their given consent to the procedure was highly questionable.

Zach needed more information to make sense of what he was seeing. What were the black strands in the injected blood? That's when the answers got even more confusing. LOT records identified them as lipid nanoparticles, meant to suppress the human immune system. He was able to observe how they bypassed defense cells, causing them to die off and allowing for the alien human-hybrid change to occur. They disengaged the cellular gatekeeper, leaving the recipient defenseless against any foreign blood invader.

He was viewing a survival of the fittest selection process. The aliens' hybridization program was targeting those of a specific gene pool—all those possessing the ERAP 2 gene which protected them against deadly diseases. Those whose ancestors had possessed this gene had survived deadly pathogens for thousands of years—bubonic plague, black death, and a host of other modern-day killers. Their genetic differences, and natural immunity to such pathogens, had eventually altered the evolution of the human genome, making their descendants the most amenable subjects for the aliens' human design.

The blood injections the aliens were giving humans caused crystalline structures to form inside the host's body. Zach watched the process on the hologram viewer as it attempted to make changes to the double helix of human DNA. He wasn't sure what he was seeing, until it hit him like a bolt of lightning. Holy shit! These forming structures were trying to insert a third strand into human DNA so that it would bond and create a triple DNA helix. This synthesized third strand, containing silicon, was attaching to genes preventing them from functioning normally.

Zach wasn't sure if the alien intent was to turn on and off switches to human disease or something else. The records, being neutral, seemed to imply it was something else entirely if one read between the lines. It was something dark. Something that could and would change life as they knew it and it was already occurring all over the world with no one trying to stop it.

The crystalline formation structures were highly communicative and capable of receiving external frequency transmissions like radio signals. This meant that instructions could be given, through transmission frequencies which had the ability to connect every human-hybrid to the hive mind of some master force which could quite possibly control their biological and psychological responses. This would cut man off from his free will divine right, thereby affecting the human angelic soul's dimensional ascension process.

As Zach could recall, this human evolutionary goal had been clearly spelled out in the Vatican Secret Archive's *Universal Covenant of Man* tablets. If the aliens' plan succeeded, they would entrap millions of human souls on Earth to do their bidding, denying them their evolution. The plan was both brilliant and diabolical. This is what Kaggen had been up to all these hundreds of thousands of years. He had just been patiently waiting to attain the numbers needed to hit critical mass where his genetic invasion could seamlessly take place without ever firing a single shot.

There was only one catch. Zach knew that if there was a frequency transmission to activate a process then there had to also be a corresponding frequency to de-activate it as well. And that he would need to find out. He looked to the LOT records for what the natural nemesis would be to destroy such a DNA deviation and came up empty. The LOT should know all this, but if it did it was not forthcoming. He pressed the issue only to learn in BIG BOLD LETTERS across his cerebral cortex that the LOT did not give out information intended for destructive purposes. Well, damn. This was something Zach didn't know. How then had Minerva gotten around this rule? They had used LOT information to overpower and destroy their enemies. Why would DNA altering, or destruction, be any different? There must be something he was missing in the equation, but the answer eluded him.

Zach knew that he would need a vial of the strange blood to take with him. He pushed through the hologram's wavering walls, feeling a tug of resistance trying to stop him, followed by a loud popping sound as he emerged through it into the cold confines of the blood freezer. The push/pull from the large magnets made his head spin with an uncomfortable pressure. There was a metallic taste in his mouth that had not been there a second ago. It made him slightly nauseous and light-headed. He swallowed hard and grunted, trying to get rid of the sudden onset of symptoms by pushing more blood to his heart. Zach knew the signs. He couldn't afford to get sick right now by being overly sensitive to a highly magnetized and charged environment. This blood bank had been intentionally set up to energetically repel human entry.

His hand patted his pants pocket, feeling the familiar weight—his very own secret weapon. Gizmo would be there by his side if things turned dicey. Still, it was hard for him to shake the creepy feeling crawling over him by being in this blood bank. Without a doubt, it was doing something to him.

What the hell, he thought. It would only be a temporary move and undoubtedly faster, too. "Gizmo, deactivate all magnets," he quickly instructed, looking up at the giant panels.

The results were totally unexpected. Zach watched in stunned disbelief as Gizmo vaporized all the magnets, every last one of them, with a bright blue laser beam. The beam turned to orange, setting up an inferno of flames that immediately spread. It jumped around as if fueled by pools of liquid nitrogen. Deafening alarms and blaring sirens went off everywhere alerting all of Malta.

"Shit, shit, shit!" Zach hissed, hearing the doors being thrown open.

"Engage cloaking protection," he screamed to Gizmo over the din as an army of Lizards, Mantis and other alien creatures stormed the room hissing at the sight. They went into immediate action to put out the spreading flames.

One of these days Zach would learn the right commands to give so Gizmo wouldn't be destroying everything in its wake. Right now, he just needed to get some blood and get the hell out of there before things got worse, which was not to be the case. Things got much worse.

"Get me a blood sample," he told the AI device. And just like that the big vats started shattering and falling like ducks in a shooting gallery. The entire freezer became a churning sea of blood, thousands of gallons washing over everything in its path. There was no way to stem the flow or destruction. It was a force of nature—a crimson tide that flooded through every corner and crevice of the room like a tsunami wave seeking ground. Zach watched creatures slipping, sliding, and being taken under by the blood bath that engulfed them, as the blood rose in depth. All the while, Zach remained untouched like Moses standing between the parting waters of the Red Sea.

Gizmo sent several ounces of untouched blood floating through the air towards them. Before it reached him the AI device had already encased and sealed it in a glass tube-like structure which morphed and rippled over it. Zach grabbed the vial and knew it was his cue to get out of there fast. He had what he needed. He turned and dived into the hologram and back into the safety of the LOT.

From inside the hologram he could see the carnage he had left behind. Their blood bank was destroyed, but somewhere there had to be other blood storages. If there was anything he had learned, the Mantis would not have put all their eggs in one basket.

~~*~~

Meghan was in a state of total awe. Beyond the Library of Truth were whole new dimensions of knowledge and thought which housed incredible and amazing things. This was a world she had no idea existed beyond 3rd Dimensional physical Earth.

It was called "Terra" meaning "new Earth" or "true Earth". Satya had explained that the 4th Universal Dimension realm had fallen in upon itself, in essence collapsing, hundreds of thousands of years ago, becoming one or similar to the 3rd Universal Dimension. With this fall it brought many of its habitants to the 3rd Dimensional realm where they found life was harder, less evolved, and filled with emotional and physical turmoil. Those that had fallen, due to service-to-self ideology, continued to cause mischief and wreak havoc still not having learned many of their soul's lessons which led to their fall in the first place. Their lust for power and control over others had been their ultimate undoing.

Satya had taken Izzie and her to 5th Universal Dimensional "Terra" for safety which still had access to the Library of Truth which resided in the 8th Universal Dimension. All this talk about dimensional mechanics had Meghan's head spinning. All she could grasp from their conversation was that there were 12 Universal Dimensions and each of those dimensions had 12 sub-level dimensions within it, much like astral planes, where one could spend many lifetimes before progressing to a higher realm—a soul's school yard of learning opportunities. Izzie was completely enthralled with this idea.

"Where were we before we came here?" Izzie wanted to know. "And where is my Pink Heaven?"

Satya had incredible patience. She knew where this was going. "Your 'Pink Heaven', as you call it, is a realm which you personally created. Others cannot access it without your express acknowledgement and permission. In the higher realms one can create anything—even their own reality. But to answer your initial question—you just came from the 3rd Universal Dimensional Earth's third sub-level. And now you're in the 5th Universal Dimension, 5th sub-level of that same dimension. And the Library of Truth can be accessed from the 8th Universal Dimension from any sublevel of that dimension."

Izzie's face lit up. The world was more complicated that she thought. But oh, so fascinating. The idea of being able to create one's own reality would be a wonderful game of endless possibilities. "That's really cool, but..." She was thinking hard. "Can I still go back to Pink Heaven to play with Caleb?"

"Who is this Caleb?" Meghan asked.

"It's a surprise," Izzie giggled, patting her Mommy's stomach. "You'll find out soon enough."

Meghan frowned. She had had enough surprises to last a lifetime and wasn't looking forward to more. The last thing she wanted was Izzie disappearing into her fantasy world again to play with imaginary playmates. It was hard enough dealing with present time reality. Satya gave her a knowing look, seeming to be of the same opinion.

"I'll show you where you'll be staying," she said quickly changing the subject. "I think you will be very pleased."

Fifth Dimensional Terra was a place of light and less density than 3rd Dimensional Earth. The skies were bluer, the air fresher, the colors more vibrant and of a higher resolution, and the sounds were both clearer and sweeter with an extended resonance range. Even the weather seemed quite moderate without extremes in temperature. In other words, it felt quite perfect.

There was another unusual observation Meghan made. Those who resided on Terra appeared to be taller in stature. Not giants, but she hadn't seen any small or little people here either, if one wasn't counting children. The effects were gradual, Meghan was told. Less gravitational density affected the body on this dimension.

Meghan quietly took in everything in her new surroundings. There were some very notable differences. There were no cars, trains, buses, or commercial planes clogging up the roads or skies. The people seemed content and happier. She saw no signs of the stress running through this society as she had so recently felt on the dimension they had just come from.

There was an abundance of different races on Terra. Human, alien, and what she would classify as "other" all interacted without any obvious class distinction. There was an open exchange of ideas which was refreshing to say the least.

"No one needs to feel right, here," Satya commented. "You will find it much different than the 3rd Universal Dimension. Here people try to find a middle ground and celebrate differences of opinion."

Meghan saw signs of unfettered creativity everywhere in buildings, parks, nature, and home design. And more encouraging was no one walked around with a cellphone obsessively texting. She wondered how they communicated.

Satya nodded hearing her silent question. "Yes. Communication devices have no practical use here. Thought exchange is instantaneous. People are aware of everyone's thoughts and actions and what they are creatively working on, professionally, personally, and socially. Because of it, lying and deceit cannot thrive. To do so, would make one an outcast and not worthy of this dimension."

Meghan was not sure how she would adjust to such openness of thought. The concept of a world without secrets and without shame because of those secrets, was foreign to her. She couldn't wait to share this knowledge with Zach. Would this eliminate the fear of being unmasked as well? Perhaps not having to hide aspects of one's life, and still be accepted no matter what, might be a wonderful liberating experience to have.

She and Izzie were shown to quarters on the top floor of a tall building, which had huge floor-to-ceiling windows looking out on their new world. Light streamed in, giving it an open and airy feeling. There had been no elevator shaft to take them to their new quarters. They just entered through a door on the main floor and instantly they were there.

"You carry your own personal portal within you," Satya explained. "You can go anywhere you like, unless you desire a bicycle or vehicle for purely recreational purposes."

Izzie's eyes grew wide. Imagine that. Her very own portal! This was all she needed to hear. "I'll be right back, Mommy." And with that she was gone, completely vanished before Meghan's eyes. Her child was off to explore her new world.

Chapter 10

Ishannika and the Universal Council of Higher Planetary Guardians (UCHPG) had been covertly monitoring Earth's multi-dimensional gridlines for some time. All aspects of the universal dimensions required that change occur slowly, seamlessly, in a flow pattern without chaos and disruption. If not, a timeline bifurcation could occur much like a train jumping its tracks and still moving forward to cause damage. But their ability to make slight correctional adjustments, and remain undetected, was becoming more difficult as time progressed.

Word was received that Kaggen had stepped up his bio-invasion plans and the signs would soon become evident. UCHPG space craft had been covertly injecting new pools of energy into the intersecting ley lines within Earth's magnetosphere to weaken and loosen their hold on the planet. These ley lines form an invisible mesh netting around Earth that serve to dampen man's divine memory of his true origins. This cosmic damper had been in put in place hundreds of thousands of years ago by those from the fallen 4th Universal Dimension to control the new denser dimension they suddenly found themselves trapped in.

Like Kaggen, the UCHPG had stepped up their efforts to thwart what was occurring on Earth's grid with larger injections of stabilizing energy. Their space craft had the ability to shape-shift, appearing like clouds or commercial aircraft during the day and night to avoid human detection. They could wink in and out of 3rd Dimensional space, becoming invisible when necessary to avoid triggering potential human panic and alarm at seeing so many of their craft in Earth's skies. If man only knew the extent of the rescue efforts that were in place without their knowledge. It was necessary to help save 3rd Dimensional Earth and all its human inhabitants, as it had such a large bearing on the rest of the multiverse.

Earth was a free will zone and had to be honored as such. It had been created as the primary dimensional level where human souls would come into matter within physical bodies. It was the first of the lower dimensional levels that allowed experimentation with free will choice and the ensuing results of such decisions.

Kaggen's erected frequency fence had served to entrap many souls on Earth's 3rd Dimensional plane, preventing souls who were ready to ascend to 5th Dimensional Terra. All this had been perpetrated in the misguided intention of preserving territorial protection and control. Soon there might be all-out war in the skies above this planet, the likes of which had only happened in the past that went beyond nuclear capability. The ancient stories and myths about fireballs in the sky and flying vimana ships were true. Those civilizations had been annihilated without barely a trace of their history remaining. This planetary war with all its weapons had contributed to the fall and collapse of the 4th Universal Dimension where such advanced technology existed but had been ultimately misused.

Ishannika knew Kaggen would soon be unleashing mass amounts of loosh energy into the magnetosphere to counter their efforts. Despite his every attempt to hide his invasion plans, he was still Mantis, and there were ways to tap into the hive mind of all the Aethien race, even if Kaggen erected a mind shield.

She was Ishannika, the Queen Matriarch, whose mind was expansive, carrying the total history of the Mantis race within her consciousness. Therefore, she knew more than the rest of her kind--both the good and the bad. She would not let some bad apples in the orchard leave a legacy that would place destructive blame on the Aethien for countless millennia to come.

Unfortunately, humans weren't aware that they freely produced loosh energy in abundance when they allowed themselves to exist in perpetual states of fear, hate and violence. It was the unspoken penultimate weapon of mass destruction, and many races, not just the Aethien, knew how to stir up and harvest such traumatized energy and blood as well.

Ishannika and the others on the Council had tapped into the holographic live stream of Zachary's sojourn into Portal 11 in Malta. This portal had turned into a place of evil and destruction, drawing all the corrupt bloodlines to its shores and underground labyrinths. Many of the satanic forces were like the hounds of hell—gathering there, lured by the scent of blood and sacrifice.

The UCHPG were watching closely each and every move of the human with the infinity mark upon the crown of his head, denoting his higher avatar soul status. Of course, young Zachary didn't believe for one second that he was a predestined spiritual warrior, one of the "chosen" ones who incarnated during planetary ascension periods every 26,000 or every 260,000 years to affect evolutionary and Galactic change. Yet he had accepted his mission without protest, prompted by his insatiable curiosity and the challenge of what appeared to be an impossible task. Someday he would learn the full truth, as well as his own personal destiny. He was in the very beginning stages of his journey, but he still had the free will to mess things up—a thought Ishannika preferred not to entertain.

Zachary had put a very small dent in Kaggen's blood storage facility. Even now, other locations had been warned and were fortifying their defenses. Would they attempt to stop him or kill him for what he had done or go after his family members? Most certainly the latter, but the records showed Zachary himself was well protected. Not by just Gizmo, whom she had personally programmed with powers only the Aethien Queen Matriarch possessed, but by other unidentified forces as well. At times the question in many Council members' minds was who Zachary Eldridge really was? The universal records were not sharing the totality of that secret. The lad had been set on a cosmic mission for a very specific purpose few would ever learn the true details of. This only added to his enigma.

The UCHPG Council agreed to dispatch one of their best planetary blood specialists to aide in Zach's process. This would accelerate his understanding of the Malta blood sample he had managed to obtain. They knew that no Earth hematologist would be able to provide him the insight he needed to speed things along. Humans had never seen synthesized alien blood the likes of which Kaggen had created. Without further discussion, there was only one person up to the task. *Gore* was selected for the job and called for. She would have to shapeshift, of course, or panic would ensue. It usually did.

~~*~~

Zach emerged from the hologram which had carried him to Portal 11. He breathed a deep sigh of relief, shaking free of the witnessed chaos and the blood bath left behind. Back in the realms of the LOT again, he felt immensely safer. It was evident that the Malta portal was highly corrupted with negative energy and evil intent. Outside of the Mantis experimental Antarctica labs, it was the first portal where he left feeling sick to his stomach. What he had seen literally took his breath away. Had it always been that way? And if not, when had it gone so bad?

He attempted to focus his breathing, recognizing it was still erratic, like his tell-tale beating heart. It was difficult erasing the memory of the floodgates of blood being unleashed like a tsunami from hell throughout the alien labs of Malta. It was a vision he would probably never forget.

Back in the LOT he felt his pulse and breathing quickly stabilize. There was such a palpable difference between the two environs. In the LOT his head was sharper, clearer, and infinitely more stable. If only he could take the frequencies within the LOT into his everyday life. Sometimes he craved feeling what other people called "normal" or anything even close to it.

His hand grasped tightly around the vial of blood which he had salvaged from his escapade. Zach brought it to his nose. The dark red substance smelled like iron shavings and old copper pennies, similar to human blood. But there was one noticeable difference—it contained an electrostatic charge. Prime numbers and other strange numerical combinations swirled from the vial telling him it was mixed with Aethien DNA and something which electrified it. Its consistency resembled creamy liquid butter. Had he been a real scientist, he might have hazarded dipping his finger in and venturing a scant taste test, but he had seen the tiny black organisms swimming inside it and wanted no part of it. There was no way of knowing how pervasive it might be in penetrating a host body and taking hold. Or if it did, it might not be reversible.

His brain craved information and lots of it. He called for all the records in the LOT on alien blood composition and saw an avalanche of holographic information move towards him in slow motion. Immediately he held up his hand, keeping it at bay, thinking fast. This would take decades to wade through. He didn't have the luxury of time on his side. Like the Vatican Secret Archive, it was necessary to call in an expert.

Before he could finish that thought, his old friend, Roone Sawyer, the former Master Librarian to the Library of Congress who had been killed by Minerva, appeared before him. For a split second he was ecstatic to see him then silently stepped back, frowning. This person did not have Roone's recognizable number signature, but a combination of numbers he hadn't seen before. These bizarre combinations crackled like fire.

"Who are you?" he demanded, wanting to know how a shapeshifter had gained entrance to the LOT.

The illusion of Roone Sawyer wavered briefly. "My name is Gore and I have been sent to help you." The voice sounded exactly like his friend's. They even displayed the exact same mannerisms.

Zach had been tricked too many times, but never inside the LOT—a place of Truth. This was strange and different. Somewhere in the LOT's records he had learned that every being in the universe had to reveal their true identity, unmask themselves, when commanded to do so. He instructed the being to do so now.

"Show me who you really are," he said, holding his breath, waiting.

The being nodded. The apparition of Roone Sawyer quickly morphed into a mammoth size creature that loomed over him, terrifyingly in size. Zach unconsciously took a big step backwards recognizing it had become reptilian in nature--a dragon creature of mottled light green with cobalt blue streaked markings down its head and back. It stretched its thick neck, adjusting back to its natural form and shape. A ripple ran through its skin from head to tail, followed by a release of breath. It looked almost relieved, if that was possible.

In front of him was the type of mythical creature only written about in ancient stories. It was beyond real—all 30 plus feet tall and several tons of it. Its eyes bulged and blinked, glowing a luminous red whose sights were locked on Zach. Its thin long tongue, a pinkish purple, hung loosely from its open mouth, which displayed sharp, jagged and spiky rows of gleaming white teeth.

Strangely, Zach felt no malice or danger emanating from the creature that towered over him. However, he felt spellbound, rooted to the spot, unable to move as the two stared eye-to-eye at each other. This was not at all what he had expected. Mantis yes; Reptilian no. Zach was the first to blink.

Gore appeared to have expected such a human reaction. As if to make its presence more palatable, less fearsome, less mystifying, Gore dwarfed down to Zach's own six-foot tall height. "Ishannika and the UCHPG Council have sent me to help you analyze the sample you hold," Gore said, looking directly at the vial in question.

Not so fast, Zach thought. He knew that even salt can appear to look like sugar. "How do I know you aren't a trickster sent by Kaggen?" he demanded to know.

Gore turned around where the LOT records on alien blood information were still being held at bay like a tsunami about to strike. "Show him who I really am," it instructed the vast amount of information suspended there, waiting to be called forth.

A ball of swirling light streaked right into Zach. Upon contact, it felt compressed at first, but within seconds it expanded. Information of a very specific nature flooded into his mind and memory. The assimilation of the truth it held was instantaneous. Zach reeled at the level of depth he now knew about alien blood and the creature called Gore. Gore was a female drakaina, a serpent dragon of the 8th Platinum Draconic True Bloodline, both a physician and scientist in her own race. She was an expert identifier at all things hemoglobin and plasma related on the multi-racial spectrum. Old beyond her years, Gore had indeed been summoned by Ishannika for her professional wisdom and expertise. Zach couldn't help but smile. She was exactly what he needed.

Without hesitation, Zach handed the blood over to Gore. He watched in fascination as the female dragon brought the vial's opening up close for visual inspection. The crystalline lens of one very large red eye quickly narrowed in and focused as it shot a beam of light directly through the blood sample like a darkfield microscope conducting a live blood analysis. The procedure was instantaneous.

To Zach's utter astonishment, Gore removed her eye from the vial's opening, looked down intently at the sample as he watched her purplish tongue dart out and lap up half of the vial's contents in one dragon slurp. A shiver ran through Gore's body as the liquid made its path through her reptilian system. Scant seconds later, the drakaina brought forth the swallowed liquid and spit it out into the air, encapsulated in a transparent bubble. It floated there, not moving. That's when Satya arrived, looking none too surprised to have a drakaina occupying the LOT. She looked to Gore and the floating bubble questioningly.

Gore nodded to Satya. "It's just as the records say. Kaggen has created a synthetic Human-Mantis blood variant. It contains messenger RNA which builds structures in the blood. It has been designed to activate cellular transformation, change mitochondria and form a new strand of DNA. The new strand attaches to existing DNA helixes by inserting itself within the structure. From there it wages a biological assault. It's an active circuitry mechanism, magnetic in nature."

Satya remained stoic. "Can the damage be reversed?"

Gore didn't mince words "It's self-replicating in nature, so it will be difficult to eradicate once injected into human subjects."

"It's already been done," Satya commented. "It's been injected into the human blood supply."

"What are you saying? How could this happen?" Zach interjected. There was a hint of alarm in his voice, he was trying to contain. He pointedly eyed Gore. "How come you don't seem to be affected."

Gore shrugged. "Dragon's blood neutralizes all other forms of aberrant bloodlines. Humans do not have such capabilities. Nor can their hematological state adapt to dragon blood. Any activator genes which can adapt and neutralize such foreign threats are not available to those with your DNA kind."

Zach didn't like the sound of that prognosis. "Then what are you saying will happen?"

"The initial human bloodline will be tainted, forever contaminated. Mantis DNA will take over and become superior. A new human-hybrid race will exist and the old one will eventually be replaced and die out."

The news just kept getting worse. "I gather you're not talking about a new and improved human version?" he asked the drakaina.

"No," Gore replied. "It will be a controlled slave race, as Kaggen has intended."

Zach looked away, letting that unthinkable thought sink in. There had to be another way. "What specifically did you see in the blood?" he asked Gore.

Gore and Satya both exchanged an unreadable look. "Kaggen inserted another component into the blood with communication properties that respond to signals. It's creating structures within the body which can take remote instruction—from external sources."

It was as bad as he suspected. This plan for man to be controlled by outside forces, creating a new species that would take orders was beyond imagination. The LOT had inferred as much, but Zach hadn't found any information in the LOT to counter such a plan. Perhaps he hadn't asked the right question.

"There must be a way to destroy the Mantis DNA before it takes over," he said, looking to them both for answers. "Just show me how to do this and I'll do it."

Satya stepped forward. "The LOT does not provide answers such as these."

It was not the response he wanted to hear. "I thought the LOT knew all things, all Truth."

"It does," Satya acknowledged.

"But it won't give me *these* answers?" he asked.

"Yes. That's right," she clarified. "Not this."

"Why not?" he shot back.

When there was no immediate response, just an all-knowing look, Zach threw up his hands in frustration and began to pace. He would have to call forth that specific information and see for himself. The very thought of overriding Satya's instruction produced a deep chill which ran through his body like a wintry warning. He didn't heed it and called forth the information needed to destroy the Mantis DNA anyway. If they wouldn't help him, he would find another way to put Kaggen out of commission, no matter what it took.

To his utter astonishment, the Library of Truth responded to his request by shutting down his view from it like a doorway being locked and closed, leaving him surrounded in a dark dense void.

Satya wore a look of infinite patience. "Zach, we *are* trying to help you in the only way allowed. There's a reason you cannot access this information, nor anyone else for that matter-- ever. All DNA is encoded with the divine name of the God Source, even Mantis DNA. It is imprinted in every cell. It's sacred knowledge. The LOT will NOT give out information intended to destroy a part of its creator self. It's just not done. This is something you need to understand. It will be up to you, with the information that has been provided thus far, to arrive at your own solution on how you choose to act upon this Kaggen situation--just like Minerva had a choice to use LOT information for either good or evil. It will always be your choice."

Zach felt frustration well up inside him. Even in the LOT there was a Catch 22. Kaggen had somehow discovered the secret to alter and consequently destroy, or re-formulate, human DNA on his own. If Kaggen could discover it, then so could he.

~~*~~

Meghan knew Zach would not be returning to their new home that evening. She also knew, with a certainty that was rare for her, that he was trying to figure out a complex problem and wouldn't rest until he did. And it would be okay. In this new 5th Dimensional reality, she realized she knew a lot of things she didn't know before. It was quite amazing. Like being plugged into a psychic hotline with unlimited data/roaming time.

Seven-year-old Izzie had wasted no time adjusting. Here one minute, gone the next and charming everyone she met during the in-between times. In the short period since their arrival, Izzie seemed to blossom, come alive like she had never before seen. Her daughter was growing up before her very eyes. She would be a good sister to her little brother waiting to be born.

Satya had already assured her that all would be okay. "She has many caretakers in this realm, so no need to worry about her safety. It's not an issue that exists here."

Meghan stopped trying to fight a need to reign in her precocious daughter. As soon as she relaxed and let go of trying to control Izzie's whereabouts, Izzie mentally checked in with her periodically to show her where she was and what she was experiencing. Meghan had no idea where the places she was being shown were. Some were stranger than strange. Perhaps it was better to not know every detail. Her child was in full blown exploratory Izzie mode. It was no wonder cell phones were not needed in this realm. Everyone was already wirelessly connected.

Knowing her daughter was safe, Meghan released her anxiety. As she did, her own creativity and curiosity begin to grow and take hold. Their quarters were generously laid out for living space. The light streaming through the floor to ceiling windows cast a geometric rainbow effect of dancing shapes across the walls. They swirled around the room, mesmerizing her. She found herself sitting back in a cushioned chair that was so ergonomically comfortable she searched for a manufacturer's tag. Of course, there was none.

For a split second she wished it had a matching footrest to comfort the rest of her pregnant body. Before even completing that thought one appeared under her feet. She just stared at it, not believing her eyes. Was this 5th Dimensional realm somewhere where thoughts and desires became real, like Izzie's Pink Heaven? She sat up with a start. If so, could she create her own little heaven? The idea intrigued her. A smile played across her lips as her mind soared with possibilities.

The freedom to create whatever she wanted was something her old life had never afforded her. She had been expected to grow up to be a well-groomed educated little lady exactly like her mother—married to the perfect up-and-coming political candidate with Washingtonian influence. On that front, Meghan knew she had failed miserably. Then when her mother died, she had been expected to be her replacement, the quintessential political hostess to her now deceased Senator father. There was never any question about what she wanted. That is, until Zach came along.

What did she want? She remembered the night coming back to the house from Izzie's birthday dinner at Il Rinnovo. Zach and she had sat on the patio swing, looking out at the Chesapeake Bay, and she had told him how she had wanted to be a filmmaker as a child. Meghan remembered it like it was yesterday.

For Christmas she had received a small movie camera after begging for one repeatedly. But no sooner did she start experimenting with creating her own colorful special effects in the kitchen, then it had been taken away from her for making a "bloody mess". Cherries in a pressure cooker, when exploded all over kitchen cabinets, looked a lot like blood. It had totally freaked out her parents.

She had never intended to cause such havoc, but she learned quickly that her artistic creativity was not something her family desired to foster in any manner and if she disobeyed she would be punished. The internal programming had been pervasive and very effective.

Unlike Izzie, she was more obedient to the demands of adults. Any rebellious nature had been disciplined right out of her at a young age. God, she hoped to heaven she would never do that to her child. Stifling creativity was like killing one's very soul.

Meghan's thoughts returned to her abandoned childhood movie camera. She wished she still had it. And magically there it was, in her hands, staring back at her—a new and upgraded version beckoning her to claim it. She glanced around the room, not sure if anyone could see her suddenly giggling like a delighted child. Christmas had come early to her world.

She extracted herself from the cushiony comfort of her chair and with camera in-hand she went out to explore her new world. Perhaps in the process, she would also find and reclaim her lost inner child.

Chapter 11

It wasn't her imagination. Something strange was happening in the U.S. Capitol. Camille Eldridge ought to know. Washington, D.C., was her backyard and while people were always a little more intense on Capitol Hill due to a plethora of power needs, there was still a palpable difference now showing itself. There were more random altercations on the street. D.C. drivers seemed more erratic with road rage rising and crime stats skyrocketing. Mostly assaults and homicides. And all this had happened in the last 10 days, like someone had flipped an insanity switch. Even the Capitol Police were on high alert after a Supreme Court Justice had been beaten and car-jacked right outside the Federal Courts Building.

Whether this sudden rage had anything to do with a multitude of world banking accounts being mysteriously frozen, including her own, was difficult to tell. Emotions were running high everywhere, for rich and poor alike. However, one would be a fool to blame it away on a summer heat wave or a full moon. Not that Camille put any stock in such woo-woo nonsense.

She had been around long enough to know something was going on and things were not getting any better. With Martin's death, the inflow of campaign cash coming into her war chest coffers was drying up as fast as she was spending it. Try as she might, she had gotten nowhere with some of the remaining Minerva board members to keep the money flowing. She was in their court and would play ball with Minerva in any shape, manner or form they wanted, if it got her the presidency.

Desperate to keep everything going, she was campaigning for her life using her own monies--temporarily, of course. Never use your own money she had always been taught, but it was too late to back out of her run for president without making herself look like a fool or worse yet, a loser. She still had hidden cash resources no IRS audit would ever find. A part of her wanted to show Martin, whether dead or alive, that she didn't need him to make her a winner. He might have rigged the steal on her other political campaign runs, but this time she would run on her own merit and Senatorial experience. Camille Eldridge could and would show them all.

The two-term president now in office would be soon gone and it would be an open playing field. The other candidates that had declared their run for office, all had skeletons in their closet. At least she had gleaned that much from Minerva intelligence sources before Martin died. If she had to, she would run a nasty smear campaign exposing all their dirty little laundry. False rumors had a way of spreading like a viral variant. It was a necessary ploy in the political playbook. Such tactics had successfully prevailed for decades. They always worked if the press was on one's side, and Camille had no reason to believe the media wouldn't be. No one attacked a grieving widow without fear of being lambasted. It was just not done, even in the most vicious of political circles.

Camille knew this was her last shot at true power. Her biological political clock was ticking, and it told her the time to act was now and never look back. "NDY" meaning "Not Done Yet" was her personal and professional motto. Change was happening too quickly, and she needed to strike while she was still hot before that changed, too.

Her thoughts returned to the mystery of what was happening in Washington and in other parts of the United States. She had seen it with her own eyes. Long-time supporters, especially those from her home State of Connecticut, seemed somewhat hostile at her recent events. Someone had even attempted to spit on her. It made her want to tell them all to go straight to hell. She was not used to being treated as such. Their anger served to ignite her. They were all ungrateful constituents. She had dedicated her life to one of public service and they were now treating her like a self-serving public enemy of the state. Was the world going utterly mad?

And if one was to believe the news, there appeared to be more turmoil and chaos in other countries of late as well. Just yesterday she heard of a fight breaking out at the United Nations between two major European powers who had been friendly allies for years. There were heated words, threats of economic sanctions and even rumblings of war. A pandemic of hot heads was spreading like a lethal virus.

Camille was from the school where one never let a good crisis go to waste. It was always an opportunity to seize additional control and power. And God knows the people needed to be controlled and led where her kind knew best to lead them. Left unchecked, she was quite certain humans would destroy themselves and everything and everyone around them--like sheep running off a cliff. They needed a smart, strong leader. Martin and life itself had taught her as much.

Years ago, they had watched the movie *Idiocracy* together and smiled at each other knowingly. If life imitated art, then the future would be theirs and belong to the genius progeny they had sired. Zach was smarter than all of them. If what Cardinal Guiseppe Cullotta had told her were true, and Zach had indeed seized dominion over Minerva, the presidency could be hers if she and her son buried the past and moved forward together.

However, infuriating as it was, Zach was still not answering her calls. But at least someone, perhaps Zach himself, had made sure her personal banking accounts were no longer frozen. Of that she was grateful. It was a promising sign. Camille was confident, as always, that she would have the last word with her son. She usually did.

~~*~~

Zach went into seclusion within the Library of Truth. Seclusion was something he had always done when confronted with a perplexing problem that demanded complete attention. He could only hope that Meghan and Izzie would understand his sudden disappearance once again. Satya would have to explain.

He had difficult work to do. Gore had laid out the cold hard facts. There was no known shut-off valve to what was taking place within human blood and mankind's genome. Kaggen had seen to that. If what was happening couldn't be stopped, the human angelic race would be forever changed and not in a good way.

Now was the time to retrieve his hidden box of portal treasures from the LOC's closed stacks—specifically the Sakya Tibetan Monastery scroll. It contained the key to the entire genetic blueprint for man that the Anunnaki and other alien races had created, revised and endlessly tinkered with over hundreds of thousands of years. The answer to his problem might be found there.

With no surviving Minerva members having access to the LOT, it was safe to bring his box of artifacts back. This might be the best place for him to set up operations. His thoughts were crystal clear in this 8th Dimensional reality. It was the only realm where he could switch on and off his numerical synesthesia at will. He could think better here and perhaps find a solution.

It was Sunday back in Washington, D.C., and the Library of Congress was closed for the day. Without further hesitation Zach popped into the closed stacks. The box was still cloaked. He instructed Gizmo to uncloak it and reached for it the second it appeared. After checking the contents, he was relieved to see it was all still there—the Minerva statues, the Covenant tablets and the precious DNA monastery scroll.

He passed his old desk, tucked away in a secluded corner between rows of bookshelves, and noticed it had a stack of work piled on it. This bothered him, as he diligently made sure his work was always done and his desk clutter-free at the end of each workday. Was no one filling in for him during his extended leave of absence?

His thoughts returned to the National Library of Russia. He hadn't forgotten that there were two Zach's in the universe. Endre's desk had been neat and orderly, like his own--not a mess of unfinished business, the likes of which he was staring at now.

He acknowledged the peculiarity that he had a twin parallel self, named Endre Zegorov, who worked in a St. Petersburg library and, from what he had seen, appeared to be a very competent extension of himself. It weighed heavily on his mind. There were no coincidences in life--at least not in his.

How it had happened continued to puzzle him. His mind abhorred loose ends and his life was now abundantly full of so many of those. Once again, he had allowed himself to be temporarily distracted. This time by the golden statues Endre had so graciously retrieved. He knew it was a poor excuse to have failed to get deeper answers.

Who was this other Zach getting his instructions from? Did he also have a Satya and access to a parallel Library of Truth? Did he know more about the portals than Zach did? There were too many variables to consider and only one way to find out. His unfinished business with Endre Zegorov needed to be seen to--now. If nothing else, perhaps it would shed new light on the problems he was currently facing.

It was Monday morning in St. Petersburg. The Russian library would now be open and, if he was lucky, his other self would be hard at work in his own stacks. The box of artifact treasures he had planned to bring back to the LOT to closely study would have to wait. He didn't dare take them with him into another foreign library. Too many unexpected things could occur, and he didn't want to chance it. He felt that he was so close to gathering all the statues and information he needed to make sense of the work thrust upon him. With a deep sigh, Zach once again returned the box to its designated shelf and re-cloaked it. He felt confident it would still be there to retrieve on his way back.

The National Library of Russia now felt very familiar to him as he emerged from Portal 10. The layout of it would forever be committed to memory, like so many other schematics he needed to view only once before being permanently stored in his brain. His sense of direction was excellent, rendering him almost incapable of getting lost.

Because he had no official ID to allow him access to restricted employee-only areas during library hours, Zach remained visibly cloaked as he moved towards the Russian stacks. Unlike his last visit, when Meghan and he were racing to locate the Golden Minerva statue before library employees started work, this time Zach slowed his pace to take in his surroundings.

The St. Petersburg library was incredibly beautiful. He meandered through the various reading rooms, noticing everything. The numerous statues and busts of Vladimir Lenin, which memorialized the Soviet Russian revolutionary leader, were everywhere like Minerva statues at the Library of Congress. Was Lenin a Minerva member in his own time, he wondered?

There were no dim rooms in this library. Overhead the brilliancy of the crystal chandeliers sparkled and showed off the luster of the rich woodwork that housed the library's world-famous collections and the colorful frescoes displayed across the ceilings. Zach itched to spend more time discovering if it had additional treasures besides Voltaire's and Emilie's secret diary.

As he moved into the library's main reading room, knowing the stacks entry would be nearby, he felt the energy noticeably shift. He looked around and spotted Endre pushing a wheeled cart down the carpeted aisle containing a full assortment of leather-bound books. Swiftly and methodically his twin delivered research materials to occupied library cubicles. A few whispered Russian words of appreciation could be heard in the quiet of the reading room.

Curious to observe both the similarities and differences of their jobs, he decided to dog Endre and observe his work routine. He suspected his duties might be very different in this country's library system. Back in the LOC, Zach rarely had to deliver such research desk materials. Lower-level library staff did such things unless the library was short staffed. He was basically a systems analysis guy.

He watched in fascination as Endre stopped at the room's main research desk to quietly flirt with a young librarian in her mid-twenties. The attractive brunette smiled back and tried to hide a laugh at something exchanged between the two. He recognized what appeared to be an intimate smile, a knowing look. Were they lovers? Zach inched closer, intent on hearing what the two found so amusing. It didn't escape him that in essence he was spying on what felt to be his duplicate self.

While he would be hard pressed to put it into words, he realized he was immensely relieved to see that Endre did not also have a twin Meghan interest. He wasn't sure what he would have done, or how he would have reacted, had that been the case. Thoughts of sharing her with his twin self was not something he wanted to contemplate.

As his twin continued on, saying goodbye to the dark-eyed brunette, Zach noticed the woman's name tag identified her as "Micha". That his twin's female interest worked in the same library and her name also began with "M" like Meghan's, only served to weird him out more. He quickly relegated that thought to an area of his mind marked, "Do not go there."

Endre abandoned the book cart as soon as he pushed through the security doors to the library's closed stacks. Suddenly, he stopped, spun around and slyly asked Zach in English: "Have you seen enough yet, brother?"

Zach stopped short. "How did you know?" he asked uncloaking himself.

Endre shrugged. "I know your energy as you know mine."

They both stared at each other, realizing what that meant. "What do you want to know?" Endre finally asked.

"Where did you come from? Who are your parents?" Zach blurted out.

Endre frowned. "They told me I was orphaned. I do not know the details of my birth origins other than I was born on the 8th of November and have a distinct birthmark, as do you. What year my birth entry took place is also unknown. I can only guess that

I am in my late twenties. I have no early memories of my childhood nor who raised me."

Zach found it extremely curious that besides possessing the same birthmark, they also shared the exact birthday. Quite possibly, even the same birth year as well. Such exact similarities were beyond coincidental. Yet, Endre had no idea who his parents were. His missing memories were even more bizarre. How had this happened?

Endre continued to explain. "About a year ago I was assigned to work at this library due to my high aptitude testing. My instructions were to prepare to help a brother 'in need'."

Zach held up his hand. "Whoa. Stop right there. Who gave you these instructions?"

Endre shook his head. "A lady came to me in my dreams one night. She awakened me, like a sleeper who had been asleep far too long. She told me it was time to do what I came here to do, and that I would know what that was at the right time." Endre sighed. "I do not know why I appear to have this selective memory of my life. I was told by this lady all about you and what I needed to do to prepare for our meeting. And I have done all that was instructed of me."

Zach suspected he knew the identity of the lady in question. "Endre, this lady you speak of--what does she look like?"

"Very beautiful," he replied. "Like an angel. I call her the 'Angel of my dreams'," he admitted.

"Did she tell you her name?" Zach asked.

Endre shook his head. "She said I would remember everything at the right time and that someday all my memories would return and reward me. This she promised."

Zach was pretty sure the angel of his dreams had to be Satya. It was the same Satya who had conveniently kept him in the dark about aspects of his own life. If both he and Endre were being played for some hidden agenda by greater powers than himself, then he wasn't sure he liked it one bit. Was this why Satya had not let him see his life file? Was he being manipulated in some cosmic game? Hadn't Satya drilled into him that it would always be a matter of 'choice'? Whose? His or hers?

Doubts were creeping in. "How did you know how to access the Minerva statues from the different portal locations?" he asked his Russian counterpart.

Endre brightened. "The information just came to me. Perhaps it occurred at the same time it was shown to you as well. One day it was all there in my mind, and I knew what to do and where to go and what to retrieve. Just like I knew you would come for it."

Zach's confusion grew. "You mean to tell me you just suddenly knew how to access the portals?"

"No. This, the lady showed me," Endre explained. "I do not think I would have stumbled upon that on my own, nor understood what it was for, without prior knowledge."

Zach was feeling somewhat miffed. Why hadn't Satya done the same for him? "She just gave you the number sequence?"

Endre shook his head. "I was not given any number sequence. I was given a key."

Zach was struck speechless. A key? Endre had been given a fucking key into the LOT when *his* entry into the place had required formulating a complex algorithm? Was this some kind of joke on him?

Endre sensed his growing annoyance. "Do not be angry," he told Zach. "Unlike your method, my key has limitations. It cannot go everywhere. However, it was given to me so that I could more easily help you when it was required."

Zach didn't know what to make of that admission. Clearly there was more to Endre's involvement than he was being led to believe and Satya was definitely behind it. For now, he would have to trust the process and see where it took him. He pushed these doubts aside for the time being, reminding himself there was still work to be done.

"Have you been to the Library of Congress portal in my country?" he finally asked Endre.

"Oh, no," Endre admitted. "I was told, or rather knew, that I was not to attempt entry into that location or the Antarctica portal. At first I did not even know they were there. But I have been to most of the others."

Zach's eyes lit up. "Have you been to the 12th portal?"

Endre nodded. "Yes. But when I got there an impenetrable wall was in place. It was not the right time to go back into the past."

"The past?" Zach prompted. "Are you saying this portal goes back in time?"

"I believe so," Endre declared. "I just knew that a certain timeline of events had to occur first before I could gain entry."

Zach was suddenly fired up. "Maybe we had to first meet, then go there together," he suggested. "C'mon," he beckoned. "Show me how you access the portals."

It had come as somewhat of a surprise that they could both read and detect each other's energy, but it came as a complete shock to Zach that he could also tap into Endre's thought processes without much effort.

While Endre didn't see the world in numbers and mathematical sequences, as Zach did, Endre had an acutely sharp and logical mind. This was indeed odd considering his extensive personal life memory lapses. Someone clearly didn't want him to remember—at least not yet.

In Zach's mind's eye, he saw Endre extract an old brass key to open the 12th portal. It reminded Zach of the key Roone had left him which opened the old clock room in the LOC's Main Reading Room. Zach watched in fascination, as Endre spun it counterclockwise in his mind. When it made a full rotational stop, they were both hurtled through the 12th portal like a spinning top on an oddly angled axis. Endre revealed that this was the only portal where this strange spin factor was involved.

Zach probed his twin's mind for an explanation to spin factor, only to learn that axial spin gave access to both past and future timelines, something he didn't know. He made note of the exact axis degree employed for future reference. This intrigued him. He wondered what else he could learn from Endre?

They spun out into a void of bright luminescence which engulfed them. "It's a veil, but it feels like a wall," Endre remarked. "I tried, but I couldn't get past it."

Zach attempted to bypass the veil of white light and was also stopped. One thing he knew for sure. The veil membrane was alive, intelligent, and pulsing with patterned energy like a 'googol'-- the number one followed by more than 100 zeroes. He could see and feel it. It was an endless stream of zeroes, the likes of which he had never witnessed. It was the closest sequence to infinity one could encounter. The thought occurred to him that this 12th portal might be a multi-dimensional keeper of all timelines, both past, present, and future. But without entry, he would never know, only be left to theorize about what lay beyond.

Endre shared his mutual disappointment. "I had also hoped you were the necessary key to unlock it," he admitted, absently scratching his head. "I think something is still missing before we can enter. The time is not yet right. Yet I can feel we're right on the precipice."

Zach's scalp was itching as well. Since his boyhood head injury, whenever he was close to figuring something out, his head tingled. It was doing so now. "Yes. I know what you mean," he said before jokingly adding, "You don't think there's another one of us out there that we need to find, like a triplet or something?" No sooner had he voiced such a preposterous possibility, than a chill ran through him.

The two silently stared at each other, mentally computing the odds of the likelihood of such a variable being true. They shook their head in unison, laughed, and immediately dismissed such a thought. What was more likely was that they needed to team up and combine their efforts to locate the needed component. "I'm going to need your help," Zach proposed. "It's time you saw what I've stored in my Library."

Chapter 12

Eric Kline drove onto the back lot of New World Studios. The guard on duty recognized his face and name and waved him through the ornate black iron gate. Over the years Eric had passed through these gates many times since landing his first job here as a writer's assistant. Straight out of UCLA Writer's School, he had been lucky to land the entry level assignment. Granted, he had to kiss up to a few people to get it, but in this business one had to do whatever was necessary to make things happen.

As an assistant, he mostly catered to the needs of established full-time TV writers who had series in production throughout the vast studio grounds. It was a highly competitive market. Hard work, a willingness to learn the ropes, and an innate flare for coming up with original story ideas were what eventually got him noticed by those who mattered. In less than two years, he was filling in at the writer's table when needed. This was his career ticket to making valuable and influential industry friends.

His first television series job eventually tanked after two seasons, but it looked good on his resume, and it gave him the start he needed to get a foot in the door. More importantly, he was well liked and known for being a reliable and fast writer. Those traits had always served him well.

Many an evening he would tap away at his computer in his small, cramped Hollywood apartment writing spec screenplays and pilot TV scripts. His UCLA professors had told him to never stop writing, no matter how bad the script might seem. And there were a lot of bad ones he had tossed in the dumpster file. But the more he wrote, the better he got. While he had never been interested in acting, he discovered he was a natural actor and salesperson when it came to pitching script ideas to producers.

Fifteen years later he had two syndicated TV series under his belt, which meant a lifetime of residual payments until the day he died. This gave him some financial breathing room. To his credit he had garnered Oscar nominations for three full length dramatic movies, with one win for Best Original Screenplay. His vanity wall in his Santa Monica home office proudly displayed this Oscar along with one Spirit and two Golden Globe awards.

In Hollywood you're only as good as your last movie or television series. If you had one or more financial flops under your belt you were instantly labeled "risky" or "past history". Eric understood this and never stopped writing and pitching. In his heart he believed that this fate would never befall him if he could prevent it. He desperately hoped today's pitch session would be successful and bear fruit. More than anything he wanted to surprise Cali with good news. They had worked so hard on making her exclusive story into something that would really sell. It had all the right ingredients, and he knew it.

After several rewrites he was feeling pretty good about their script collaboration. It would undoubtedly go through more rewrites once it got into pre-production, but it was a sound piece of work in his opinion. It was currently untitled, but he was kicking around the working title of *Hacked Truth* or *The Minerva Files*. He kind of liked that second one.

Eric was determined to produce this dramatic, mystery thriller himself with New World Studios funding. He personally knew Bianca LaShea, President of Entertainment, and he was confident that she had his back. Several years ago they had a brief liaison, nothing serious, but they had become good friends and it helped to have a real mover and shaker in the industry who liked you and your stuff, although of late he hadn't seen or heard much from her.

So it came as somewhat of a surprise to hear through the industry grapevine the allegations she was under some kind of federal criminal investigation. Consequently, she was taking a brief hiatus from her executive position at the studios until the "misunderstanding" was cleared up. No one seemed to know the legal details of what her alleged crime was. That alone was unbelievable in a town where mouths forever gossiped, and tongues wagged with a never-ending stream of soap opera details. The industry thrived on the blood of personal and professional drama both on and off the big screen. But Bianca had somehow managed to keep the raps on whatever was going down. She was well connected and had her ways.

Whatever the story, it came as an even bigger shock when Eric walked into his morning pitch meeting and there she was, sitting all business-like on a padded leather couch off to the side, her long shapely legs crossed in front of her like she had just come off a fashion model shoot. In contrast, her God-awful horn-rimmed glasses, perched at the end of her sharp-pointed nose, gave an air of condensation which served to perfect her "Don't dare fuck with me" look. That legendary look was now directed at him.

Why Bianca LaShea had decided to look in on an initial pitch session was puzzling when she was officially supposed to be on hiatus. He knew for a fact that LaShea rarely sat in on meetings at this level. She silently watched him under hooded lids. He felt a slight chill run down his spine. In the past she had always been friendly to him. Something had changed.

"Bianca. Good to see you again," he said acknowledging her presence with a slight nod in her direction before being introduced to the two unknown dark suits. He shook their hands, searching his memory for who they might be. He didn't recognize either of their names. Where were the producers he was expecting to meet with--Guy LaSalle and Seth Manckin? They were nowhere in sight. Something felt off—way off.

The cut of these guys' suits gave them the air as if they had just come straight from an FBI central casting call. His pulse leaped a notch when he spotted another anomaly. Was that a shoulder holster bulge under one of the guy's jackets? WTF? Was he carrying a piece?

They motioned him towards a rather uncomfortable looking straight-backed chair placed before a carved mahogany executive's desk. Clearly, they meant for him to sit his butt down there. It looked like a wired hot seat which he wanted no part of. He instinctively moved away from them and plopped down on the couch next to Bianca. They looked none too pleased.

"I thought I was meeting with LaSalle and Manckin today," he casually said. "What's with these guys?"

He smiled for good measure, flashing her one of his most charming smiles. Bianca frowned, removed her ugly glasses and gave it to him straight.

"Eric, who's your source for this screenplay?"

He didn't like the sound of her voice. It had a slight menacing undertone. "It's confidential, I can't…"

The guy with the hidden gun immediately cut him off. "Are you in contact with or know the whereabouts of the fugitive Cali Cavaleri?"

He looked at them blankly, trying to keep the panic off his face. Fugitive? Cali was no fugitive. The only crime she had committed was revealing the cold hard truth. No crime there.

"What's this all about?" he hedged.

Had his agent or someone in his management agency leaked a copy of his story outline to the wrong person? Had these guys read it? He had hoped to keep the completed script under wraps for a while and just give the studios an in-depth overview pitch until he could gauge the receptivity to his little bombshell story. If he didn't, they might use his idea and run with it themselves. Stealing other people's story ideas was rampant in Hollywood. Fuck! It was hard to keep anything a secret in this goddamn town. But right now, he had more important things to worry about—like Cali. They were on to her.

"Listen. I don't know this Cali Cavaleri person," he blatantly lied. "The story information came from an anonymous source."

Bianca sighed in that exasperating way she did when she was annoyed. "Eric, darling, you better tell these gentlemen everything you know about the information you obtained, or you will be prosecuted for aiding and abetting a criminal—or quite possibly worse."

Eric wanted to slap her. He who had never laid a hand on a woman ever before. She was referring to the woman he loved, who was no criminal. Why was she so irritated? It felt personal. Did this have anything at all to do with her own criminal investigation?

"Am I being threatened?" he asked looking to all three of them for confirmation. It sure sounded like it. They silently stared back at him, dead serious.

"I think there's been some kind of mistake," he began trying to keep it light.

"Tell us your source and where she is," the guy with the hidden gun repeated. "And we'll leave you alone."

Eric felt like he had stepped into a hornet's nest. "Listen, guys. I'd like to help you, but I don't know what you're talking about."

"Okay," Bianca chimed in, with an almost imperceptible nod towards the men. "Have it your way."

One of the two suits got out his phone and texted a few ominous keystrokes, before slipping it back into his jacket pocket. He crossed his arms over his broad chest, staring intently back at Eric. There was a hint of supreme satisfaction on his lips. "Done," he replied to Bianca.

Who were these guys? Hired guns? And what the hell did they mean by "done"? He felt evil in the room. It angered him. Against his better judgment, Eric didn't mince words and came right to the point.

"Are you involved with Minerva?" he asked the woman he had once fucked who was now fucking with him.

In the very briefest moment of unguarded honesty, Bianca attempted to hide her surprise. But he had been in bed with this woman and knew all her subtle looks. She was clearly taken aback—almost scared. He had hit a direct bullseye, shown his hand, which meant he was now dealing with the enemy. It was a stupid move. These guys didn't mess around. He and Cali were in real danger.

As if on cue, inside his jacket pocket, his phone started buzzing like mad. He glanced at the barrage of text messages coming through, one from his cleaning woman who had just arrived on the scene, others from concerned neighbors. There was some kind of an explosion and now his home was on fire.

What the fuck? His first and only thought was of Cali. Had they found and killed her?

~~*~~

Cali was jogging down San Vicente Boulevard on her way back from the 4th Street stairs when she heard the loud explosion. The rumble shook the quiet tree-lined street under her feet like a rolling wave of thunder. This was no Southern California earthquake. She knew immediately what it meant when she saw smoke and plumes of fire shoot up from the direction of Eric's house only a short block away. They found her.

Panic coursed through her veins, propelling her into hyper-vigilant survival mode. She ducked behind a coral tree, plastering her spine up against it to regain control over her labored breathing. One quick glance around told her she was not being overtly observed, but there were overhead street cameras everywhere in Santa Monica. One couldn't be too certain. Eyes were everywhere. People started opening windows and sliding glass doors to see what had happened. Others streamed out of their homes as gas mains blew, causing a series of mini explosions. Smoke filled the air and sirens were heard blaring in the distance.

It was only a matter of time before she would be spotted. Cali pulled her baseball cap down lower over her face. Flying under the radar was paramount to staying alive. Instincts told her this explosion was no accident, but deliberate sabotage. Something had changed and they were on to her and Eric. Fuck!

There were so many protective measures she had taken besides carrying a hidden gun in the back of her running shorts. She had changed her hair color from blond to brunette as soon as she and Eric had returned to LA. Whenever asked, she gave her name as "Vicki Vale", like the photojournalist bombshell from the Batman comics. That had been Eric's idea, natch. So far no one had called her on it. Like everyone else, they assumed she was just a wannabe actress who had changed her name to something catchier. In LA she was just another pretty face in a sea of beautiful women.

The fire engines were already speeding down the boulevard, stopping traffic, and causing a snarl on cross streets. Cali cautiously stayed her distance from the scene, covertly watching from behind a bushy hedge as the flames engulfed Eric's home, destroying everything despite firefighters' best efforts. Whatever had been used, it was a quick accelerant. It spread like a California wildfire to adjacent properties, already dry from severe drought conditions.

Cali knew she was responsible for bringing this devastation upon Eric and his neighbors. It wasn't fair. They didn't deserve it. If it wasn't for Eric coming to her rescue, she would probably already be dead. But they had prepared ahead in the event an unforeseen calamity took place and they were separated from each other when that time came. A safe meeting place had been arranged. Phone communication would be too dangerous. Ditch all electronic devices. Minerva could easily track them anywhere. Even with all the safeguards they had already taken, their house had still been marked and fire-bombed.

With a heavy heart, Cali turned around and quickly jogged towards Ocean Avenue and Palisades Park, blending in with other runners as she made her way south towards the tourist populated Santa Monica Pier. Her mind was running through dozens of different scenarios, focused on carrying out Plan B or moving quickly to Plan C if something else went wrong. She barely glanced at the beautiful blue waters of the Pacific Ocean in her determination to escape.

The park was in full swing. There was the usual assortment of boot camp fitness instructors setting up business on niches of green grass, discreetly away from any signs of the homeless vagabonds sleeping on nearby benches. Cali sped past street performers displaying their talents--break dancers, 3-card Monte cons and musicians belting out tunes from their mobile stereo speakers. Washington, D.C., and Santa Monica may have seemed like worlds apart, but in the end, everyone was trying to hustle and make a fast buck. No one noticed her frantic pace.

Her feet instinctively sped up as she rounded a curb and ran down the concrete ramp leading to the pier, the aquarium, and the amusement park below. It was open 24 hours, which is why she and Eric had picked such a spot. Like most days, with today being no different, it was filled with arcade vendors selling their wares to a never-ending parade of photo-snapping tourists. She reminded herself to slow down and not draw undue attention to herself. Instead, she did a fast walk past the brightly lit Ferris wheel, the Mexican Restaurant and the Harbor Masters' Office, heading for the west end of the pier.

A continual spray of ocean waves crashed up against the thick wooden pilings. There was rough water out there today and with storm clouds slowly rolling in, she knew she didn't have long before the rain swept in with it. If she was lucky, it would blow over with only a sprinkle.

Cali leaned over the railing to look down on the smaller deck below. It extended 1000 feet beyond the tide line, providing deep water access. On any given morning, one could find die-hard anglers down there casting their lines and trolling for whatever the ocean would offer up. She noted that only a few were out today, which was good.

From the first time she had come here, Cali had observed that these men of the sea were a superstitious lot possessing their own unique style of fishing. Some had good luck talismans, special home-made lures, and didn't take well to strangers approaching their multiple fishing-pole locations. Tourists rarely ventured down there. It was much easier observing them from up above. But she was no tourist—not today.

Cali ventured down the side stairs into their domain and frowned. Off in a secluded corner a fisherman, wearing a worn straw cowboy hat, was hard at work shucking mussels and clams at a metal cleaning station. Eric had told her that rear wash-station was rarely used, which meant the two other sink stations had to be plugged up with fish and guts debris. She sauntered over and flashed the cowboy a brilliant smile.

"Hey there, little girl," the old man said with a sly smile and wink, as he continued cleaning his haul. "You aiming to fish today? If so, they're biting."

Cali leaned up against the metal table, one hand poised on its overflow lip, the other slowly running underneath its length, searching. "No. Just passing through," she replied before adding with a slight drawl, "You're doing a good job there, cowboy. Where you from?"

"Texas via Arizona. Gonna have me a good lunch today," he proudly declared reviewing his day's catch.

"No shit? I'm from Arizona, too," she said, smiling. And just like that her eyes lit up as her fingers found what she sought hidden in an underside corner of the table.

The cowboy mistook the spark in her eyes for something else. "Want to join me?" he asked eyeing her shapely runner's legs. "My name's Eddie. You ain't tasted nothing until you've had old Eddie's seafood jumbo. I live a stone's throw from here. What do you say, pretty lady?"

Geez, Louise. Why did old men always hit on her when she was nice to them?

"I'm so sorry, Eddie," she said tightly clutching the small magnetic box in her fist. "That's a mighty tempting offer, but I have to run. Maybe next time."

Cali did an abrupt about-face, calling over her shoulder as she raced for the stairs. "Nice meeting you, Eddie. Good luck with those fish!"

~~*~~

She and Eric had planted several keys in locations around LA in the event one was found and compromised. The magnetic key holder had a trick mechanism and would be rendered useless unless you knew how to open it and what the key inside unlocked. The Santa Monica Pier had been the closest location, affording some protection from recognition among the masses.

Inside a 24-hour public Luggage Stasher facility, located not far from the Third Street Promenade, Cali used the key. From a small locker she extracted the backpack containing everything she and Eric had thought would be important. Cash, fake passports and credit cards, a USB backup drive of their work, a small laptop, two burner phones and a change of clothing for each of them. It was the total extent of their worldly belongings. Now there was only one more place to go and wait, hoping he was still alive and would come for her.

Chapter 13

Meghan was in love with the 5th Dimension. It was a creator's paradise where she felt free from the restrictions and overwhelming responsibilities of her old life. Here she had total control and acceptance over what she thought and what she wanted to do. Not a soul she met told her she was wrong or that she should think differently. There was no forced conformity, secrecy, or political correctness like she had experienced growing up in Washingtonian circles. She spent the day documenting everything she had experienced, as well as meeting different races and people. It was fascinating to interact and connect with their knowledge, wisdom, and for some—their abundant sense of life humor.

These individuals weren't driven by conventional standards, yet ironically, they were more productive. Freedom and self-expression made them flourish. Here they were co-creators with each other. They thrived on discovering new ideas and concepts to put into form. Their unique inventions were everywhere and some she had yet to understand. The advanced sciences were alive and well in this dimension.

Meghan wandered through open air museums, parks, neighborhoods, farms, and markets. Not a convenience store or strip mall was anywhere to be seen. Traffic was unnecessary as people were their own transport. It was as different as night and day, almost a dream fantasy world, compared to the life they had fled from. It didn't take long to start learning how to maneuver in this new world. What she didn't know others readily helped her with--one had only to ask.

Happiness was the noticeable underlying factor. People warmly greeted her and either wished her well or pointed her towards some stunning landscape her photographic eye might enjoy or find interesting. The air was sweeter, the waters clear and bluer, and the plants larger and healthier. Life was simpler here, and so much freer. People took the time to enjoy themselves and talk with each other, openly expressing divergent ideas and thoughts.

There were no cell phones incessantly ringing or cell towers marring the landscape. People were instantly connected to each other, like Izzie mentally checking in with her from time to time. Telepathy was the norm and since everyone could easily tell if a person was lying or not, no one attempted to deceive others. Like Satya had told her--dishonesty became unnecessary.

Men and women seemed quite ageless, too, which puzzled her. Youthfulness was on abundant display everywhere she looked. She met a few individuals who appeared older, but upon questioning they told her it had been their choice. Age was a choice?! Had she heard that correctly?

Meghan learned this revelation on her very first day. She had been the recipient of the strangest conversation with a grandmotherly figure, attending her garden on a grassy knoll, only to learn that without the environmental pollutants and toxins from the lower dimensions, aging pretty much slowed down or stopped altogether.

Life span could be within hundreds of years until one was ready to move on to the next dimension. Death and transition were one's choice? Meghan's head was reeling. This was the land of anti-aging. No wrinkle creams, no facelifts, just nature slowed down. Had she died and gone to heaven? Perhaps so.

There were no hospitals here either--just wellness and healing centers where sound, color and light were used in combination with nature's bounty. When someone became 'unbalanced and out of harmony', as they called it, this is where they went to be "re-tuned" before disease set in.

"For thousands of years these modalities were what the ancients practiced," the woman informed her, "only to be forgotten and replaced by unnatural means on the lower dimensions."

There was so much Meghan didn't understand. "You can see these lower dimensions?" she asked, seeing the woman immediately nod and smile.

"But why can't these lower dimensions see this place and learn from it?" Meghan added.

The woman, who called herself Gertrude, attempted to explain. "That's part of the process, dear. If you don't vibrate at a higher frequency, then you can't see through the veil. Some access this dimension in the dream state, but essentially when individual souls are ready, they find their way here—like you and your daughter, Izzie. We all know why you've come. It's no secret."

Indeed, everyone did seem to know why Meghan was there and why she was so amazed at what she was currently experiencing. No one stopped her from filming this new Shangri-La. If this is a dream, she thought—please don't ever wake me up. She couldn't wait to tell Zach the extent of what she had uncovered. Perhaps, he already knew.

Izzie, on the other hand, had accessed that special place where her waiting-to-be-born little brother Caleb was hanging out. Like a psychic detective, she was getting good at following his unique frequency signature. He certainly moved around a lot, but she finally found him in what appeared to be a private library with golden walls displaying markings that looked similar to the Sanskrit symbols Zach had once showed her.

Izzie was shocked to find that Caleb no longer looked like the little brother she had met and played with in Pink Heaven. He looked to be almost as old as her mother and Zach. At first she felt confused, wondering if she had somehow followed the wrong frequency. How could she have been that off?

This man was reviewing small holographic images--taking in the information through his eyes like a viewing scope. And he looked so serious. This couldn't be her "Caleb". Izzie backed away, prepared to leave this strange man alone with his studies. That's when the man turned his head and gave her a lopsided grin.

"Hello, big sister! Spying on me?" he asked, as the images he was studying suddenly retreated from view.

Izzie's eyes grew as big as saucers. Yep, it was Caleb all right! "Oh my God, what happened to you? You're so big!"

"And why is that a problem?" he asked, amused to see her look of disbelief.

Izzie put her hands on her hips and stared him down defiantly. "Because it's not fair! I'm your big sister and I can't take care of you, like big sisters are supposed to, when you look as old as Zach!"

Caleb laughed. "You know you can grow up too—if you want to."

His words stopped her dead in her tracks. She could grow up? What did he mean? "How?" she demanded to know.

"Use your imagination, Izzie," he grinned, his eyes sparkling with suppressed laughter. "I know you certainly have an over-abundance of it."

She sized him up. "How old are you?"

Caleb shrugged. "How old do I look?"

"Very old!" she pointed out. "Almost ancient."

He chuckled at her answer. "Okay. Let's say for your sake that I'm 21."

She hmphed and thought about that. Just like she figured—old. "Then I want to be 22, so I can still be your big sister!"

As that desire became firmly entrenched in her mind, Izzie felt her body instantly morph in form and shape. Her initial and immediate reaction was one of complete shock. Oh. My. God! Her body was doing strange and bizarre things. She glanced down at what was once her flat little chest only to realize that she now had grown up boobies like her Mommy. She tentatively patted them in place to see if they were real. Just like huge mosquito bites, they were very real. OMG, she was even wearing a big girl bra, too!

Her torso had lengthened, her arms had grown, and her short little legs were now both long and shapely. She lifted one long and graceful bare arm only to realize she had more hair, too, everywhere, not just on her head where her long blond tresses flowed down her back, but on her arms and *under* them as well. How very strange. In this transformative child-to-woman process she had somehow thought to attire herself in skinny blue jeans and a pink form-fitting tank top like the grown-up doll figures her mother had once played with when she was a child.

As a 22-year-old, it meant she could go anywhere and do everything grown-ups did. It didn't occur to her that her mind had not matured as fast as her now adult body. She still felt like seven-year-old Izzie inside, despite her appearance.

From the look on Caleb's face, both eyebrows raised in stunned surprise, she knew she had impressed him. "You're going to be trouble for our parents in a few years," he commented, before adding, "more so than you are now."

"I want to see. I want to see," she repeated aloud, as her wish was instantly granted. Her new countenance stared back at her from a floating holographic mirror. She carefully examined herself from all angles with growing fascination. So this is what she would look like all grown up. She had to admit she was rather pleased with what she saw. Her mother, however, probably wouldn't feel the same way. Just picturing her face, and her shocked look, brought forth a fit of unbridled merriment.

"Oh boy, Mom is really going to be pissed!" she said laughing aloud. "She won't know what to do with me. She'll be so..." Izzie stopped mid-sentence, suddenly debating the merits of her transformation. She frowned. "Maybe I had better change back before she finds out."

Caleb shook his head. "Don't worry. In her eyes she will still see you as little Izzie."

Izzie's eyes danced in delight. "Really?"

Caleb nodded. "People can see you however you want them to see you. Young or old."

God, how she liked this place! She walked her new grown-up body around to get the feel of it, as Caleb returned to making notations in a sheath of documents he was studying. No longer having an attentive audience, Izzie soon lost interest in how cool she looked. She peeked over his shoulder at the pages of written symbols, she could neither distinguish nor read. "Whatcha doing?"

Caleb's face grew serious. "Dad's going to need help. I'm preparing."

"Dad?" she asked, finally realizing who he was referring to. "Oh, you mean Zach." She had yet to think of him in such definitive daddy terms. Of course. He would soon be Caleb's father.

He nodded. "Yes, Zach. The Council asked me."

Izzie frowned. "What are you talking about? What Council?" she questioned.

"It's complicated," he said, which made her throw up her hands in utter frustration.

How she hated that adult phrase. To her ears, it sounded like a ridiculous answer anyway. "You're not even born yet, Caleb!" she pointed out. "You'll be a baby for years. How are you supposed to help anyone?!"

"There are some future unknown factors," he began, not wanting to directly point out to his big sister-to-be that he knew more about the matter than she did.

Izzie was not buying it. "Just tell me and let me decide," she shot back. "I want to know everything you know. I want to help, too."

He hesitated; she persisted. "Who do I have to speak to? Satya? Is she the one in charge?"

Caleb shook his head. "There are many involved. That's why I'm here now."

Again, he hesitated. "You know, you really shouldn't be here, Izzie," he pointed out. "This is a private place."

A random thought popped into Izzie's head. Where exactly was this *'private'* place he was referring to? She spun around taking in her immediate surroundings. While it felt somewhat like the Library of Truth, it also felt different in a way she couldn't quite put her finger on. The frequency of it reminded her of someone. Someone who...she gasped. Could it be?

"You should go," he quickly advised, reading her formulating thoughts. Izzie was a clever one. Much too clever.

Her blue eyes brilliantly lit up like she had just figured out the answer to the million-dollar jackpot question. This was Satya's personal domain, her very own private library. Izzie had been too distracted finding her brother all grown up to initially connect the dots. No, she would not leave. How private could it be anyway? If Caleb could be here, then so could she. This place might have answers about Satya, and everyone connected to her, including this mysterious "Council". If it was anything like the Library of Truth, then she, too, knew how to access information.

Before Caleb could stop her, Izzie called forth the secrets she desperately sought. A hologram within a hologram of information surrounded her. She heard Caleb's distant warning in her mind as she stepped into it, realizing immediately that it was not at all what she could have imagined. It was far worse.

Chapter 14

Endre had never "officially" travelled outside the Russian City of St. Petersburg. Despite having been to portal sites scattered throughout the world doing his Minerva statue "retrieval" work, he had never made it through to "Portal 3" located inside Washington's Library of Congress.

With Zach beside him he was now able to break through the barrier that had barred his entry in the past. He suspected that the powers that be had prevented him from accessing this portal until the timing was right, which appeared to be the case now under Zach's direct invitation. The LOC was clearly his twin's domain, and he could not go it alone.

Endre wasn't sure why Zach had been able to access his library portal in Russia while he had been placed on standby with regard to the LOC. They had both discussed it at length and knew there was some greater mind at work in this grand plan which was slowly unfolding. Whether it was Satya, Ishannika, or the Universal Council of Higher Planetary Guardians orchestrating it all was anyone's guess. It might be one, or all of them, or someone else that had yet to make its presence known.

Endre desperately wanted to see Zach's world to help him make sense of his own. The time difference between their two worlds helped make that possible. It was pre-dawn on Capitol Hill when they came through the portal into the perpetually illuminated bastion of the Library of Congress.

This was indeed Zach's world on so many levels. When the Library closed its doors each night, welcoming silence into its empty halls, an eternal peace swept clean the cacophony of energy left behind from the daily parade of visitors. It was during these times when Zach felt the books and their knowledge speak to him without the interference of employees, researchers, and tourists adding in their own mathematical signatures. Numbers danced throughout the spacious halls, rooms, and shelves in concert with each other. It was their time to sing before the people came in and drowned out their unique literary song.

Evening time was when it became a concert hall of knowledge where every book, touched or untouched that day, could breathe a deep sigh of relief and let go. Zach had discovered this secret from doing Qigong in the Great Hall one night. As he moved the energy around him, he experienced the connection to the books. It was instantaneous and powerful, both visceral and physical, catapulting him into a sublime state of consciousness. The books spoke to him, spilling forth their secrets and hiding places. He became the conductor of information in an orchestra of ideas. Gratitude flooded through him at such times, causing his heart to open to the abundance of energy flowing through his being. It was a drugless high where he felt omnipotent and capable of doing anything.

Zach would have loved to share such a sublime experience with Endre, but now was not the time for it. Besides, explaining such a contact high to his twin just wouldn't be the same. One had to experience such things for oneself to know, to understand, as he had.

Endre insisted on seeing everything, not knowing if he would have the chance again, which Zach understood. Their steps softly echoed through the Great Hall and Main Gallery, past the grand marble staircase and the detailed multi-colored mosaics. Not a word was spoken as Endre noted the larger-than-life Minerva statues that graced the interior hall. Fascinated by all there was to see, his eyes darted to every scientific inscription emblazoned on the walls to read and reverently commit to memory. Zach felt like he was observing himself when he, too, took in the magnificence of this place for the very first time.

The one item Endre insisted on seeing was the Golden Minerva statue tucked away in the hidden balcony of the private Congressional Reading Room. Zach led him down a long empty corridor, making sure they remained cloaked to security cameras. When they arrived at the very last door, he quickly inputted the keypad access code and opened it to a dimly lit room. Street lighting showed through a tall window that fronted Capitol Hill, serving to illuminate the room's cozy living room style. There was no need to turn on overhead lights. They could see just fine.

Like a homing pigeon, Endre went straight for the balcony stairs, taking them two at a time. When his eyes gazed upon the LOC's Minerva, he marched right up to it, grasped the golden figure with both hands and with one swift movement soundlessly extracted it from its secure pedestal base. He immediately turned it over, searching for its "P3" marking. The moment he identified it was there, his face registered complete satisfaction. "It's real," he grinned, holding it up like an award.

Zach was struck speechless at his twin's brazen action. He braced for an immediate security response, but no alarms went off, nor flashing or blinking lights. Silent sensors had to be transmitting the theft right now to a vast security monitoring system. Any moment now agents would be swarming the place. But nothing happened.

A faint energy imprint of the statue wavered atop the pedestal base. It was as if the statue energetically existed there in time and space but no longer did in physical form. This had somehow tricked the sensors into believing the illusion. Despite the prospect of buying them time, Zach wondered how long it would take before people noticed the real statue was missing. Not long. That was for certain.

Endre found Zach's shock somewhat amusing. "It will take several hours for the imprint to dissipate," he explained. "They all do that. I'm not sure why. It's the strangest thing."

Zach shook his head, trying to make sense of what he knew had to be one of the best security systems a museum could possibly have, and yet it failed to identify the treasure had been taken. Were the statues made of more than just gold to leave such an energy imprint behind?

"Don't worry, brother," Endre assured, seeing his continued uncertainty. "It was time, or it would not have allowed me to take it like all the others."

Endre foolishly grinned, enjoying himself. "Now, what's next on the tour?"

Zach collected his wits. Endre was clearly a doer, while Zach was first and foremost an analytic thinker. Endre's strategy was to simply take the bull by the horns and then deal with the aftermath. So far, he had been lucky. The two of them would have to find how their strengths fit together. "This way," he instructed, quietly closing the Congressional Reading Room door behind them and leading Endre towards his domain in the stacks.

~~*~~

"This is amazing!" Endre said pouring over the Sakya Monastery scroll, his eyes scanning the lineage notations. "It goes back hundreds of thousands of years ago! Who would have thought humanity was that old?!"

Obviously, Endre had never seen the LOT's hologram of Ancient Antarctica when 10-foot giants once inhabited the fertile continent. So much history had been lost, covered up or denied. Man had destroyed and restarted civilization over again so many times—sometimes due to his own foolishness, other times to the planet's tectonic pole shifts.

The Sakya scroll reminded them of man's long hidden history. They spread out the parchment genome map on the largest flat surface they could find, a long table under the dome of the Library's Main Reading Room. Together they examined every detail of the genetic blueprint. Deciphering its hand-scrawled notations was not easy. They put it under a magnification lens to make it more legible. So many alterations had been made to man's DNA that it would make a geneticist's head spin. No wonder someone had squirreled away the damming evidence inside the old Tibetan Monastery. Had it not been for Gizmo, it might never had been found. The AI was proving to be worth its weight in gold.

Zach had instructed Gizmo to cloak the entire Main Reading Room so they could move around freely and avoid alerting any guard making his nightly rounds. Witnessing objects moving around would certainly spook anyone. Being extra cautious, they spoke in hushed tones as they continued their search for answers.

Pinpointing where and when Kaggen had inserted his own human-hybrid DNA alterations into man's genetic code was not an easy task. Some coding strains made absolutely no sense. It was a complex puzzle and neither of them were DNA experts. Zach pointed out what he could be sure of thus far.

"This 'K' strain here belongs to the human purebloods the Anunnaki Race created, thereby eliminating the *homo habilis* neanderthal man," Zach pointed out. "They must have discovered this earlier primitive race wasn't evolutionarily viable and kept tinkering. I think they eventually decided to create an entirely new race from their own genetic code, knowing it was stable. This has got to be the unexplainable jump in evolution, the missing link, which has stumped our geneticists."

Zach was following the numbers. He zeroed in one particular coding sequence marked: "-K-". "I believe this is where the alteration was made to their new human model. It's got be the genetic sequence the Anunnaki employed to turn off several other DNA strands they themselves possessed. I have no idea what human potential they turned off nor why, but it shows here that they did do it. Perhaps the LOT can shed some light on that."

Endre looked up. "Did you run this sequence through all the databases and see if anything comes up?"

Zach nodded. "I did and it's a genetic non-sequence. It's not even listed in The Genome Project database where there are billions of codes. It's like it doesn't exist."

"It has to--somewhere," Endre pointed out.

Zach's reminded himself of Satya's advice. He already possessed all the answers he sought. The database inside his head was not only linked to the Library of Truth but also Kaggen's hive mind space craft. The answers had to be buried somewhere in there.

Movement always helped him gain greater clarity, bringing information into focus. His Master Qigong instructor had reminded him countless times throughout his years of training that distraction is the tool of one's enemy. He immediately moved into "heaven to earth", an age-old position which had served him well in finding inner truth.

He breathed in deeply and allowed the numbers in his head, all linked to information stored in short- and long-term memory, to spiral forward with each breath. He waded through them, letting them stream past on waves of light information. They kept coming and he fought the warning signs of neuronal overload that usually brought on a seizure. The last time this had happened was when he discovered who his father really was—the Governor of Minerva. This had caused him to black out in Antarctica and somehow land up in the Bodleian Library at Oxford with missing memory. He was determined not to allow that to ever happen again.

It was like grasping at fly-away numbers. He struggled to rein then in to put them together. Out of order and form he could harness their intent. It reminded him of the task Ishannika had given him on the dwarf planet of Nordekka where he had to liberate *The Minerva Files* Nehemiah had locked away. This mental exercise felt vaguely familiar. He felt pressure in his head, meaning he was coming up against inaccessible information. He tabled the thought and went back to the task at hand, moving around the mind obstruction.

Endre silently watched Zach's movements, completely fascinated and transfixed with witnessing such fluidity in motion. While he wasn't sure what his American counterpart was doing, as it did look rather strange, Endre could feel the energy difference that surrounded them in the Main Reading Room. It was palpable. The air pulsed with an electrical charge. It was as if Zach's movements had become a human particle generator of energy. And it appeared to be growing stronger. Endre knew many things, but this man he called "brother" was indeed unusual on so many levels. Yet, despite the strangeness he now witnessed, he hungered to understand the reasons which had brought them together.

From a sitting position, curiosity drew him to his feet. He had waited and watched for a sign—any sign which would explain what Zach was doing. Suddenly he felt swept into the circuitry of whatever it was Zach was formulating. Without hesitation, he joined his own energy into the mix, not even knowing it was his to give his twin. It flowed freely, like an offering. He realized, too late, that it was too much for him to handle without such experience. Seconds later, Endre felt himself drawn into a mental void, causing him to slump to the floor unconscious.

Zach continued to move his body throughout the Main Reading Room bringing the necessary numbers together, as the patterns built into a definitive sequence. He was oblivious to all else, knowing that Endre's added energy had staved off his own oncoming seizure, but not realizing it had caused his twin to pass out because of it.

His own mind was crystal clear as he came out of Qigong. The numbers had been tamed and given him answers. Zach glanced around to find Endre asleep. No, not asleep but slumped in an odd position on the room's dark red carpet. Zach rushed over to him and shook him once, then twice. Endre's eyes finally fluttered open, looking somewhat dazed and confused. He hadn't known he had passed out, nor why. He took Zach's outstretched hand, and slowly rose to his feet.

Endre shook the cobwebs from his head. The first words out of his mouth were, "Bro, that was one fucked up head trip!"

Zach knew what he meant only too well. Since childhood, he had gotten used to living in his strange numerical world. Others might find it the stuff of nightmares if they could see and experience what he often did. But to him, the numbers spoke a logical language, a familiar tongue that was both reliable and consistent.

Endre put his hand on Zach's shoulder. "How about you? Are *you* okay?" he wanted to know.

"Yeah," Zach answered. "Thanks for your help. I was close to overload."

Endre shrugged and got to the point. "Did you learn anything?" he asked, hopefully.

Zach grinned from ear-to-ear. The "head trip" as Endre had called it, had been worth it. The patterns had finally come together. "I believe so," he told Endre. "Now I understand why and where the Anunnaki altered the human genetic code and how Kaggen capitalized on it. It's really quite brilliant."

Chapter 15

Eric had never been so scared in his whole entire life. Sweat poured off him like a red hot sauna. When he literally ran out of the goon squad meeting and raced through the gates of New World Studios, he was ashen faced. He drove like a demon West on the 10 Freeway heading towards Santa Monica. Was he being followed? He kept looking in his rear-view mirror but couldn't tell. He got off at the Second Street exit ramp and took a hard right into the first public parking structure he saw, watching for any cars entering behind him.

"C'mon, c'mon," he impatiently yelled at the ticket machine, waiting for the entry gate to go up and allow him in. He zoomed into the first available parking spot and silently waited, holding his breath wondering what to do next. The sound of his heart beating wildly in his chest was like thunder to his ears. It occurred to him he was now living his art—the very things he wrote about in thriller scripts, and at this moment it didn't feel thrilling at all. It was a goddamn nightmare!

There were a few cars that came in after him looking for spots, which passed him right by. People were coming and going in the busy garage. It was the usual pier and lunch hour traffic. There was an overwhelming urge to get out of the car and get away from his vehicle as fast as he could run. He left his phone behind, knowing they would use it to track him, and grabbed a jean jacket and baseball cap from his back seat. He quickly donned them, along with dark glasses, hoping to disguise himself. At the last second, he remembered a gym bag he always kept a change of clothes in and grabbed that as well.

His thoughts ran to the garage's security cameras. Minerva operatives would undoubtedly check them. He slowly opened his car door, ducked down and crawled between parked cars to avoid detection. Cautiously, he made his way to an open stairway where he hugged the wall and kept his head low. He looked for surveillance cameras everywhere. One couldn't be too certain. They might find him despite all he was doing, but at least he wouldn't make it easy for them.

The lunch crowd was out in force filling up the restaurants and cafes along Second Street and Eric took advantage of it. He attached himself to small clusters of people, skirting their periphery, where he might blend in and not be easily identified. Those surveillance street cameras and spy satellites in the skies above monitored everyone and everything night and day. They needed at least six feet of distance space between persons to make clear facial recognition and positive ID. How did he know this? He had learned it from an NSA consultant on a TV series where he had been the head writer. In times of terror, buried and obscure information finds its way to the surface and lets itself be known.

He knew Los Angeles alone had over 35,000 surveillance cameras. It was a Trojan horse allowed in under the guise of being for the people's security and safety, like China had done. Santa Monica couldn't be far behind in how many they, too, had erected. Eyes in the sky were everywhere. The primary purpose was data gathering and spying, not safety. If he wasn't careful, they would use this data against him and track him as well.

There was no doubt in Eric's mind. He couldn't return to his non-existent house, much as he had loved this crowning achievement—a successful writer's gift to himself. It had become a little love nest for him and Cali. He kept telling himself that she had escaped and would go to the first place they had decided upon. He prayed she had made it.

Having spent his childhood playing on the Santa Monica Pier, Eric knew every nook and cranny, every hiding place a kid could find and explore to play free games, steal vendor food and avoid getting caught. All of which he utilized now, weaving in and out of arcade back entrances, behind the Ferris wheel pit and onto the lower deck of the fishing pier. He went straight for the cleaning table, not missing a beat, and ran his hand over the underside surface searching for the hidden spot. It was gone.

Inside he felt a mixture of profound relief. She had either found it or someone else had. Which would it be? There was no way of knowing. He was betting everything on the former. He had too. Any other option he found totally unacceptable. In his mind, it meant she had retrieved their hidden stash and gone directly to the jump-room portal Zach had opened for them. It was their backup should the time ever come when they needed to make a quick escape--like now. They had planned for all contingencies.

"Don't worry. I've taken care of it," Zach had reassured them. Being he was now privy to so many of Minerva's deepest portal secrets, they believed him. "No one knows about this jump-room, or at least not where it goes or how to access it. I made sure of it," he added.

Zach had left them with a set of specific instructions. Under no circumstances should they write down such information anywhere. Instead, he schooled them on committing it to memory. They had obediently done what they were told.

Eric hoped Cali had gone directly to the jump-room where, if separated, they had agreed to wait 24 hours for the other person and no longer. If the other didn't show, they were to leave without them. Hope coursed through him as he made his way there now. Would it be too late?

The two-story warehouse off Sepulveda Boulevard near LAX Airport had been shuttered for years, at least for as long as Eric remembered living in Los Angeles. It was believed some corporate entity owned it and kept paying property taxes on it, year-after-year, never having made any attempt to sell the valuable property or tear it down. After a while the abandoned building just seemed to blend into the urban landscape and people forgot about it or why it was still there. Eric now understood why. It was owned by Minerva and housed an incredible secret.

Drops of rain started coming down, releasing the city from a long overdue dry spell. Eric glanced up at the threatening dark clouds overhead. The heavens looked like they were about to open and dump a deluge of water any minute. Without wasting time, Eric stole his way to the back of the building where he saw a shattered window that he didn't remember from the last time they had come through the portal. Had Cali broken through it or were there squatters inside? His uneasiness ramped up a notch. He climbed through and hugged the shadows.

It was dark, musty, and the air inside the place was rank and fetid. The smell of dead animals, possibly rodents, assaulted his nostrils. A few live ones scurried overhead on the second floor above him. If Cali was up there now, he was certain she was probably shitting bricks having encountered the vermin infestation. If there were any human inhabitants who had taken up residence in the abandoned warehouse, he certainly had yet to see any evidence of them. That at least was reassuring.

The rain started pelting down outside, the wind whipping against the windows like the sound of small hail. Cali was nowhere to be seen on the first floor, so he stealthily climbed the steps to the second floor when a loud clap of thunder rocked the building. He heard a shriek behind him. He swung around to see her crouched, with an iron bar in her hand ready to swing it at his head. He instinctively ducked and jumped out of the way.

"For fuck's sake!" she said, throwing the bar down and launching herself at him. "I thought you might be someone else!"

"Yeah, I got that," he said hugging her close and feeling her breath coming out in short little gasps. He came clean. He had too. "I was ambushed at the studio. Somehow, they knew about you and me."

She leaned back, searching his eyes. "How?" she asked.

"I don't know," he admitted, seeing her confusion. He decided to omit anything about his past relationship with Bianca LeShea, things were complicated enough. "I had an initial pitch session and was met by a goon squad. I told them nothing about by you, but I'm sure they were the ones who gave the order to fire-bomb my place while I was there."

Her next words spilled out in a gush of terror. "Oh, Eric. I saw what they did to your house. It was terrible. If it had happened 15 minutes earlier, it would have taken me along with it."

He couldn't find words to express what he as feeling right now. Destroying the house was bad enough, but the thought of her going up with it struck him with terror. He grabbed her arm. "C'mon babe. Let's get out of here!"

The portal jump-room was located on the second floor in what appeared, for all practical purposes, as a small freight elevator shaft in the far corner of the empty space. At first glance, it looked like a closet until you opened the door and realized it was a one floor elevator that didn't move or go anywhere. Inside was a hidden floor panel, which slid back to reveal a locked keypad, just as Zach had instructed. It took them a few minutes to locate it and input the 8-digit code they had memorized then reverse the number sequence in the exact order.

They waited. Nothing happened. Cali swore under her breath, her hands trembling. They tried the code again, painstakingly slower this time, while they held their collective breath. It had to work. There was nowhere else safe for them to go.

Another loud bolt of thunder struck somewhere nearby. All at once a low rumble was felt from the floorboards under their feet followed by the shaft's walls rippling in watery waves all around them. Cali clutched their survival backpack containing all their worldly belongings, while Eric grabbed her to him. There was no turning back—only forward, wherever it took them. A second later they vanished into thin air.

Meghan observed that Izzie had been unusually quiet since returning to their new quarters. They both had separately explored this 5th Dimensional world they now resided in, and each had made incredible discoveries. This was a whole other realm they never knew existed. There were so many possibilities open to them that their old world lacked. But regardless of such vast differences, Meghan sensed an unanticipated change in her young daughter. She was encountering a look she couldn't identify, despite seven years of becoming an expert on identifying her child's many and varying mood shifts.

"What's wrong, honey?" Meghan finally asked. "Did something happen that made you sad?"

Meghan wasn't even sure the identified emotion she was witnessing on her daughter's face *was* sadness, but she threw it out there anyway hoping for a bite. Izzie didn't answer at first. There was a contemplative look on her face, that held a fleeting sense of maturity.

"I'm not sure I want to grow up, Mommy," she finally blurted out. "It's not as much fun as being a kid, is it?" she asked looking to her mother for confirmation.

Meghan had not anticipated that particular response coming out of the mouth of her seven-year-old. Whatever was going on in Izzie's head? "Well, being an adult certainly entails more responsibility," Meghan admitted. "But then again there's more freedom to make your own choices and find your own way as well."

Izzie nodded, before coming right out with what was weighing on her mind. "Satya will be leaving the Library of Truth," she said. "It said it was her destiny—her time to go."

Meghan didn't know what to say to such a sudden and strange announcement. She finally shook her head to clear it and find her tongue. "Ah, okay," she began cautiously, "And how do you know this, honey?"

"I peeked," she said sheepishly, before admitting, "She has records, too, Mommy. She's older than anyone knows, hundreds of years old, maybe even going back to the dinosaurs. But her records said she is leaving, moving somewhere else. It's a place I never heard of and I can't describe it either. And I think it's happening soon."

Meghan's mouth hung open in semi-shock. She gulped hard before shutting it. If this was true, what did it mean for Satya and them as well? They were safe because Satya had given them sanctuary.

"What else did you learn?" Meghan prompted, as she felt there was more to this tale.

"I can't say," Izzie said, hanging her head in shame. "Satya found out what I had done. I told her I didn't mean to snoop, but I couldn't help it," she admitted. "I think she's disappointed with me. I promised her I wouldn't say anything more about her destiny."

Meghan was in a dilemma. She wanted to know Satya's destiny, which might give clues to their own, but Izzie had clearly done something wrong and as a mother she needed to make sure she understood such things. "Did you apologize to Satya?" she asked her daughter.

"Yes, Mommy, I did," she replied. "I'm really sorry. I apologized to Caleb, too. I didn't want him to think I was a snoopy poopy sister. And I don't want to grow up and have boobs either!" she finally declared, before stalking off.

Meghan shook her head. Izzie had totally lost her. Boobs? Where had that come from? And there was that Caleb stuff again. She wished Zach was here to help her make sense of it all. Where was he?

Zach was still in the Main Reading Room trying to explain to Endre the revelation which had come to him. When engrossed in finding a solution to a difficult problem, he would often lose all track of time, like now. He forgot about eating, about sleeping, and in this case, that there were two people who loved him who were awaiting his return. It wasn't something he was used to having in his life. It still felt so foreign. And now the insight he had retrieved from the Mind of the LOT and the alien space craft, gave him tunnel vision. His mind dwelled on nothing but the plan, or rather the blueprints, which were all laid out in his head. What he saw *was* brilliant and Zach thrived on brilliance.

While it was true that the Anunnaki had created man from their own genetic code, they had also made some key alterations. They deactivated certain DNA strands that would have given their human creations the understanding of all things in the multiverse. The Anunnaki knew how to access Universal Mind and find solutions to all things big and small. They were master geneticists, seen as gods in the cosmos—their evolution going back millions of years. They created humans, not to enslave and manipulate like Kaggen, but to study and watch how they evolved over thousands of years, much like a pet experiment.

It was therefore agreed upon that it was necessary to slow down the evolution of humans, by simplifying their DNA, so they would not surpass their creators. There were bets placed on the outcome of whether man himself would find a way to unlock his evolutionary potential.

They had intentionally turned off all telepathic and psi capabilities, the knowledge of transmutation of energy and matter that effected alchemy, the ability to shapeshift, jump timelines, and teleport one's mind and body from one realm to another. Man would not be privy to the secrets of extended life without aging. Nor would he have access to ultimate Truth.

As parental creators, the Anunnaki thought they were doing the right thing in their experimental tinkering. They recognized there would be some rogue pureblood human souls who would evolve faster and master what the Anunnaki had taken as God-given abilities by their own angelic creators, but the human race, as a whole, would move forward at the slow pace they had set out for it—meaning a prolonged evolutionary process. This would make long-term study of their creations possible without constant intervention.

Eventually the Anunnaki would return to learn what had become of man's process. To the Anunnaki it was a just a grand experiment. They had seeded other races in the multiverse as well. The question would become--which of their test groups would evolve the most and fastest over time.

Zach learned that the Anunnaki would return to Earth to evaluate man's progress in the year 2569. He saw and understood it all, down to the sequencing these master geneticists had employed in their subjects to deactivate more evolved DNA strands. It was, in essence, genetic psychic surgery. Man's extra DNA strands were energetically still there, like the Minerva statue's energy imprint left behind in the LOC's Congressional Reading Room after Endre had extracted it from its base. Was it too late to transmute and re-activate these dormant strands after all this time? This, Zach was not so sure of. Based on information he had learned it would entail generating a unique frequency transmission to get the process started. Once activated, he had no idea what would or could happen after that.

There were so many variables in play. His mind jumped to the matter of Kaggen's part in this complex problem. He had inserted Mantis DNA into thousands, no millions of pureblood humans through his abduction experimentation with the Grey beings. Their blood was now tainted, compromised, and those black nanoparticles appeared to have magnetic bot-like properties that made them respond to transmitted direction. This he had learned from the mind of the alien space craft that recorded everything.

Kaggen had cleverly re-worked human blood to make it possible to control his human-hybrids. And why not? He felt he had created them. His power over them was much the same as the Anunnaki towards their pureblood human creations. The question on Zach's mind was whether Kaggen was controlling human-hybrids already via some communication signal device or was he waiting for some bigger event to take place before unleashing his Earth domination plans?

If Zach were to generate the frequency bandwidth needed to help restore de-activated human DNA, what might the effect be on Kaggen's hybrids? It might cause an even greater race of monsters to take form. The answer to this problem was not to be found in the Mind of the LOT or from what the organic memory the alien spaceship held. It was an unknown factor of larger proportion which had never been attempted. It could be the definitive answer he sought, or it could also bring about mass destruction, like a deadly directed energy weapon. He had to think out all possible outcomes. There was no room for guesswork. It would have to be done in calculated stages.

Zach turned to Endre and shared his thoughts. "They're showing me we need to use a high-power microwave source in the 'KA' bandwidth focused in 40 GHz, including the addition of several sound harmonics. The problem is that it could knock out satellites—theirs and ours."

Endre frowned. "Does Minerva have KA band satellite communication capability?" he asked.

There was so much technology Minerva possessed, Zach really couldn't say. But he would certainly find out.

Chapter 16

Like the true puppet master he had become, Kaggen watched his creations do his bidding with the utmost fascination. It was his hour upon the stage after thousands of years of paving the path for his human-hybrid invasion. He had come to thrive on chaos and disruption. The "loosh" energy produced by the human aggressive response to such upheaval, drove their ego fear state into hyperdrive. The loosh output was abundant everywhere and growing stronger.

Internally, the altered blood of his hybrid creations was now boiling with the red lust of rage he had set in motion. It responded to unique programming which had lain dormant by design, just waiting to be activated—by him. The growing army of hybrids looked human, but they were walking, breathing receiver stations. Even now his hybrids were forging a new biological network that linked them all together like a hive satellite.

The hybrids were coming online with each other faster than he had anticipated. Their deeds were becoming more noticeable by the day. Violence was escalating across the globe. It was as if there had been a sudden release of all the world's asylum inmates. It was beginning to affect all races, ages, businesses, countries, economic backgrounds, both poor and rich, and within the very circles and denizens of the power elite themselves. Few understood what was happening—and how or why it had happened so quickly. To the keen observing eye, it was as if someone had flipped a switch and thrown the world into a realm where darkness and evil flourished.

Once-beautiful cities were turning into cesspools of crime with rapidly escalating killings. In the streets, in homes, in stores, restaurants, businesses and governments his hybrids went about doing his work. They hunted down human purebloods who they then attacked, tormented, and destroyed. It was a thing of beauty to watch. Kaggen's Mantis brethren, who had heralded and supported his plan, were enjoying the slow internal destruction play out in front of them. It was the ultimate show of shows. Loosh energy was flowing freely--dividing and conquering these stupid gullible humans. They became so easily confused, like sheep. This planet would eventually belong to the Mantis and it now looked to be sooner rather than later.

Mysteriously docked within the Rings of Saturn, near the tiny icy moon of Enceladus, and unknown to most everyone, an undetectable Mantis satellite beamed down these high-speed impulses to the internal programming of his army network of human-hybrids on Earth.

Minerva ships had been given limited access to Saturn, giving the Mantis plenty of cover. Even NASA's Cassini-Huygens probe had been scrubbed of any revealing pictures of the large space station and satellite hidden in plain sight. Eventually the NASA probe was forced offline and conveniently crashed on the surface of the planet, where it was promptly blown up and disposed of by alien forces. The Mantis did not want the truth out there. The human-hybrids that infiltrated such space agencies had been programmed to make sure of it.

In Kaggen's humble opinion, the blood composition which he had developed and formulated for his human-hybrids was beyond genius. It had taken decades of experimentation in finding the right properties which a hybrid's body would totally accept. His lab workers had terminated many a hybrid life that had completely failed to biologically accept the new DNA properties. There was to be no genetic room for error. All had to be perfect before he connected them en masse to the Source Hive Mind. Once done, they would slowly build into a hybrid communication receiving structure.

Personality changes would eventually take hold, never becoming zombie-like, but instead functioning as cunning, diabolical, and threatening entities when necessary. This last step in the process would forever cut off his beings from any potential higher guidance that might hijack them from their true purpose. Independent thought would not be capable outside the rules of their assigned programming. These beings would eventually become soulless creatures, keeping them forever locked into his slave race. He had made sure of that. The Saturn satellite ray beam was now fully operational and sending out pulses, night and day, at specific intervals to avoid total chaos.

Kaggen could switch hybrid behavior on and off at will to avoid detection by curious health and medical professionals. If their suspicions were aroused, they might indeed start doing blood tests and find strange properties as well as unusual cellular behavior. But he was confident few would listen to their warnings if they found such things. These men of science would be vilified, ridiculed, and dismissed by other human-hybrids scientists until they shut up out of fear for their lives and careers.

When Kaggen had gotten word of the destruction of his hybrid blood banks in Malta, he had seethed with unrestrained rage. This was compounded by having also lost his experimental labs at the Antarctica Base when he had been forced to flee. After consulting the Oracle, he knew who was to blame on both counts. He had under-estimated the lad, Zachary, just like he had under-estimated the child Izzie and her ability to escape him. Kaggen did not like being bested by anyone. This only served to spur him on and set in motion a plan for revenge.

First off, he activated the human-hybrids he had in place infiltrating world governments. By design, he had planted a greater number of his minions within the circles of influence inside the U.S. Capitol. They would eventually wreak havoc on the laws and rules which human purebloods lived by, crumbling the internal infrastructure that was based for centuries on right versus wrong. Governments would eventually fail and fall. Their country's borders would dissolve and there would be a breakup of the States. Division was always key to conquering.

Kaggen's hybrids had been programmed to maintain allegiance only to the Mantis group mind. This meant the good of the hybrid hive and their hive master. They would find and gravitate towards other human-hybrids, like homing pigeons, coming home to roost. Together they would work as one and become as strong as Kaggen wanted them to be to protect the hive. In his hands, he maintained the controls. All was as he had planned. Mantis history would be rewritten, and he would redeem himself in the eyes of his race. This had always been his intention.

Kaggen had been manipulating human-hybrids for years on a much smaller scale, slowly trying out different methods and tweaking it to perfection so that the changes would be imperceptible from human pureblood observation. He had finally arrived at the stage where his experimental trials were now ready for primetime. A new race was being born with Mantis lineage and it was all his doing. Even the Mantis matriarch, Ishannika, would in all certainty be impressed.

However, this morning he had consulted the Oracle once again and it showed danger looming on the horizon. What form it would take wasn't entirely clear. All he could gather was that Zachary Eldridge had stumbled upon a secret. He cursed the lad for his continued interference. His sudden appearance on the scene had coincided with Kaggen's visions of the future becoming less vivid and the Oracle not always cooperating with him. The Higher Council of Planetary Guardians had to be behind the lad and, of course, that meddlesome recordkeeper of the Library of Truth.

It was time to send a strong message to his young nemesis-- one that would hit home in retribution for his getting continually in the way. Zach had taken something from Kaggen and consequently something would be taken from him in return.

~~*~~

Camille Eldridge had taken special care with her dress and appearance for tonight's classy black-tie fundraiser for her presidential run. Hosted by billionaire hedge fund mogul, Jeffrey Carlton, tickets to the New York Plaza Hotel event had gone for a cool $25,000 a plate. Every table had sold out quickly, not an empty seat to be found, even after adding last-minute extra tables. The main ballroom of the Plaza Hotel would be packed with Connecticut and New York high society matriarchs and patriarchs that influenced the political scene outside Washington.

The wife of Martin Eldridge, former Governor of Minerva, had diligently amassed a war chest of donations, now in the millions, on her own. "Money is Power" had become her personal mantra. Fundraising was the key. One could never stop. Camille had gotten good at asking for money and promising whatever was necessary. The tides were changing. Six-figure and million-dollar donation checks were now flowing into her coffers. A fortune would be needed to buy her way into the White House.

It became abundantly clear that Camille could not count on Elizabeth Vandam of Cornerstone Media Enterprises to help her keep the media networks in check. The woman was currently drowning under lawsuits and multiple legal investigations for FCC violations that had seemed to materialize out of nowhere. Vandam was focused solely on saving herself from fraud charges and bankruptcy court. Powerful people were suddenly finding themselves in hot water, which Camille found strangely curious. So much had changed after Martin died. But their fate didn't concern her in the least. She, too, had to think of herself first and foremost. All the rest of them be damned.

Truth be told, she was quite proud of her efforts in representing her party--the Party of the People. Fuck Martin, she thought, remembering his taunting reminder that she was nothing without his help. She didn't need her son's help either. In her mind, Camille was quite confident she would rise to the true power she deserved.

Tonight's entertainment, *Falla*, was a rising young star in the rock music world, with her hit songs stationed at the top of the charts. It was only expected that who's who in the celebrity and political world would be in attendance and want to be seen at such an event—her event. Behind the scenes she was already making her deals, cementing her alliances, making the necessary promises to the usual jungle of corporate heads, lobbyists, and political bedfellows. After all, she was quite good at it. James Talbot had taught her more than he ever knew.

There were brief moments when she almost missed having him around to talk shop with and learn who was compromised and who still needed to be compromised from his insider view. "If you're going to do shit in Washington, make sure you shit vanilla ice cream," he had crudely told her. "Remember--white cream always rises to the top."

Yes, she was determined to come out smelling sweeter than the rest. Along with Jim's sage advice, there was a part of her who also missed the rough and regular sex she had with him. It was more an emotional than physical outlet for her--especially towards the end when she just wanted to smack the hell out of the male race and he loved her for it. These days, she was either too busy or too bone weary to cultivate new lovers. She was a widow now, so anyone was fair game, but men could be so distracting. And, truth be told, she didn't know who to trust. Loose tongues wagged and she wanted to avoid all forms of gossip that might taint her personage. She had the presidency to win, and campaigning was an energy-demanding job. It was the only job that mattered.

Camille was prominently seated at the head table with the Mayor of New York, her generous host Jeffrey Carlton, two New York State Senators, the Governor, and their respective spouses. This would be a lavish night to remember. Waiters in white tails made the rounds generously pouring bubbly champagne. Overhead the chandeliers were brilliantly lit, dispelling any shadows, and bathing the room in a warm welcoming glow.

Security was tight as luminaries from both the entertainment and political world were out in force dripping with expensive jewelry and toting along their own private security details. Metal detectors had been set up outside the main door, which was now standard practice at all these type of events—especially with the recent rise in crime that was becoming prevalent everywhere. Safety was always of paramount concern.

Camille was thoroughly impressed by tonight's turnout. Her eyes scanned the room, taking in everyone and everything. Her people had done well. She had meticulously planned for this gala like a bride arranging a five-star wedding. While she had been a stickler for details, her staff had carried out what looked to be a flawless event. It would be her biggest fundraiser to-date and she wanted it to be something everyone would talk about for some time—like a presidential inauguration ball. Her path to higher power was destined. Satisfaction and pride flowed through her with each sip of her Moet champagne.

Camille wore a signature bright red gown intended to make a definitive powerhouse statement. The lightly-beaded, hourglass-hugging ensemble had been designed to display her years of dedication to staying youthful and fit. She didn't look her age and longevity counted in Washington. The people wanted someone who could stay the course and not age like so many others had after only a few years running the country. Camille Eldridge would be different.

A quick glance in the mirror before departing her hotel suite told her all she needed to know. Her makeup and hair were perfect, her skin flawless. A sly smile appeared on her lips. Yes, she would take their breath away. The world was waiting for her, and she knew exactly how to deliver what the people wanted. Her speech had been written by the best money could buy. She had practically memorized it to make it seem spontaneous and heartfelt. A little humor had been inserted as well. People loved to laugh and be entertained. This she knew how to do.

The Cartier double diamond strand worn around her neck sparkled in the spotlight that lit her as she was introduced. Like a queen ascending her throne she rose from the table and walked onstage, smiling and waving. There was the deafening sound of thunderous applause in her ears. They loved her. She tried to look humble from all the adulation. That, too, was important. A radiant fill light from the stage gave her a glowing aura as she stepped behind the podium and gazed out onto a vast sea of welcoming faces.

Why had she never done this earlier, she thought to herself? Did it take Martin's death to give her the courage to go it alone and seek out a higher office? Camille pushed such doubts aside. She was a strong and powerful woman in her own right and tonight she would prove it to the world or, at least, to the influential and powerful New York and Connecticut political scene.

She spoke eloquently about her humble roots as a young woman growing up in New York City, conveniently omitting her job as a phone sex worker that lucratively paid the mounting bills, before she could make a modest success in the high-end world of modeling for some of the world's top designers.

She had caught the eye of Martin Eldridge and from there Martin had helped use his money and influence to launch her successfully in the political world, after an almost failed congressional run in her Upper East Side district. Unknown to her at the time, he had fixed that race to guarantee her win. This, too, she failed to mention to her audience, instead telling them about how she had struggled and worked hard for her congressional district for so many years before launching her Senatorial run. She was, and would always be, a servant to the people.

"Together we will forge forward to create a new world," she told her audience upon closing. "With your generous support, I promise to secure our borders from all foreign and domestic threats and to strengthen our military to ensure our continued world-wide dominance and protection. I will move to enact strong legislation to enforce the safety and security of our neighborhoods and cities from the crime that has been allowed to steal over what we have cherished and built. I will work for transparency in government and fair and equal justice for all. And, yes, we will bring prosperity and integrity back to this great country of ours. As your humble servant, I ask for your support and generosity in bringing Truth & Freedom back to America."

A large, patriotic red, white, and blue "Eldridge for President" sign was unfurled behind her, expanding the entire length of the stage, as the orchestra started up the night's rousing theme song—Carly Simon's "Let the River Run". Camille held up both arms in the air, did a little shimmy dance, showing she could still shake it along with the best of them, and waved a few grateful kisses to the crowd as she mouthed a silent thank you to all her many supporters.

She slowly walked towards the stage steps, where she took the offered hand of an elegantly attired gentleman waiting to help her safely navigate the stairs in her long gown. Camille Eldridge was beaming. This was her moment. She allowed herself to enjoy every second of it. There would be many more like it with even bigger ones to come once she was president. The applauding crowd cheered her on. *They love me*, she thought ecstatically. *They really, really love me!*

She took another step and had the wind suddenly knocked out of her. The adulation briefly faded as the room watched her falter and sway. A look of stunned surprise spread across her face. The crowd collectively gasped as she fell down the stairs, dragging her escort with her. The music came to a complete and sudden halt. Everyone stood up, their mouths agape as they silently watched and waited for the drama to play out and see if she was alright.

Camille Eldridge did not stir from where she landed on the ballroom's plush red carpeting. Her escort tried to help her up only to register a look of total shock when he glanced down to discover there was blood on his hands. A dark stain covered the front of Camille's red dress, displaying the last drops of blood from a heart forever stopped. It was clear to anyone within close range that she had been shot.

Too late, Camille's own security detail rushed forward in stunned disbelief. The hotel venue had been thoroughly checked and secured, as was their job. Someone had carried out the impossible. The place was dripping with private bodyguards for the rich and famous who were now in terror that a skilled psychotic killer was in their very midst. While some pushed closer to get a better view, others discreetly made their escape, sensing an incoming wave of doom and wanting no part of it like rats fleeing a sinking ship.

Everyone was shouting orders at once for 911, for an ambulance, for someone to do something. "Is there a physician in the house?" one of Camille's security people shouted out. A retired surgeon pushed his way forward through the crowd and knelt down beside the unconscious presidential candidate where he felt for a pulse. The man shook his head telling the crowd all they needed to know. Camille Eldridge was dead. Any attempts to resuscitate her would be futile. It would take a coroner to discover the ballistics that had made the direct hit to her heart, stopping it dead.

Pandemonium and chaos ensued throughout the room as the news of her death spread. Fear registered on everyone's face. The police arrived and were barring anyone from leaving who had not already taken flight earlier. Hundreds were now left to deal with the messy interrogation process. Camille Eldridge had indeed made it a night the rich and famous would forever remember.

~~*~~

Zach heard the news of his mother's death upon his arrival back into the LOT with Endre. A hologram shot out towards him, giving him an instant replay of the entire fundraising event. Everything inside him felt compelled to watch it, despite having not summoned it up or known why the LOT was showing him what he was now viewing. The Mind of the LOT felt it important enough for him to see the truth for himself. And he did, until the very bitter end.

He felt the wind knocked out of him as if the bullet had gone through his own heart. The hologram viewer swept through the area searching until it revealed a lone marksman, hidden in the shadows of a backstage lighting catwalk. The sniper had taken careful aim and silently hit his mother from the rear where she was most vulnerable. The shot had instantly killed her. The LOT identified the killer's name and that he was a special access program sharpshooter in the space fleet--an accomplished assassin. Seconds after successfully carrying out his mission, her killer simply vanished and disappeared without a trace. Someone with AI or alien technology was behind this, and Zach knew who it was—Kaggen.

An emotional wave of anger and sadness flooded through him. He and his mother had not been close, and their issues had been vast, but she had not deserved to die like this. Despite her not wanting the burden of being a mother, his mother, there were some memories he possessed of her having shown love and concern for his welfare. She was not all the monster he sometimes painted her out to be and now that she was gone, he reminded himself of this.

Zach was surprised to feel tears running down his cheek. Quickly wiping them away, he was at a loss to find words for what he had just learned from the hologram. It was beyond comprehension. Both his parents were now gone—wiped out by unnatural means within two months' time of each other. Like Meghan, he too was now an orphan.

Zach glanced over at Endre who was silently feeling his grief. His twin's eyes were filled with tears for Zach. Quietly Endre moved towards him and slowly wrapped his arms around his brother.

"I'm so sorry," was all Endre could continue to say. "This is a terrible thing. Just terrible."

Zach's chest heaved with silent rage causing numbers to explode inside him like a numerical war of the worlds. Endre released him and knew it best if he retreated.

"I will leave you now and start working on what we discussed," he muttered barely above a whisper. "You will require time to deal with this, but I am there if you need me," he added before turning and disappearing back through the Russian portal.

Zach had not failed to identify that every time he got close to making real headway, another obstacle or distraction appeared in his path slowing him down. He was averse to seeing his mother's death as a distraction, but he knew Kaggen had killed her to send him a clear message to stay out of his business. Since Meghan and Izzie were now safely beyond Kaggen's reach, the Mantis had taken the next living family member of his with which to extract revenge.

Now more than ever he wanted to get back to Meghan. It felt way too long to be separated from the ones you love. He craved her comfort, like a homeless person seeking shelter in a storm. She was his rock—his family.

~~*~~

Kaggen's eyes were glued to the Oracle, mesmerized as he watched Camille Eldridge's last moments on the face of the Earth. Such high drama from these humans. Little would they know that the attendees at her lavish fundraiser were infiltrated by his human-hybrids. Some sat at the head table right next to the Eldridge woman. They were undetectable but could be activated if needed. He had programmed different level tiers of operatives who could be prompted to act and carry out special tasks, like the Eldridge woman's assassin.

Upon discovering the destruction of his prime hybrid blood bank, the Mantis leader's first preference had been to rip the very soul out of Zachary Eldridge and take away his precious Meghan and her little girl. However, much to his dismay, the Higher Council was hiding them somewhere out of his reach. He was confident they couldn't hide forever and would eventually slip up, making themselves known to him. It was only a matter of time before he struck. They, like many others, were on his growing termination list.

Kaggen regretted not disposing of the two of them sooner, especially that little snot of a girl, Izzie, who had bested him. He would not make that mistake again. He grumbled under his breath before a sly smile spread across his face. His long pink tongue shot out and he licked his lips in gleeful anticipation of the oncoming devastation that would take its toll. Zachary's mother was only one of many to come. Soon people would be dropping like flies from sudden and mysterious heart attacks. Crippling death frequencies, tuned to the human pureblood frequency would soon be beamed down from his Saturn satellite base to aid his hybrids. Human purebloods would be none the wiser. The world would eventually turn AI with only one puppet master among a slave race of Human-Mantis hybrids.

The members of the Inter-Planetary Consortium of One Mind (IPCOM) had taken up residence on the Mantis space station within the Rings of Saturn where their long-range ray beams were undetectable. It was the best vantage point with which to watch the final act play out on Earth.

The space station was a city within a city, with docking capabilities for scores of large intergalactic space craft. Here the rogues and renegades of the cosmos found a safe haven. They, along with other members of IPCOM, openly mocked the U.S./Russian Space Station which to them was nothing more than a floating Motel 6 for children in space. IPCOM made sure it stayed within its limited orbit around Earth and never ventured further out. IPCOM was well aware that the astronauts onboard the U.S./Russian station occasionally observed one of their craft, but mostly they remained publicly silent to preserve their reputations and appease their superiors. Minerva, preserving its collaboration with the alien races, had seen to that cover-up. But they could no longer count on Minerva. All human/alien treaties had now been broken upon the demise of Martin Eldridge, the late Governor of Minerva. His surviving son wanted no part of them and the feelings between them were now mutual.

It was a time of great change—the change they had in many ways been expecting. Hadn't the Oracle predicted as much? It was the harbinger sign that marked the time when their bio-invasion plans would need to be stepped up and set in motion.

The Oracle had told them some time ago that an "infinity being" of a trinity nature would come to shake the world and they would shake right back. War would be the outcome. Kaggen was not clear what the Oracle meant by an "infinity being" and no explanation was forthcoming when they asked the Oracle for clarification.

Members of IPCOM had discussed it at great length. Did it mean the being was infinite in nature and could not be destroyed? Was the being even human? And what did the Oracle mean by "trinity nature"? The Oracle had inferred it was not a biblical term, although biblical changes would occur. It was confusing and although many theories had been expressed regarding this being that was destined to shake up their world, they had yet to arrive at a definitive answer to this puzzle. They were essentially flying in the dark, something Kaggen proudly refused to admit to anyone.

Chapter 17

Meghan felt Zach's presence before he made himself known. She had been inside his mind; he had been deep inside her body, and they had somehow forged an energetic connection that left no distance between them despite time and space. Lately she had come to recognize when he was internally stressed. She saw it now written on his face. It had taken up residence in his body as well. Meghan was certain he was being overwhelmed with a synesthesia response that would have brought most normal people to their knees. But Zach was anything but normal. The numbers which possessed him would be waging an internal battle within the man she had come to love. He might not believe in his own strength, but she did.

Someone of significance had died. It came to her immediately, like an energetic live newscast. How she knew his mother had been killed, and in a most violent manner, had to be due to the all-knowingness of her having taken up residence in the 5th Dimension. Telepathy was a common ability in this realm, and she was aware that her own was rapidly developing. At first it had felt strange to openly know such things, but it came as no surprise that now she could easily read him. In fact, she cherished it, as she did him.

Without a word, he heard her thoughts and simply nodded. Meghan knew. For the second time that day, Zach felt comforting arms wrap around him. She drew him close and cradled him.

"Don't go back," she whispered, perhaps a bit more urgently than intended. "They will try and kill you, too."

She drew him tightly against her, as if she could physically and mentally will him to stay. "I can't imagine any kind of life without you. You know you'll be safe here, Zach. Please don't go back there," she implored him again, but already knew what he would say.

Zach kissed her face, her neck and the hand that had just lovingly stroked his head like a child needing comfort. "I need to take care of some things first," he said, softly in her ear. "Endre and I may have a solution to what Kaggen is doing. I can't walk away without at least trying to stop him."

She was crying softly now, fearful of never seeing him again. It was his turn to comfort her. "I'm so sorry, love," he whispered, his fingers caressing her head, running through the soft red strands of hair that framed her face. He looked deep into her eyes. "This is something I must do."

Yes, she knew this but hated to admit it. They had been through so much together, she felt married to him in every way already, especially with their child on the way. Clearly the universe had brought them together for a reason and his destiny was part of something bigger. It was not her role to stop him. But it didn't make it any easier to let him go to do what was expected of him. She, too, had to be strong and support this man as he had always supported her.

"Marry me," she boldly proposed, watching his face intently. "Tonight, before you go."

Immediately he knew it was the right thing to do. "Yes," he responded without a moment's hesitation. The simple request brought forth a tenderness inside him that threatened to bring tears to his eyes. "Go get Izzie. She will forever be a part of this union."

They both went to wake her, only to find her sitting up in bed, cross-legged and diligently drawing figures on a large pad of paper, as she often did. She looked up and smiled when she saw Zach enter the room with her mother.

"This is for you," she said, immediately handing her picture to him.

Zach took it and examined it. Izzie had drawn three figures riding rainbows as they emerged from a bright, shiny, triangular-shaped sun. They could see what appeared to be tiny space craft hovering in the skies above them.

"It's very colorful and imaginative," Meghan commented.

Zach looked at it questioningly. "What does it mean, Izzie?" he asked, knowing Izzie often drew from her inner eye where she saw things that had a meaningful message.

Meghan immediately saw where he was heading. "Is that you, me and Zach?"

Izzie shook her head. "I don't know who they are." She turned to Zach, "I thought you would know."

Zach kept his thoughts to himself. There was something that rang familiar about the scene, like the time Ishannika had taken him through the Sun to Nordekka where he had freed *The Minerva Files*. But for the life of him, he didn't know what the drawing meant either. He filed the picture away in his mind, hoping to later make sense of it.

Meghan and Zach sat on the bed and looked knowingly at each other. "We have something special to tell you," Meghan began with a radiant and happy smile.

Izzie's eyes lit up. "Are you going to have another baby?"

Meghan laughed. "Oh God. No, honey. One baby at a time is more than enough for now. We wanted to tell you that Zach and

I are getting married. Tonight. And we want you to be there with us."

They waited for her reaction. It was surprisingly matter of fact. "Okay," she responded, putting aside her pastel pencils and drawing pad. "Can I be the flower girl?"

Zach ruffled her hair. "You can be whatever you like, Izzie."

"Can I pick the place, too?" she asked, becoming more excited.

Zach nodded. "Sure."

The ceremony was a simple one that took place in the Library of Truth, with Satya presiding. Satya called forth a hologram of the little Wedding Chapel on the grounds of the Grand Wailea Beach Resort on Maui, where both Izzie and Meghan had stayed. That was Izzie's idea. To her the island chapel was an adorable little dollhouse—the stuff of heavenly dreams. As part of their new family, the decision was made and Izzie's wish was granted.

The small foursome stepped inside the hologram Wedding Chapel. Sunlight streamed through its stained-glass window, bathing them in dancing rainbow-colored flecks of light around the room. There was no time or need for lavish wedding gowns or formal attire. It was a simple affair like the day they had first met in the Library of Congress' Great Hall. That day Zach had known that the beautiful red-headed woman with the swirling number eights around her was destined to be someone significant in his life.

As their flower girl, Izzie picked bright red Torch Ginger and Birds of Paradise to carry in her little outstretched arms. She beamed, knowing that her dream was finally coming true. The angel that had been sent to her would now be her daddy, just as he would be Caleb's.

Izzie continued to spin her dreams for her fairytale family, while she quietly listened to her mother and Zach exchange their personal vows. She hung on their every word--to love and cherish each other as equal partners, to be good parents to both her and their new child to-be, to bring joy and comfort to each other in the wake of adversity, to be truthful and open in all things, and to support each other no matter what. Then they just talked to each other, declaring all the things they loved about the other. Total mushy stuff.

Izzie finally sat down in a chapel pew and waited it out. It was a lot of promises. Grownups could talk forever. But she sensed she needed to be patient and let them get all these promises out of their system. All she cared about was that Zach was going to be her daddy and she would finally have a real father for the first time in her short life—just like other kids did. That thought alone filled her with immense pride and satisfaction. She loved Zach and he loved both her and her mother. That was good enough for her.

Satya had produced two gold rings and pronounced them husband and wife. Izzie watched Zach kiss the living daylights out of her Mommy. Geez. Izzie finally looked away. It was embarrassing seeing grownups kiss like that.

Seconds later, Zach scooped up Izzie in his arms and promised to be the best father to her that he could possibly be. She put her arms around both of her parents and hugged them. They were a threesome now, like the people in her drawing. They would go everywhere together, exploring and learning new things, like families were supposed to do. Right?

~~*~~

Zach hoped it wasn't their last night together. He knew his future was uncertain. Gizmo could only protect him so far in his old world that was fraught with danger, especially now with Kaggen most likely having placed a target on his back. A bullet could easily strike him dead, and Meghan would once again be a widow. Everything inside him fought that outcome. He couldn't do that to the woman he loved, just like he knew he would never ever want to intentionally cause her pain. Perhaps if she had never met him her life would be a normal one, not one that had catapulted her into a dangerous alien world where she was running for her and her daughter's life. With their respective families now vanquished, all they had left was each other.

Thoughts of possibly never seeing her again, or feeling her love, brought forth strong emotions that threatened to spill over and overwhelm him. His heart opened and flooded with such a deep response it made their night of wedded intimacy one which bordered on the spiritual. Zach made love to his new wife as if it was their first time again and quite possibly their last. Meghan sensed it, letting his urgency feed hers and sweep them both along.

"I'll always love you," he told her, tenderly kissing every inch of her lush, beautiful body, memorizing it, forever immortalizing it in his mind. He paused at her stomach, placing both hands over the small mound of her belly where new life grew and kissed it reverently. There was nothing he desired more than to live to see his son born and someday grow to manhood. Learning to be a good father, and being there for his son, unlike his own father who had failed to do so for him, was an experience he longed to have.

With each passing thought of his own mortality, burning desire coursed through him. Whatever it took, he would make this experience between them one that neither would ever forget.

His manhood wanted to explode the second he plunged into her pink wetness, while his mouth and tongue ravished hers. But he forced himself to slow down, wanting to savor it, to make it last. It became even harder to do so as she wrapped her long legs around him and tightly clutched him to her to deepen his penetration. For a split second he felt there was no line between him as she welcomed him in further. His conscious awareness slipped inside hers, experiencing her own desperate fears that their time together might be limited.

When they had tethered their minds together to remote view and find Izzie, a bond had been established that he had never experienced with another human being. They instinctively did so again now. Without the normal human barriers, he could no longer tell where he ended, and she began. They reveled in the feeling of what was going on in the other's body and mind. The mutual love between them joined and merged, creating immense energy.

His mind and body could feel her release coming on like a fast-rising flash flood. When it struck, it was like a bolt of lightning. He succumbed to her release and allowed his own to join hers, leaving them both shaking from the intensity. They had never done that before—being inside each other's head during such a physical and emotional release. It made mere physical sex pale in comparison. Was this what humans had always strived to attain during sexual union, never quite reaching the penultimate satisfaction, because without consciousness merging it stayed in the lower dimensional realm? That realization hit them both. If the powers that be allowed him to remain alive to completely feel and experience this woman again, it would be as they had just done, without barriers. That knowledge was now a mutual revelation.

Neither of them had yet to disengage consciously or physically. They just held each other, suspended in this unique blissful state, basking in the feel of each other, mind-to-mind, skin-to-skin. That night they had attained a very different kind of love union. It was a heavenly gift.

They didn't need to make love all night. They had attained a soul-to-soul satisfaction. Zach covered them both, his hand caressing Meghan's back as he had learned to do to help quiet her energy. He slept curled up around his new wife, feeling complete.

In the middle of the night, he awoke in a state of high awareness, knowing the time for his departure was fast approaching. He extricated himself from the warmth of Meghan's body, left their bed, and moved to the bay window that looked out upon this new 5th Dimensional world. The sun was rising on the horizon to a new morning. Streaks of light peeked through, bathing his naked silhouette in its illumination. He was simply a man meeting the new day and preparing to go out in the world to do his work.

Zach felt a moment of nostalgia and doubt. Was this the third act in his life where the hero dies? Had his spiritual journey come to this end, or would he rise above it? There was a prayer on his lips when he thought of Meghan—an old song he had always loved which never failed to move him. He heard the words in his head like a mantra...

'...And I remember when I moved in you, and the holy dove she was moving too, and every single breath we drew was Hallelujah.'

He whispered to himself, "Hallelujah, my love."

From behind he felt feminine arms wrap around him, and a head rest against his shoulder. She had felt it, too. Whatever it took, he would find a way back to her.

~~*~~

Zach had cleanup work to do. There was his mother's murder, the resulting homicide investigation which he was quite certain would come to nothing, and the Eldridge's vast financial estate to deal with. He left it all in the hands of their family's estate lawyer who was more than capable to see to all their holdings. Zach had laid out what he wanted carried out with implicit instructions. Since it was no longer safe for him to be seen in public, the official face of the Eldridge family was now handled by a law firm which was only too happy to take on the mammoth task and be paid royally for the privilege.

His mother's body didn't need to be identified. Hundreds of ringside witnesses knew it was Camille Eldridge and no other who had been shot down. But the lawyer took care of those coroner formalities as well. There was a film crew at the lavish fundraising event that night, documenting Camille's presidential run, as was the norm. Every candidate running for office retained their own media crew for promotional purposes. Camille's death was immortalized in living technicolor, as the cameras never stopped rolling throughout the unfolding drama. They recorded his mother's very last moments alive followed by her sudden and dramatic exit from this world.

Inevitably, a trove of graphic videos leaked to all the media outlets. Snippets were played and replayed on newscasts around the world. So many of the event's attendees had preserved the horror on their cellphones and were only too eager to share their ringside view of this historical political bombshell on their social media accounts moments after it occurred. The massive internet hits of the murder made the tragedy go viral in no time. Camille Eldridge became more famous in death than in all her years of public service. The irony of that was not lost on her son. His mother always wanted to be remembered, to be part of political history, and she had gotten her wish in spades.

Camille Eldridge had made her after-death plans already known years before. "They won't have me rotting away in some box underground. I want my ashes scattered over the goddamn Capitol where I belong," he had once overheard her tell a friend. He would make sure of that, as well. It was the least he could do as he closed the last chapter in the Eldridge family saga. A cremation and simple memorial service would be arranged prior to her last flyover the Capitol.

There was, of course, all the money to deal with. Zach arranged to have the Eldridge estate holdings, comprised of extensive commercial and residential properties, liquidated and all monies put in a trust fund for Meghan, Izzie, and his future heirs in the event of his demise. He had decided to keep the flat in Dupont Circle for sentimental reasons. It held the cherished memory of his first intimate experience with Meghan. He felt himself rouse at the memory and schooled himself to focus on the matters at hand.

The lawyers would be paid dearly to expedite his instructions in a timely and immediate manner. They were only too happy to comply. The Eldridge estate was worth hundreds of billions on paper. A few billion tossed to the lawyers would not make much of a dent in his overall plan.

It was also decided that all campaign fundraising monies his mother had amassed would be returned to their donors. Her staff would be paid, terminated and given letters of reference. Zach wanted everything wrapped up in the event he and his family did or did not return to this world. He left no stone unturned in his cleanup process.

When he felt satisfied with the dissolution plans for his estate, his thoughts returned once again to the matter of Kaggen and Antarctica. The Base Commander of the continent's underground operation had been holding down the fort way too long. Zach needed to see for himself what had taken place since removing Meghan and Izzie from the frozen space base. Zach was aware that he had been remiss in not keeping a closer eye on what was left of Minerva's hold on the place. There had been too many fires to put out everywhere else. He hoped the DOLARIS software he had installed on the Base's security system was keeping things in check, but he knew anything could have happened after he departed for the LOT and the 5th Dimension. A power coup was not out of the question in the resulting leadership vacuum. There were still eight existing Minerva members after the Gizmo holocaust that had wiped out his father and several others. Those that remained had all been too scared at what they had seen in the LOT concerning their own futures. Zach was counting on their being too wrapped up in putting out their own fires to think about seizing control of Minerva. One could only hope.

He weighed his priorities as he was prone to do when he was overwhelmed. His mind always felt sharp and relatively calm during his time in the LOT. Back in his old world, like here in Antarctica, he felt his number synesthesia more profoundly than ever. If only he could rewrite a programming script for his brain to turn it on and off at will. There were definitely times when his unusual abilities played to his advantage, but this was not one of them. Zach moved into an old familiar Qigong position which helped quiet the number patterns demanding order. They followed the flow of energy, riding it as they settled down into numerical bundles that defied chaos. The ancient meditative practice would forever be his salvation.

Chapter 18

Bruno DiMaglia had been fighting his own internal and external battles. As Antarctica Base Commander all departments reported to him. It was imperative he take stock of what was necessary and still operational in this once mammoth operation, as he felt his career days might be numbered on this icy continent.

Duty and honor bound, he was entrusted to keep the Base and its varied functions going strong until given orders otherwise. It had been his job for so long, he knew no other life. But after seeing the factual evidence inside the Library of Truth, and how he himself had been so easily compromised, he felt a disconcerting mind shift. On many an occasion during his years of service he had looked the other way when witnessing what he thought was a bad decision by his superiors. He had always told himself that it was not his place to judge. As a military man he had been raised to ask no questions and follow orders. Disobedience meant dishonor and termination. That way of thinking was now over.

Witnessing the horror and the extent of the alien's experimental hybrid labs, the creature abominations, the blood manipulation—all of it had served to open his eyes forever. This alien/Mantis agenda had intentionally been kept a secret from so many, himself included. As Base Commander, he should have known. It made him question his own complicity, something he had thought bred out of him as a career military man.

The new Governor was a breed apart and DiMaglia recognized and respected this. As Commander he needed to make critical adjustments to accommodate a newer way of thinking which he was told would be more open and transparent. DiMaglia was determined to give the new Governor the benefit of doubt, along with a chance to prove himself.

After Kaggen and his race fled the Base, most of the other alien races had made their mass exodus shortly thereafter as well. Once they departed, their ships had remained untraceable on all tracking satellites. Consequently, they had become a clear and dangerous threat to the Minerva space force. The Mantis had regrouped somewhere in space cleverly evading human detection. But DiMaglia knew they were just waiting and plotting, as was their nature, before returning to reclaim the Base. He was determined not to let this happen. Not under his watch.

It had become necessary to temporarily shut down all access points into and out of the Base to prevent them from become sitting ducks for any alien weaponized retaliation. DiMaglia knew what their capabilities were and now that all treaties between the humans and their kind had been broken it wouldn't take much for them to take over. That had been the purpose behind the treaties in the first place, to stem off an invasion by forces technologically more advanced and diabolical. Humans were catching up, but not fast enough to make a difference.

His thoughts kept returning to the discovery of their hidden biolabs and human-hybrid experimentation which had shaken him to his very core—more than he cared to admit. The scenes had invaded his nightly dreams, making sleep elusive. There was a lot he had witnessed and been privy to during his years of special military service. Out of necessity, one quickly develops a thick skin for scenes of blood, death, and gore. But what he had experienced in their sub-level labs made his very skin crawl. The Mantis had experimented on every type of living form that moved and breathed--children, men, women, animals, and creatures that one couldn't even identify. Some were still alive when his crew had fire-bombed the last vestiges of horror the Mantis had left behind.

Whatever they had succeeded to create for their purpose and satisfaction they had clearly taken with them. Any documentation or evidence of what this might be was now missing. Even the blood samples they had preserved and locked in an evidence freezer had mysteriously disappeared.

There were human traitors on the Base, and DiMaglia had done his best to ferret them out. When he discovered many of the culprits, he had responded accordingly. Instead of having them shot on the spot, they had been ejected out onto the frozen tundra of the continent to survive by their own means. Most died within hours or less, being instruments of their own demise. No one could last long in sub-zero temperatures without adequate shelter and supplies. Did he care? Hell no. It sent a clear message to anyone else contemplating going rogue.

The Governor's son had done strange things to the Base's DOLARIS Security System, including preventing any changes or shutdowns of the software by anyone trying to override or hijack it. As Base Commander he and his tech team had tried to break the system to test its parameters. It had been unbreakable. It did allow them to shut down access points into and out of the Base, but only because the Governor's son had instructed them to do so when he was last here. It was Zachary Eldridge, the new Governor, who had inputted the necessary override code, then quickly deleted any reference to it should someone try to locate it in the code files. The only one who had access to the Source Code was, of course, the new Governor.

Like his nightly dreams about the alien lab atrocities, DiMaglia also found it hard to forget that fateful and last Minerva board meeting when all hell had broken loose. In the aftermath the new Governor had taken him and the eight remaining Minerva members to a Library of Truth location he hadn't known existed. Here he learned some disturbing facts. The incident of his being drugged and compromised at the hands of the old Counselor still angered him deeply. No one would ever trick him again to retrieve confidential information.

Observing the fate of the eight surviving Minerva members told him they would be hard pressed to attempt a power coup. He knew fear when he saw it and there was plenty of it to go around when the strange holographic truth had revealed itself about the future—their future.

Minerva's cherished jump-rooms, which afforded quick entry from different points in the world to the Antarctica Base, had been de-activated. The Governor's son had seen to that as well. There would be no more spur of the moment secret meetings with other members from across the globe. Whether temporary or permanent, Minerva had been unofficially disbanded until further notice.

There was only one jump-room that remained online. The new Governor had insisted upon it. It was an obscure access point located in an abandoned Los Angeles warehouse that hadn't, at least to his knowledge, been used in years. DiMaglia wasn't sure where this specific jump-room led, and he didn't ask. The security system wasn't reporting data on its accessibility, so he understood it to be a topic not open for discussion. His instructions were that this jump-room would remain forever open, protected, and confidential until further notice. DiMaglia honored that request.

News always traveled with lightning speed to the farthest reaches of Antarctica. Information was routed there first through the vast Minerva satellite network. DiMaglia learned of Camille's Eldridge's death within minutes after she had been shot, so it came as no surprise when the new Governor returned to the Base directly through the LOT. What did come as a shock was to see he had an identical twin accompanying him.

Endre saw the man's shock upon meeting. There was no hiding it. He acknowledged DiMaglia when introductions were made but remained cautious as he shook the Commander's hand. Was he someone Endre could trust? The Base, its inhabitants and all its workings were foreign to him. Endre was scrambling to put all the new information coming at him into perspective. Like a 1000-piece puzzle, containing nothing but white pieces, it became challenging to see where everything fit together. Gaining access to the Library of Congress and now the Antarctica Base opened the parameters of his world. The picture it presented was much bigger than he would have ever thought. That Zach trusted to share it with him filled him with new determination to do right by him.

Endre knew he was smart. Russian aptitude and intelligence testing, which separated those best suited to the trade schools from those smart enough to go on to higher education, had proven this repeatedly. His high scores showed him best suited to academia and the sciences. His mind was sharp and solution focused. While he was unfettered by the number synesthesia condition Zach experienced, he knew his own hidden talent lay in having read so many of the advanced science books available in the National Library of Russia.

A voracious reader, Endre had always maintained an interest in space exploration. That his mother country had led this race from the beginning filled him with national pride. It wasn't well known but the National Library of Russia was a depository for aerospace documents from Roscosmos, the Russian space agency's equivalent of NASA, located in Kazakhstan. It contained a wealth of information, not accessible to the general public. But this had not stopped Endre from pouring over every item in the vaults within the time he worked at the library. It was fascinating information which he found himself craving to examine during his daily employee breaks.

That being the case, he was naturally inclined to make a concerted effort to understand the secrets of the Antarctica Base and its advanced space technology as well. He believed that was why he was here. If there was a way to help his American brother, he would do it or die trying. In many ways, he too was on a mission. Why he had been chosen to play a role in this unfolding drama was something that continued to intrigue him. Until he understood it completely, he would follow the path to truth. Perhaps there the answers which eluded him would also reveal themselves.

Endre took in everything he saw at the Base down to the smallest detail. This was not just the work of the Americans. Every major power on Earth had bases in Antarctica. They were all connected and of a mutual purpose, something that shocked him to learn. From the very start they had all been in on the alien-human treatises and agreed to keep it hidden. The sovereign nation status was a fallacy. The only time his country and the U.S. had openly cooperated for appearances sake was on the U.S./Russian Space Station. Despite all the documents Roscosmos had archived, Endre now knew they didn't portray the whole picture. What else had they covered up about the frontiers of space and the extraterrestrial presence? Had they told the people anything true? Endre remained silent, putting aside his doubts for the time being and instead paid close attention to the discussion occurring between DiMaglia and Zach.

"I need to talk with the Base's science teams. All of them," Zach told the Commander. "Assemble what's still left of them. I gather by this point many of them have fled, but they aren't all gone, are they?"

DiMaglia frowned. The ranks had indeed thinned considerably. The Base was operating at less than 50%. After securing the return of the child from Kaggen's clutches, many changes had taken place since Zachary had abruptly left the icy continent. No one knew if he would return or whether Minerva would cease to exist. It came as no surprise when Base personnel secretly, and some openly, questioned the safety of their jobs and what role they might still play. Many feared they would be terminated like what they had heard happened to other Minerva members. Only DiMaglia held firm. No one had given him his dismissal orders, so he stayed put. His instincts told him the new Governor would eventually return and set things right.

"There are several still here from the Space Force, sir," the Commander replied. "They have been busy working on the Mercury fuel propulsion project you set in motion when you were last here. I believe they are close to a prototype from the detailed specs and formulations you provided."

Hearing this news greatly pleased Zach. These men were the best of the best. His father had picked well. That they had stayed on and not left for greener pastures told him they were driven more by science than fear and greed. It would be unrealistic to think that there were not a few good men amongst the evil Minerva influence that ruled Antarctica. DiMaglia was certainly proving to be one of them.

Zach soon found himself back in the Minerva boardroom, the scene of his father's death, sitting in the seat reserved for the Governor. The déjà vu of the moment was not lost on him. In his pocket, Gizmo rested quietly, which gave Zach some semblance of relief. He knew all too well what the AI's capabilities could do when a threat was presented. But the faces of the scientists, physicists, and mathematicians seated before him, all 10 of them, stared back without hostility or malice. They seemed more curious and expectant than anything else.

Zach had already proven to them that he possessed complex knowledge and definitive scientific answers to problems they had been attempting to solve for some time. The specific data the new Governor had provided them on the alien's Mercury fuel propulsion systems made it easy for them to quickly replicate such a system without the necessary trial and error testing periods that took considerable time. This knowledge, in itself, commanded their attention and respect. The old Governor had not been nearly as forthcoming with concrete answers, despite his astrophysics background. They were open to hearing what his son had to say before making any judgmental decisions.

Zach sensed their tentative acceptance. He nodded to Endre, who sat off to the side observing, while he got down to business. The scientists would have to know what was at risk if they failed.

DiMaglia had documented everything before destroying the Mantis biolabs. The graphic images, projected onto a large screen behind Zach, spoke a thousand words. There was dead silence as Zach explained what he had witnessed, which they were now viewing.

The Commander nodded in validation. "I have seen this human-hybrid lab with my own eyes," he confirmed. "It is now destroyed, but their work has not ceased. They have taken it all with them and it is my belief that we can expect a counter-offensive. These aliens are not done with us."

There was dead silence around the table when the gruesome images stopped. Not a man there had known what the aliens had been doing right under their very noses all these years. They had been told and assured that their scientific contributions were for the greater whole of humanity and that their efforts would foster planetary harmony and peace between all human and interstellar races. As participants in the Special Access Space Force, they had come to expect truth and transparency in the details of their space mission, no matter how disturbing those facts might be, so they believed what they were told.

Zach assessed their level of shock. It was fairly high. "We have all been lied to, gentlemen," he admitted. "They not only deceived you but those who came before you as well. However, we have a chance to change that, knowing the truth. I firmly believe the truth will set us free to take back our planet from these dangerous beings."

"What are we to do?" one man spoke up, looking around the table to his colleagues who also looked doubtful. Their faces seemed to agree with him. They all knew what they were up against. "These beings are so much more advanced. They've had millions of years to perfect their technology and experimentation. With all due respect, sir, we are still in the infancy stage."

Zach had been expecting such a response. "What's your name?" Zach asked the man.

"Lieutenant Colonel Grant Walker, sir," he replied.

"And your role here? On the Base?" he prompted.

"I'm Senior Astronautical Engineer for Cyberspace Effects Operations, sir," he quickly answered.

Zach went around the table asking each man's name, their rank and position. The majority were military men who knew how to follow orders, whatever the mission. It was a small group, comprised of source intelligence analysts, a few technology and logistics engineers, but more importantly space system specialists that would know how to implement his plan, if indeed possible. He came back to Lt. Col. Walker. "How many satellites do we have orbiting Earth," he asked.

The Lieutenant knew the exact count. "We have exactly 9,381 as of today and approximately only half of them are currently active," he responded.

"And the aliens?" Zach asked. "Do we know how many they have?"

This time Lieutenant Walker hesitated before speaking. "To my knowledge, sir, I believe they have at least 16,000 that we know about. Some are inter-species jointly owned. They were tight-lipped about who and what they were capable of monitoring from deep space, as well as what satellites belonged to whom. At best this is a guesstimate on my part."

Captain Torie Gregory, a Space Operations Officer from the Base's Quantum Physics Division, chimed in. "We also have reason to believe they have a large spaceship parked near Saturn, but we have been unable to confirm this rumor. There may be more. The Cassini probe was sabotaged before we could transmit back confirmative details."

"The Cassini probe was a number of years ago. Why are we still unable to verify this?" Zach wanted to know.

Captain Gregory shook his head. "The aliens have erected some kind of frequency fence in areas of space where we suspect they've set up hidden satellite outposts. This frequency wall has been weaponized in successfully deterring closer examination. It scrambles our communications and short-circuits our probes."

None of this surprised Zach. The aliens were masters at deception and sabotage. They were so much better at hiding information than Minerva. "Have you isolated the frequency band they're using?" he asked Lt. Col. Walker.

Walker leaned forward in his chair. "We've tried, sir," he admitted. "But every time we think we've pinpointed their band, they change it, like they're tracking *us*. All we have been able to ascertain thus far is that they transmit in the high frequency section of the microwave spectrum. They're strategic experts in evasion."

Zach agreed. He had come up against that very problem trying to locate where they had hidden Izzie after abducting her. The Mantis knew that other galaxies and deeper parts of space were still inaccessible to human space travel.

There was a consensus throughout the room that they had a big problem, as everyone started sharing what they, too, had discovered or had come up against. Zach held up his hand to bring the meeting back to order. "You've all done incredible work and I sincerely thank you for all your continued efforts. But we're going to have to expand our thinking moving forward. We need to function outside the box for what I'm about to propose."

Once again, he had their undivided attention. Every eye was upon him. They were ready to listen as Zach continued. "I have new information which may make a difference in overcoming these obstacles you've encountered," he began. "Our problem is two-fold. Over-riding their frequency fence is key. But our primary goal right now is de-activation of their human hybrid program before it becomes the bio-invasion of this planet they always intended it to be. Unfortunately, it's already happening. And it's spreading quickly."

There were grim looks all around. Zach had waltzed in proposing to solve a problem that had evaded some of the best scientific minds in the room. Did they think him cocky and arrogant? Was it any wonder their looks of confidence had fallen several notches since the start of the meeting? Nevertheless, Zach undauntingly forged on.

"Kaggen has corrupted the universal blood supply with thin, black, snakelike particles, that are magnetic in nature. This nanoparticle slowly builds crystalline structures within the host body, leading to the formation of a 3rd strand of DNA which responds to communication signals..."

He paused, knowing what he was revealing was bad enough, but there was worse to come. "I can only assume," he revealed, feeling his own dread, "that Kaggen is using his vast satellite network to transmit frequency signals capable of being received through electronic devices which are everywhere--cellphones, computers, television, cell towers, and so forth. These devices continue to receive signals whether powered on or off. Kaggen is activating his soldiers to create havoc and crime sprees across the globe. I believe he is behind the sudden increased anger and violence now occurring globally. His purpose is to de-stabilize all systems before taking over."

A single voice in the room was heard expressing the question presently on everyone's mind. "Do you have a solution to prevent this, sir?" The man had a faint yet undisguised glimmer of hope in his eyes.

Zach hoped so. Nothing was certain and he didn't want to deceive them with false expectations. He attempted to lay out his plan, letting them decide. "All their ships contain organic memory, holding vast amounts of data. They believe we are unable to access this information, but this is no longer true. There was a singular communication breach before they departed the Base. This is how I knew about their Mercury fuel-propulsion system."

In unison, the group appeared to sit up straighter, leaning forward waiting. Zach unfurled the Sakya Monastery scroll, the genetic blueprint Zach believed contained a big part of the DNA puzzle. "Gentlemen, what you see before you has been buried from human consciousness for thousands of years. I believe it holds the creation key to human DNA activation and correction, as well as deep clues into how Kaggen might have used this information for his human-hybrids."

Zach explained the "K" strain of DNA. While his small group of Space Force scientists pored over the data display trying to make sense of it, Zach nodded to Endre, who stood up and came over to the table.

"Endre Zegorov will share with you what we learned from the organic memory of one of their ships and the frequency band we believe might be weaponized against them." Zach motioned to Endre who stepped forward and started making notations on a large whiteboard.

"It appears we have been looking in the wrong place," Endre informed them. "All our efforts should now be focused in the 'KA' Band and above, utilizing a specific range of harmonic frequencies that are unique to our experience. If we build smaller steerable beams for higher capacity density, we can transport high-speed data back at them without degradation and bypass their frequency fence. They won't be expecting this and the way we will do it will certainly never have been done before."

Endre now knew what Zach knew. And the beauty of it was, that not having the equivalent higher education degrees as the scientists in the room had, Endre understood the information in a way that opened his mind to greater possibilities. It was no coincidence that life circumstances had provided him the opportunity where he had access to examine space exploration documents from the Roscosmos Russian space archive. Destiny had prepared him for this moment.

Then divine intervention stepped in. "Sir," Walker interrupted. "If memory and data was obtained from the organic skin of one of their craft, and it's possible for certain human readers to decipher it, would it not stand to reason that all their craft might be capable of divulging this same information as well?"

Zach's ear picked up. "Why do you ask?"

"There's a compounded craft of theirs on Level 7, that's been mothballed for years. They probably forgot about it when they hastily departed."

Zach and Endre smiled in unison. The devil was always in the details.

Chapter 19

Washington was still reeling from the very public and tragic murder of Camille Eldridge. Why had her security failed, they wanted to know? That one of their own political bedfellows could be picked off so easily sent fear into the hearts of everyone who held office, including those candidates who had been running against Camille Eldridge.

The media and nightly news would not let go of the story, despite hitting a roadblock for new clues to her killer. The story was going nowhere but it was still a ratings bonanza of speculation and finger pointing. An unsolved crime of such notoriety fueled the conspiracy theorists. Was it a cover-up by those in power? Was someone important being protected? The people wanted answers. They would not put the matter to rest until someone was arrested and paid for their crime. NYPD, working in conjunction with the Feds, had no suspect to pin it on, so the stories continued, growing in fanatical proportion. The truth was out there somewhere, but it remained beyond everyone's reach.

It did not go unnoticed that the only surviving son of Camille Eldridge had not stepped forward to make a public statement about the grievous incident. The public wanted to see personal human drama played out on their news feeds, not an attorney spokesperson for the family reading a prepared statement. Where was this wayward son, they wondered? No one had those answers either, which only served to fuel further speculation.

Camille's untimely death served to deflect attention away from other important news stories, including a valuable theft that had been discovered inside the Library of Congress. Very little had been publicly reported on the incident and the Library seemed to prefer it that way. The Library's Communication Dept. released a short, brief statement revealing only that a "small statue" was missing from inside the private Congressional Reading Room and authorities were looking into it. There was no mention that the statue in question was solid gold, quite old and valuable, and was from before the time of the Library's founder, Thomas Jefferson.

Neither was it revealed that there was no forced entry into the room and that security cameras were all functioning at the time of the theft. The recorded footage had been carefully examined for edits, but there was no evidence of digital tampering. Yet the fact remained--there were no visible signs of human entry. The mystery only deepened. The statue seemed to have just disappeared into thin air like Camille Eldridge's killer.

Everyone suspected it was an inside job. It had to be. There was evidence that someone had used a key code to gain access to the private Reading Room in the early hours of the morning before the Library opened. The input code used had been a universal one that many Congressional representatives knew about. But the thief in question knew how to bypass the security cameras, which was secured information. And to make matters even stranger, several hours after the thief gained access and left, only then did the security alarm identify there had been a burglary. The system had failed on all levels.

Investigators continued to be stumped as to why there was no visible damage to the pedestal stand securing the statue, or how it had been extracted. It was simply baffling. How such a crime had been pulled off was the question on everyone's mind. The facts just did not add up. The only real clue had been the use of a key code by someone who knew what they were doing.

But who had time for such things? An escalation in crime was occurring everywhere and law enforcement was spread thin on Capitol Hill. The investigation was not a high priority in the eyes of the U.S. Capitol Police (USCP) whose jurisdiction included all federal buildings on the Hill, including the Library of Congress. They were confident the insurance claim companies and their adjusters would come in and do their work for them. The USCP had a hell of a lot bigger fish to fry.

Thousands of miles away Zach saw the news come in over the private feed that concerned all portal locations. This was how the Counselor had learned of the strange power loss in Cairo, Egypt the night he and Izzie had breached the Great Pyramid portal. Anything that concerned portal locations was always of prime importance.

Zach handed the report to Endre. "You've caused quite a stir in my Library," he grinned. "The police are calling you the 'Phantom Thief'."

Endre grinned. "Were they all that easy. This was the only Golden Minerva statue sitting right out there in plain sight. Most of the time I have to track and search to locate these statues."

This intrigued Zach. Gizmo had led him to the Sakya Monastery and the Baalbeck statues, both hidden deep underground. "How do you find them?" he asked.

"I hear them," Endre revealed. "They speak to me."

Was Endre clairaudient, Zach wondered? Did he also have hidden talents Zach had yet to learn about? His curiosity grew. "Tell me. What do they sound like?" he asked.

Endre thought about it for a moment. "It's almost like a melody, but not quite. More like a tonal sequence that grows louder as I hone into the statue's location."

"Can you sound out those tones for me?" Zach inquired.

Endre produced several tones then repeated them. Zach listened and watched in fascination. Musical tones were like math to him. He could see them dancing around Endre as Zach told him to keep repeating the sequence. Suddenly it dawned on him what the numbers meant. They were the electron configuration for the element of pure gold.

Zach understood, but not completely. "How do you distinguish statue gold from all the other gold out there?" he wanted to know.

"Statue gold has a higher pitch density," Endre replied. "It sounds quite different."

Zach had to ask. "Can you find the Antarctica statue right now? Or should I ask for Gizmo's help?"

Endre shook his head in the negative. He was up for the challenge. "No. I've got this."

Zach watched Endre go into bloodhound mode, listening attentively with an acute ear. He quietly followed him throughout the entire Base and all its many levels. An hour later Endre stopped. He frowned. "I don't hear it. It's not here."

They silently looked to each other, the same question on both their minds. How could it not be here? And if so, where was it? Without all the statues the alien portal entries into Earth could never be successfully closed. Their mission would be a failure.

Zach's face revealed his disappointment. As if to brighten his mood, Endre had an idea. "While we figure out where it might be," he suggested, "let's go retrieve the Malta statue. I'll show you how I do it."

Like before, they accessed the Malta portal through a holographic vehicle within the Library of Truth. As they traveled deep into the Earth's interior it became immediately clear that despite Zach's inadvertently destroying their blood bank operation on his last visit, there were still traces of the Mantis presence. Were they rebuilding their hive and attempting to re-salvage their operations? Endre remained quiet, listening intently. "We need to go deeper," he instructed.

The 11th portal Minerva statue was also a difficult one to locate, according to Endre. "Unlike the other portals, the evil of this place is very strong. There is much more going on here than just alien involvement," he remarked, as a shiver ran through him. Zach felt it, too.

"There is dark energy everywhere," Endre continued. "Death and sacrifice have taken place here. This has weakened the statue's tones. I can hear it, but it's very faint."

After his first visit to this island, Zach had delved further into the placement of the mysterious 11th portal. Malta remained an enigma to the world. It was an independent island republic off the southern coast of Italy, which claimed allegiance to no country and made its own rules. What went on below the surface of its beautiful and picturesque landscape was hidden to all but those in the know. It had become a perfect base for the alien blood labs.

The hologram took them below the labs, deeper towards the Earth's core than Zach had thought possible. He had lost all concept of distance, but it had to be hundreds of miles down. Zach did a quick mental calculation. The Earth's core was approximately 1,800 miles from the surface. If they didn't stop soon, they would be within its fiery hot core, the heat of it as intense as the Sun itself.

"I hear it!" Endre shouted. "We're close."

The hologram moved sideways through a solid dense wall, then abruptly stopped. In front of them was not at all what they had expected to find. It was a tropical land with rivers, mountains and trees, and blue skies above. "Holy shit!" Zach breathed, in barely a whisper. "Where the fuck are we?"

Without another word, Endre took off running. Like a bloodhound he had only one purpose. Find the statue. Zach lost sight of him, leaving him alone in this strange land wondering what to make of it.

He called on LOT information to identify his current location. The hologram displayed even more puzzling data. It marked the coordinates as a planet within a planet, designating it as AG-19281.

"Is it inhabited?" Zach asked.

"Yes. It has 9.1 million species," he learned. Zach realized that probably included all plant and animal life.

"Does AG-19281 have human inhabitants or is it occupied by an alien species?" he questioned.

Zach breathed a deep sigh of relief when he saw the readout inform him: "Only human inhabitants". Was this some kind of parallel Earth of humans or something else? He tried to bring up more data, only to discover that it was a different year here altogether. The year on AG-19281 was 2252. Things could not get any weirder. Had future man transitioned to inside the planet, abandoning its exterior? If so, what had happened? Had nuclear war decimated the species or had he failed and an alien invasion been successfully carried out? Zach wasn't sure he wanted to know. Knowing the future could color the present. If he had failed, he didn't want to face that fact just yet.

Endre had still not returned from what he assumed would be a quick extraction of the statue in question and then a swift departure from this strange otherworldly place. Another 15 minutes passed and still no sign of his twin. He was itching to get back to the Antarctica Base to continue working with his science team on the problem at hand. They had finally located the mothballed alien craft on Level 7 and were "preparing" it. Zach had yet to engage with it and see what information it held, but hopefully soon they would know more.

This trip to Malta and the unexpected discovery of AG-19281 had been a spur of the moment decision—something Zach had estimated to be nothing more than a quick retrieval mission at best. It was turning out to be just the opposite. The universe seemed to always be finding ways to slow him down from his true purpose. Zach knew he needed to stay focused on what was important--thwarting Kaggen and his mission.

Where the hell was Endre? His impatience and now concern regarding Endre's whereabouts grew with each passing minute. "Fuck," he swore under his breath. It was time to go looking for him.

Zach wasn't sure if the humans on AG-19281 were friendly, hostile or a de-evolved primitive lot despite the future year of 2252. At least there *was* a future, he reminded himself. Playing it safe, he took the protection of the hologram with him, scanning the land from within its close confines. Two small drone-like space craft buzzed over him, curious to see who or what he was.

"Go away. I mean no harm," his mind silently called out to their operators. And to his amazement, they did. They simply turned tail and sped off.

Zach now knew that the humans on AG-19281 in the year 2252 were both intelligent and advanced. Their space craft were small, fast, and able to maneuver and navigate with quick precision. That they had read his friendly intention told him that they had to possess telepathic abilities.

He was getting nowhere fast in this fertile new land that had hills and valleys for miles in every direction. He had yet to see a city or town. "Find Endre," he finally told Gizmo, who immediately pointed them in an entirely new direction due northeast. There was a large mountain range up ahead that light was streaming from. As Zach got closer, he realized with a start that---damn, it was not a mountain at all. It was a freaking pyramid. Bigger than the ones he had seen topside on Earth and this one was covered in gold. Outside this incredible edifice he spotted Endre eagerly conversing with a group of three very tall, thin men who were dressed in white. They looked to be wearing flight suits that hugged their body like a biological second skin.

Endre looked up when the men did and waved excitedly. His face lit up, beckoning Zach to join him. The hologram came to a stop and he heard one of the men speaking to Endre in his native Russian and gesturing towards Zach.

"Are they Russian?" Zach questioned.

Endre laughed. "No not at all. They say they are Melchizedeks and can speak any language necessary."

"Melchizedeks? You mean like the cosmic priesthood?" Zach asked. The Ancient Egyptians referred to the Melchizedeks as the healer magicians, the futurists, the keepers of the secrets of the cosmos. Were these men from that ancient order?

"LOT data says this is the year 2252," he told Endre. "Did they tell you that?"

Endre nodded. "Yes, and more. They knew my name and asked where you were. They have been expecting us."

Zach was taken aback. "What do you mean?"

Endre was spilling over with excitement. "They showed me ancient documents that had our names on it and today's date in the year 2252."

Zach found that hard to believe. "You're joking with me, right?"

The three men found that amusing and laughed in unison. "Welcome Zachary Eldridge," one in the group said in perfect English. "We are the keepers of the statue you came to retrieve."

Zach stared at him curiously. All three men were radiating 8s from the middle of their foreheads, in an area some had come to call the "third eye". These men were eights like Endre and himself. It was strange to come across so many eights in one place. And they said they had the statute?

He raised a questioning brow. "Where is it?"

"I will bring it to you," another man replied. Saying no more he then vanished.

Endre could hardly contain himself. "Zach, they know the secrets to transmutation. These men tell me they are hundreds of years old and they have stopped aging. It appears they can affect cellular regeneration."

Zach saw for himself that they were able to shift matter in ways only dreamed about or they would not have been able to pull off that vanishing act. And just as quickly as the man had disappeared, he was back again, holding a Golden Minerva statue. He placed it in Endre's outstretched waiting hands.

"It has been kept safe and is all yours again," he said with a reverent nod. "We have been honored to serve." The man looked to both of them for affirmation.

Zach found the man's choice of words odd. Serve whom, he wondered? Instead, he thanked the man, feeling a need to say more, but not knowing what that might be. Now that they had the statue and a glimpse into this future world, Zach was less eager to leave. He wanted to know more. The walls of the gold pyramid were filled with engraved writings, as the Pyramid at

Giza had once been rumored to hold on its white limestone outer walls. What did they say of the past and the future?

"Can we go inside the pyramid?" he asked the men for he might never get the chance again. He wanted to see for himself what other wonders this future race had attained.

"This is not possible," the man told him. "This might affect your future, should you know what we know. The ancient writings were very specific. Once you return to your world there will come an earthquake upon the land above us, deep and penetrating, and that portal will forever be closed and the evil within it destroyed. Do not be alarmed when this occurs. It is meant to be. We have been waiting for the sign of your appearance to set cause and effect into motion."

Zach was now even more mystified. Their visit had been predestined, but by whom? The Melchizedeks? And once they departed there would come a planet-altering earthquake—and not to be afraid? Right. Endre seemed to read his mind. This white puzzle they found themselves assembling just kept getting harder and harder to piece together and make sense of.

"Are you the three men who planted the golden statues in all the portals?" Zach questioned, recalling Izzie's recent drawing and the vision he had seen at Baalbeck.

"No," they said in unison, slightly amused. If they knew who was responsible for the statues, they weren't saying.

The three men stepped closer and placed their hands on Endre and Zach's shoulders. It generated a distinct tingling effect which rippled throughout their bodies, right down to their toes. "Go and do what you must," these mysterious men told their visitors. "Our work here is done."

Endre clutched the Golden Minerva to him and stepped back into the hologram with Zach following behind him. Zach hesitated. There were too many questions he had hoped to have answered by this ancient mystical order. There was something still pressing on his mind which, like a dog with a bone, he couldn't let go of. "Who brought your civilization to this place? And how long ago?"

They seemed to have been expecting the question, from the knowing look upon their faces. "We are merely an ancient outpost from a pre-Atlantean civilization, brought here to guarantee the future," they informed him.

"By whom?" Zach wanted to know.

The ancient one smiled. "By Nehemiah, of course."

~~*~~

Zach and Endre felt the earthquake erupt from the very depths of the planet, as their hologram exited the 11th portal, returning to the LOT. The island of Malta was rocked to its very core, registering 8.8 on the seismic Richter Scale sending shock waves that rippled across the ocean, setting off tsunami alerts on multiple distant shores.

The megaquake was felt thousands of miles away in neighboring countries where the ground rolled, and the Earth rumbled in response. Some thought it was the end of times and fell to their knees in prayer, much like the Tibetan monks had at the Sakya Monastery when Zach had extricated the Minerva statue from the ground underneath. Yet, oddly enough, only a moderate amount of damage occurred in the towns and cities inhabiting Malta's surface infrastructure. Strangely, human life was spared.

The Melchizedeks from the year 2252 had kept their word. Everything hidden underground on the island, alien and otherwise, was instantaneously wiped out. Nothing of evil separated those on AG-19281 from life on the surface.

In the Antarctica Base Systems Room, the 11th portal went offline ceasing to exist. Neither Zach nor Endre were surprised to see it happen. It signaled to them that they were closer to their goal.

Change was occurring rapidly in unexpected ways. DiMaglia brought word of an urgent new development. "Sir, you need to go down to Level 7 right now. Our tech team reports that old space craft the aliens left behind has suddenly come alive. They say it's spinning like the devil."

Endre raced behind him as they hopped into the mono wave transports that took Base personnel to all levels. Zach felt it before he saw its pulsing blue rays sending out bolts of light. The entire area felt charged with energy. The air fairly crackled with static. The men stood back with uncertainty.

"What happened?!" Zach shouted out.

Lt. Col. Walker had also been called to the Bay which housed the old Antare704 auxiliary craft. "We don't know, sir. It began shaking and then something triggered the craft to turn on. It appears to be emitting a signal pulse."

Zach could see that for himself. It was spewing out garbage numbers without a sequence, which meant nothing to him. "Is it registering radiation?" he asked, for the light spectrum rays had an unearthly glow about them.

One of the technicians shook his head. "It's within normal range."

Endre voiced what he was thinking. "Do you think it has anything to do with the 11th portal destruction?"

Admittedly, the timing of the two events was highly suspect. Zach didn't believe in coincidences. They didn't jive with the laws of the universe. He knew there was only one way to find out for sure. To the surprise and subsequent shock of all who witnessed it, Zach went over and put both hands on the skin of the auxiliary craft. The unearthly blue glow went through him like greased lightning, illuminating him from within. Gasps were heard all around.

Inside Zach's pocket, Gizmo's reaction to being plugged into a larger AI system caused him to immediately turn on and start conversing. Gizmo craved data, like humans crave food. He began downloading the memory within the craft's internal hive mind into his own at a rapid pace, while simultaneously analyzing the information spewing forth. There was an instantaneous mind meld.

When Zach managed to pull away from the craft, he was aware of his body still pulsing, then ebbing, before finally quieting altogether. It had been an intense experience, just like before. But this time Zach felt infinitely stronger. There was no oncoming seizure to stave off. With each new discovery in this ongoing life experience, he was aware that he was changing. In many ways the old Zach was dying and being re-born.

As he embraced this awareness, the space craft shut down as suddenly as it had started up. However, in his pocket Gizmo was alive, thriving, and amped up wanting more data to take in and analyze. Zach ran his hand over Gizmo attempting to reassure the AI that he could come down from this information rollercoaster ride. It immediately responded and went silent.

A sea of faces waited for Zach to speak, wondering if he still could. To all who had witnessed the unearthly event, it looked like a heart-stopping experience--as if the god of lightning had run electrical current right through him.

Endre was the first to speak, taking his usual practical approach. "What did you learn?"

Zach took a deep breath. There was good news and bad news. "The Mantis know that Portal 11 is lost to them. This sent out an emergency distress signal to the hive mind intelligence of all their craft," he told the group. "The signal sent was activation instructions to download all off-site stored memory to the hive mind for preservation. This is what triggered this craft into life. The good news is that I was able to learn something that might help us."

What he failed to tell them was that Gizmo had gotten it all—the entire hive mind intelligence of Mantis technology. Kaggen and his lot had made a fatal error in neglecting to destroy this old ship before departing to deep space. However, soon they would realize there was one ship transmitting information back to them which was unaccounted for. But it would be too late to retrieve unless they had the remote capability of signaling it to self-destruct.

"Seal up this area immediately," Zach instructed the Base Commander. "And evacuate all personal in adjoining sectors for now. Kaggen will soon realize his mistake. I'm sure he will attempt to eliminate this craft."

~~*~~

Kaggen swore vehemently. He was being plagued with unforeseen obstacles. His antennae lashed out like whip cords ready to strike. Something diabolical and sinister had obliterated their Malta hive. Not just disabling their blood banks like before, which could be replaced, but the entire underground operation. All the levels had collapsed in upon themselves, like some controlled demolition, forever sealing in the doom of his Aethien brethren. He felt and heard the wretched high-pitched screams of countless members of his race as they slowly suffocated and died. Rebuilding would be impossible.

The emergency distress signal alerting them of a portal hive being destroyed set off warning signals heard throughout his fleet of spaceships traversing the galaxies. It was a signal rarely, if ever, heard. It put everyone on high alert, causing their hive mind intelligence source to go into survival protection mode.

Kaggen continued to swear loudly. His anger was legendary, and his crew knew someone's head would be picked off that day, because the bad news just kept getting worse. Their leader abhorred loose ends and leaving one of their craft behind in Antarctica, even one barely operable, presented a real risk if it landed up in the wrong hands. Someone had failed to take the old Antare704 totally offline. The abandoned and forgotten craft was now sending out signals awaiting further instructions in the very heart of enemy territory.

While Kaggen was almost certain the humans were not clever enough to access the impenetrable hive mind intelligence banks the craft was linked to, it was best to take necessary precautions anyway. He pulled the self-destruct signal, which instantly reduced the craft to a pile of metal dust. This was sure to get the humans' attention but, as always, they would be clueless as to what they had sitting right under their very noses.

The only good news was that the satellite transmission frequencies streaming from Saturn to Earth were performing brilliantly. Kaggen's long planned for goals were being achieved with little effort. It was covert warfare at its best. His creations were hitting their targets with missile precision. Hybrids everywhere were becoming increasingly more active with each passing day. Some had turned into killing machines, as their self-assembled 3rd strand DNA was activated and received instructions. Since this mixed race was physically indistinguishable from all others, no one was the wiser of the true agenda. The hybrids began viciously targeting human purebloods with an obsession. Terror soon spread far and wide as cities became overrun with urban warfare. The human loosh energy output was off the charts.

All of Earth's electronic devices were now receiving and transmitting a signal to the digital identities of Kaggen's human-hybrids and their new and improved offspring. That they were, in essence, locked into his digital prison system gave him no cause for concern. They were a necessary means to an end. Earth would be totally overrun and conquered from within. This had always been the master plan.

Chapter 20

Meghan felt the baby move within her, reminding her that this child would be part of the new life they were starting together as the Eldridge family. Zach hadn't been gone more than a week, but it felt like a veritable lifetime. It left a profound sense of absence inside her which at times bordered on melancholia. She fought it as well as the tears that often slipped out at night with the emptiness of their marriage bed. Meghan told herself that this bout of emotional incontinence was nothing more than mommy hormones and that it would soon pass. Deep in her heart, she knew he would come back to her. He had to. She wanted more than just being mentally connected to him. She wanted his physical presence as well.

Every day she ventured out to capture on film the heart and life of this other world she found herself occupying. When he returned, she wanted to surprise Zach with the images that had inspired her reawakened creativity. Even with a critical eye, she knew they were good. The eyes of the people in this dimension spoke volumes, telling a different, more interesting tale. They were open, clear, and filled with such knowledge and wisdom. But more than ever they exuded a deep satisfaction with life.

At times it almost seemed that their bodies radiated light as well. Perhaps this was just her imagination, but then again, maybe not. She found herself often having to adjust aperture lens exposure to compensate for too much subject light. She knew this was unusual under normal lighting conditions, but then again nothing was normal here either.

The farmland she came across was lush and ripe with all varieties of fruits and vegetables. Tropical and non-tropical species existed side-by-side. The plants grew bigger, the fruit was sweeter, and instrumental music was played throughout the fields both night and day. Thriving vegetation appeared to grow towards the source of the sound like an invisible nutrient. Meghan learned that the food which grew was pest-resistant due to the melodic soundwaves fortifying the plant's ability to ward off insects. Pesticides and toxins did not exist in this realm.

Walking through a vineyard field one day, the purple grapes bursting off the vine, she came upon a small group of women. They were enthusiastically discussing grape harvesting strategies for producing the smoothest varieties of wines. This was a subject Meghan knew little to nothing about. Their talk fascinated her. She asked if she could join them. Without a moment's hesitation, the women welcomed her to sit down amongst them. It was a horticultural group, yet their interests were varied. They talked openly about spirituality, love, death, and subjects Meghan rarely, if ever, heard discussed where she came from. They seemed so well-informed—and they laughed a lot. More than anything else, she loved that. It was infectious. Before long she itched to photograph their animated faces as she listened to them share their other-worldly experiences.

Being in a place where there were no secrets or lies, a woman named Anne spoke up addressing her words to the other women. "I can see that Meghan wants to preserve this moment. Shall we invite her to take our imprints?" The request was met with mutual enthusiasm.

"Oh. Yes. Please do," she heard chorused all around. "But only if you come back and then share them with us," another woman suggested.

Incredible colors appeared around each woman when she developed her prints. They were astounding and beyond beautiful. She took a picture of herself and was shocked to see she also had colors emerging. The next day Meghan brought them her photos and every day after that she found her way back to that vineyard haven. These women soon became her support group and awakened in her the infinite possibilities of this unusual realm.

Of course, they were interested in her story and how she was adjusting. Surprisingly they knew everything about Zach, their recent marriage, and their baby on the way. That knowledge was a little disconcerting, but in a place where everyone knew what everyone else was spiritually working on, it didn't seem to be a negative privacy factor.

"Your daughter Izzie is very precious," one woman remarked. "She certainly has made a name for herself here. I find her abilities quite astounding for one so young."

Another woman was quick to chime in. "Caleb simply adores her. She never ceases to make him laugh, which is good. Sometimes he can be too serious."

There it was again. Caleb. Exactly who was this Caleb she had yet to meet? Izzie had been somewhat tight-lipped about her new friend. The next day Meghan was determined to find out. "I want to meet your little Caleb friend," she informed Izzie.

Izzie gave her mother's request a moment of thought. "Well, sometimes Caleb is little and sometimes he's very big. I never know what to expect," she admitted before pausing. "He's way more fun when he's smaller than me."

This response totally confused Meghan, throwing her for a loop. What kind of creature was this Caleb person that he could be both 'big' and 'little'? "I want to meet him," Meghan insisted. "Today."

And so that very day Izzie took Meghan to Caleb's secret office hidden away inside the Library of Truth on the 8th Dimensional realm. "Hold my hand, Mommy," Izzie instructed. "I know how to pop into the LOT. Zach showed me."

Meghan shook her head trying to understand what was happening. Why did her daughter feel like she was growing up faster than warranted for a seven-year-old? She seemed so at home in this new realm, so much more knowledgeable and adaptive than her own mother. Izzie seemed to be speeding right past her, evolving right before her eyes.

Izzie took her hand, holding tightly, and within seconds Meghan found herself in a small library she had never seen before. And in front of her was a young man, approximately her age, studying a very large tome with ancient symbols.

He looked up, just as surprised to see her as she was to learn that this was Izzie's friend Caleb—apparently the "big" grown-up version. Caleb respectfully rose to his feet, affording her an up-close look at him. This was no kid, but a good-looking young man in his 20's. The fact that he was hanging out with her precocious young daughter did not sit well with her. Her protective instincts kicked into overdrive. If it wasn't for the women having spoken so highly of him, she might have given him a little piece of her mind. But something stopped her, seeing the incredible loving and endearing look on his face.

She was completely taken aback when he stepped forward and hugged her. The baby inside her kicked with the contact. "I've looked forward to meeting you," he told her, taking her hand in his. "Thank you for having me."

Meghan frowned, more confused than ever. Having him? What did he mean? Izzie giggled. She gave Meghan's growing tummy a little solicitous pat as she danced in place between the two of them. "Shall we tell her?" Izzie asked excitedly, looking to Caleb for confirmation.

He hesitated, weighing the possibilities. These things usually were not done this way. There was a procedure involved with entrance into one's soul grouping. He knew he was being born into a very unusual family and that his father would be exceptionable. This was an honor for him. Caleb knew more about that honor right now than they did. Yet the fact remained that it was his role to make sure nothing jeopardized his own mission. Little Izzie had already opened a Pandora's Box and now Caleb had to put Meghan at ease. He could see alarm and suspicion in her eyes.

That was true. Meghan felt like she was the last one to the party. "Tell me what?" she demanded looking back and forth between the two of them. For some reason Izzie was enjoying this meeting immensely. Caleb looked slightly pained.

Finally, he stepped forward having made his decision. "I am the soul embodiment of the physical son you now carry within you. Towards the end of your final trimester, I will enter your womb and take living form. When born, you will be my mother. I cannot adequately express how grateful I am for this honor."

Meghan was struck speechless. Izzie continued to giggle away with pure delight.

~~*~~

Separated from the Council and support of his new family, Zachary Eldridge had just made a strategic move which, for him, had been a rather difficult life and death decision. There was no turning back. The order had been given.

Ishannika, who maintained access to his life file, as was afforded her leadership position, knew so immediately on many levels. She could see the evidence of it. Zachary was contemplating a bold move and she liked that. Bold moves were called for when it came to dealing with the likes of Kaggen. But she also knew that his move could backfire resulting in game over.

Holographically, she called all the other members of the Universal Council of Higher Planetary Guardians together for an urgent meeting. They came from all corners of the multiverse to hear her pressing news. They had seen for themselves what was recently occurring on Earth and knew they couldn't make their next move until young Zachary made his first. That was part of the Covenant agreement. The waiting had seemed like an eternity and every one of them knew the stakes.

Ishannika stepped aside, revealing the room's multi-dimensional holographic chess board which she had guarded over for thousands of years. Each move was carefully recorded on all its levels, each play locked in until the final outcome. It was the end game that signaled whether humanity would be released or not from its battle for freedom and truth.

The Mantis matriarch had been alerted the second a piece made its move. This was no simulated AI game, where thousands of possible moves were known, and the most intelligently programmed computer won. This was a real-time life and death run out, as young Zachary was now learning. Only the strongest would persevere and survive the final outcome.

RoyDol could see what the move meant within the bigger picture of the chess board, but he wanted details. "This decision he made... Tell us more," he requested.

Ishannika reviewed his recent records wanting to be thorough in her reporting. "Zachary has penetrated the memory of the hive mind. He now has access to the creation elements of Kaggen's hybrids. This is something no human pureblood has ever been able to do until now. This opened his Queen to capture on the board but forces a checkmate in several moves."

Milchris, from the Orion constellation, raised a hopeful brow. "What has Zachary decided to do with this knowledge?"

Ishannika got right to the point. "He has reprogrammed several online Minerva satellites to start transmitting a nullifying frequency. Somehow, he was able to isolate the exact harmonic frequency and wave band necessary to deactivate a hybrid's 3rd DNA strand. This will sever them from Kaggen's signals once and for all. The boy is clever but perhaps too clever as well."

RoyDol frowned. "Does he understand the repercussions of such a move?"

Ishannika was not so sure, as there were several pressing issues at stake. "Zachary doesn't want to kill, only deactivate," she reported. "But he does understand that letting Kaggen's abominations proliferate would ultimately mean the end of his race. This has caused him somewhat of a moral dilemma. However, just within the last hour he did make his final decision. The records show he gave the order to start the deactivation transmission, but only at 50% capacity."

They could see for themselves that pieces were starting to move on the chessboard's other levels. Young Zachary was being cautious with his transmission. The boy did not know if it might have a negative impact on human purebloods as well. Only time would reveal this.

~~*~~

The alien races monitored all corners of deep space in their intelligence gathering quest. They usually knew who and what was transiting through portals from outside galaxies into this one, as well as their purpose for being on or near Earth. While the Sun portal was the major stable entry point, there were others. Some were random and spontaneous in their opening, but most alien ships had detection technology of where and when these portals opened and for how long.

Neutrality was something many of the alien races had agreed upon many millennia ago. They had their own treaties. Without them they would be at war with each other, ultimately destroying their space playground. The large Federation and Higher Planetary Guardian ships were given wide berth by all. Most did not want to mess with the big guys. They could wipe one out in a nanosecond and had when circumstances called on them to do so.

With their normal level of space surveillance, Kaggen's people did not miss the sudden and unexpected onset of transmission signals coming from a Minerva communications satellite. Since these satellites were mostly benign and posed no directed threat to their satellites or ships, they overlooked it without closer scrutiny. That soon changed as reports started coming in about some strange interactive behavior occurring on Earth.

Behavior monitoring was the Mantis' forte. All human-hybrids were digitally connected to the hive through their 3rd DNA strand bio-chipping. Millions of them were routinely monitored and remotely tweaked for specific missions. History and data were collected and stored on each of them. It was a mammoth operation.

Kaggen knew how many were at the top of the corporate and political structure in every country, as well as how many graced the arts, sports and entertainment fields. In the U.S. alone some states had a heavier concentration than others. Wherever they went his hybrids caused both overt and covert disruption that deviated from the accepted norm. It was an emerging new race—and in time it would be openly recognized as his creation—an incredible tribute to the brilliance of the Aethien Mantis mind.

Mapu was the first of the Greys to point out something was amiss. "Sir, there appears to be a glitch in the system," he reported. "We are getting feedback from our world-wide surveillance network, showing some strange anomalies."

Kaggen scoffed. "Impossible," he replied. His system was flawless.

"See for yourself, sir," Mapu said, bringing up the evidence.

A checkerboard of screens came up across the expanse of the room showing thousands of camera frames displaying where hybrids stopped whatever they were doing and just seemed to stare out in frozen confusion. Some had stopped their vehicles while driving, blocking traffic or causing an accident. There were those who had just sat down in the middle of roads and streets, getting hit or run over.

Mapu offered a theory. "The transmission signal from the Saturn satellite appears to have gotten weaker. This could be affecting behavior in some of the older hybrids. What would you like me to do, sir?"

Kaggen was not so sure. Something like this had never happened before. If the signal was weak, there was only one thing to do. "Ramp it up, until we can figure what's causing it and fix it," he demanded. Power and more of it was one thing he understood.

Mapu nodded. "Very well." It was as he would have done so himself. He turned to his team of Greys and gave the order. Transmission was bumped up, just shy of full spectrum capacity.

Within hours they could see their strategy had helped, but not solved the problem. There were still hybrids glitching out. Kaggen sent an army of his best satellite techs to investigate further. They reported back news that sent panic coursing through him. The Saturn satellite was functioning properly. The signal was strong and had not weakened one bit. Some other signal from space had to be interfering and causing the havoc.

Chapter 21

Zach hadn't slept in days. His brain was wired for action and because of it the Antarctica Base was abuzz with tactical activity. They were launching another satellite for a secondary mission. If all went as planned, it would hopefully be the final nail in the coffin of the Mantis.

A call for more force was always the first line of defense in any battle and Zach knew this was a battle. Kaggen's counterattack had been immediate. From what they could detect, the alien transmissions were coming from a rogue satellite parked inside the Rings of Saturn. Low frequency microbeams were bombarding Earth's hybrids at a rapid rate. Zach was positive the information being transmitted to Kaggen's creatures was aimed at continued compliance and control. It appeared to be working.

The ball was now in Zach's court. Should he counter and ramp up his transmissions to override Kaggen's? Uncertainty regarding the potential negative side effects of all these transmissions on human purebloods was of paramount concern. No one, to his knowledge, had ever attempted such a thing before. Zach consulted with the Library of Truth, hoping for a definitive answer. His answer was less than definitive and open to interpretation.

"Human purebloods do not possess Kaggen's 3rd strand DNA," he was informed by LOT memory. "The frequencies you are utilizing have a specific target, as do all frequencies."

Zach took this to mean it wouldn't affect purebloods, but he had to be sure. Being a pureblood himself, he gave the order for Base personnel to test their stronger counter frequency on him first. Someone had to be the guinea pig. He couldn't very well ask others to do what he himself wasn't willing or ready to do. It was decided that the medical safety team would monitor all his vitals throughout the experiment just in case something went wrong. For one hour, he sat alone in a containment room where the frequency beams used on the human-hybrids slowly penetrated his body from head to toe.

Initially, Zach felt only a minor buzz course through him as his body decided how to react to this new intrusion. It was much like a jolt of caffeine one downs to start one's day, but then it just died out as suddenly as it came on. There weren't any noticeable side effects. If nothing else, Zach found himself desperately fighting off sleep. But he wasn't sure if this onslaught of tiredness was the result of not having slept in days or the effects of this test transmission.

The medical tests were analyzed and evaluated. It was a relief to learn there were no discernable anomalies. His heart was strong, his overall brainwave activity was well within the normal range, despite his synesthesia, and comprehensive DNA testing showed no foreign abnormalities. Zach gave the order to ramp up their transmission frequencies as well. Over several hours his team watched and waited. Information from the global networks started rolling in, but it was the incredible raw video footage which told the real story.

~~*~~

Kaggen was closely monitoring the situation as well. And he did not like what he saw. Hybrids had rallied after his escalation transmission then suddenly many of them were plagued with a bout of dizziness, followed by a seizure which caused them to spin around and fall to the ground where they thrashed and flailed, before going still. The reports coming in told of how thousands across the globe were also dying of sudden and inexplicable heart attacks. Medical experts were calling it a bacterial virus for lack of a better explanation. But with no known cure, the death toll was mounting.

More accidents were occurring. Car and truck drivers, airplane pilots, and train operators were dying while doing their jobs. Senators, congressman, world leaders, and even the President of the United States were not spared. Throughout this strange "virus", statisticians quietly observed that the good news was that crime and murder rates were quickly dropping with the sudden drop in population. Those who publicly tried to point this out were laughed at or dismissed as fools.

The dead were piling up faster than the professionals in the death industry could handle. Mortuaries, funeral homes, and crematoriums were backlogged, and huge freezer trucks were brought in to accommodate the dead. The world braced for what looked like a deadly pandemic.

Some brave medical professionals performed autopsies on the dead and what they found baffled them. Those who died had a rare Rh negative blood factor that was abnormal by all standards. Strange black threads had been detected in their blood which could not be written off as any known virus. These mysterious organisms appeared to respond to spoken words when placed under a microscope. They evaded capture displaying a rare form of biological intelligence. Whatever they were, they were foreign and alive.

Someone had thought to perform a DNA test on several of the dead. What they found struck fear into them. While many of the dead looked human by conventional definition and standards, strangely they were not. They had extra vertebrae in their spine for no apparent function.

Like their blood, their DNA was also abnormal. It contained a self-forming triple helix. While forensic pathologists discreetly shared this knowledge amongst trusted medical colleagues, they learned that their peers had also observed such mutations. It was generally decided to publicly keep their mouths shut. The truth would be beyond unfathomable, and who would believe them anyway? What they were dealing with was something of an alien nature that appeared human. That alone would cause fear and panic. They were smart enough to know they would be the ones professionally attacked if they suggested such a scientific absurdity.

Kaggen had counted on the established medical community saying nothing should they ever realize what they were truly dealing with. But he had never planned for such a negative development occurring in his human-hybrid agenda, the likes of what was happening now.

Something or someone was targeting his hybrids' 3rd strand DNA and the very blood that ran through their circulatory system. The realization that it had spread so rapidly made him boil with rage. Clearly it was not some rogue virus doing this damage to his hybrids, but an intentionally directed energy weapon aimed at biological warfare. He knew a pureblood had to be behind it and he suspected he knew whom. Who else would be so brazen and bold to come up against him? Yet, he didn't want to entertain the notion that by increasing his transmissional frequencies he himself might have precipitated the overload leading to so many of his hybrid's seizures and death.

The members of the Inter-Planetary Consortium of One Mind (IPCOM) were clearly angry with him. An assemblage of over one hundred high-ranking officers who ran the mammoth Saturn Space Station, as well as their Consortium superiors, had called for this unscheduled meeting. The room was packed with several rogue species. News of what was happening on Earth had quickly spread, as bad news often does. Clearly, they blamed him for this folly.

Kaggen was met by a sea of judgmental faces. He didn't like it one bit. Beloved when victorious, how quickly they could turn on you at the least sign of trouble. But this was just a temporary setback and they needed reminding of this fact.

Kaggen knew how and what was needed to do damage control. He shape-shifted to appear larger than he already was. This served to reinforce and re-establish not only who he was, but his power and authority in the multiverse. If it wasn't for his brilliance all these years, surpassing even the Anunnaki in their genetic manipulation skills, the Mantis might never have gotten this far in their bio-invasion agenda.

He told them of his counter-attack plan. "We are currently trying to identify the direct wave source of the transmission countering our own. This has been difficult as we believe an existing satellite may have changed its frequency band. Whether this was accidental or intentional is not certain. However, I believe the latter. When we increased our transmission strength, one particular satellite did so as well. This is more than coincidence."

"Who operates this satellite?" he was immediately asked.

This was the part Kaggen knew they wouldn't like. "It's very likely coming from a Minerva satellite," he responded. "But we're unable to confirm that at the moment."

"And why not?" came a litany of indignation. They all knew they were far superior to anything Minerva or the human's possessed.

Kaggen could feel their anger swelling and he understood it. "This particular satellite is shielded," he tried to explain. "We don't know how they were able to block us, as we've never shared this capability with Minerva. Unfortunately, it prevents our weaponry from targeting this satellite for destruction."

Kaggen hesitated, offering new hope. "But there are other ways..."

There were dubious looks exchanged all around. He sensed they did not believe him and was sure of it when someone rudely interjected: "Enlighten us then. What exactly is this plan of yours?"

~~*~~

Zach left Endre in charge of *their* plan. The need for sleep was overwhelming him to the point he could barely keep his eyes open. For someone who needed less sleep than most, this was highly unusual. Even a round of Qigong could not replenish the energy loss he was experiencing. He could only hope the test transmission he had received would not affect the energy levels of human purebloods if that *was* indeed the cause of his own exhaustion. If so, they would become complacent and unable to fight back if and when it became necessary. No matter what, he couldn't allow that to happen. They would be sitting ducks. He would know soon enough whether he had made the wrong decision after getting some restorative sleep.

Within minutes of lying down, he felt himself slide into a deep REM state where his dreams became extremely vivid. Unconsciously, he found himself searching for Meghan in her dimensional world, wanting and desiring her closeness like they had shared their last night as husband and wife. To his surprise, he found her in a library conversing with a young, attractive man who, from all indications, appeared to be very much taken with Meghan. In turn, he could see that she welcomed the animated exchange and was also totally captivated with him and by what he was saying.

Zach strained to hear their words, but frustration quickly set in when he was unable to do so. This was promptly followed by a stab of jealousy when he witnessed the young man move forward, warmly embrace Meghan, and see her hug him back in the same familiar way. Who was this person? The pressing need to know filled him with intense emotions, causing him to immediately awaken from his deep sleep. His heart was racing wildly. Sweat beaded his brow.

Zach felt an internal war waging within him of whether to return immediately to the 5th Dimension and never leave Meghan alone ever again. What was he doing here when the people who were most important to him, those he dearly loved, were somewhere else? He knew that if he went back to her right now, he might never return to finish this thing with Kaggen, important or not. Could he leave Endre to do the job for him, he wondered? Or could humanity fend for itself and let him live and enjoy his life and let the pieces fall where they may?

This intense moment of reflection filled him with existential self-doubt. Had he been fooling himself to believe he could do something to make a difference in this world? Would people even accept the truth after being misled for so long? He recalled the words of the great Mark Twain: "It's easier to fool people than to convince them they've been fooled."

Maybe he, himself, was just another fool amongst the masses. More than anything he wanted to be back where he belonged with Meghan and Izzie, where he felt loved and accepted for who he already was, not for what he might be able to do for humanity.

Struggling with such thoughts, he remotely connected to her, like he had done before--mind-to-mind, heart-to-heart. She had gone off to think after having the strange encounter with the man. He felt her dismay and pushed forward to merge with her mentally, letting her know he was there. There was an immediate smile from within as she recognized his presence. Yes, she missed him, too. There was no doubt about it. Her excitement was evident. She brought forth images of their last night together, recreating the intense emotional experience. He could have gotten lost in it, in her, but he sensed she had something of importance that weighed on her mind.

Zach was unexpectedly taken aback when she shared that she had just met the son that would soon be born to them. His name was Caleb, and it was Izzie who had introduced them. At first, she had found such a revelation difficult, if not completely insane, to believe. How could this be true? He was a grown man already. When she questioned him, he had enlightened her on the mechanisms of a soul's entry process prior to birth.

Meghan shared that Caleb had thanked her for the honor of becoming her child. *Can you believe this,* she silently mused? She hadn't even known she had any say in the identity of the soul coming through. Apparently, it was all arranged on some higher level. Zach listened to her internal thoughts about how amazing their son was and would, in all likelihood, be as a grown up. And there was the Izzie factor as well. She was completely enamored of her brother-to-be and they had become fast friends. Izzie was already acting like a big sister.

After learning all this, Zach felt more foolish than ever. His moment of jealousy had stemmed from seeing a handsome stranger who he now knew would soon be his own son. Meghan's amusement was evident when she picked up his self-chastising thoughts. In his mind, he felt her kiss away any lingering fears. Meghan let him know their son would be quite brilliant. He found it even more curious when she conveyed Caleb had told her that Zach and he already had many past lifetimes together—some as colleagues.

Zach was not aware of any prior lifetimes, and he wasn't sure what to make of such a claim. Although it sounded quite fantastic, his thoughts ran to how best to raise this child to bring out the best in him. What would his individual talents be, he wondered? Meghan had an answer for that as well. Caleb had told her he was by nature a mathematical physicist. This news made Zach's heart fill with parental pride. Yes, his son would be like-minded. They would have much to discuss and share. His heart beamed with pride and gratitude. This was the life he had fantasized about having, the family he had always wanted.

Zach found himself sharing with her what he and Endre were attempting to do to de-activate Kaggen's human-hybrids. He also revealed the doubts he was having. Meghan's words of support and encouragement to keep going, not give up and how proud she was of him, made his confidence soar. What lingered in his heart and mind was that she was proud of him. And that meant more than anything outside of the fact that she loved him. Had anyone in his life prior to Meghan ever truly expressed how proud they were of him?

There was something else she wanted to share which Caleb had revealed. "He said that the 12th is now open and there you would find *your* truth. Do you think he meant the last portal?" The mind connection between them began to sever. Izzie had just entered the room wanting her mother and presenting a distraction. Zach let her go. He was now more confident than ever that he could reconnect with her whenever he needed to.

Their connection had brought him new resolve, along with a deeper sense of partnership. Bonding with Meghan had recharged him and at the same time provided unusual information that left him reeling. His son would be like him in many ways. The craziness at learning they had worked together in the past was strange enough by itself, but that Caleb somehow knew the 12th portal was now accessible, and what he might find there, told him he was closer to an end point now more than ever. Yet the question remained whether or not he would be successful.

Chapter 22

Endre had closely monitored the tense situation in Zach's brief absence. "They tried to break through our satellite shield," he immediately informed Zach. "When they couldn't penetrate it, Kaggen started targeting all our Minerva satellites looking for a weak link to counterstrike. They know who they're fighting," he said, before adding. "I anticipated they might do this, so I had DiMaglia run up extra shielding on hundreds of our critical space structures."

Zach was more than impressed. It appeared he had left things in very capable hands. Endre's knowledge of Russian space technology was vast. He had instinctively known what to do. If something happened to him, he trusted Endre would step in and see this enfolding drama play out to its end.

"Better to make those shields reflective," Zach added. "Neutralizing them may not be enough. Let's send their ray beams back at them if they attempt it again. That will send a very clear message."

Endre liked that idea. The coding for such a retaliatory maneuver was not something the Mantis had openly shared with humans, but this information was stored in the hive mind of the space craft Zach had accessed. The physics of such things were new to him. He had to rely on the expertise of his Minerva science team to employ this offensive maneuver. And throughout this waiting game to see what Kaggen would attempt next, the Antarctica based frequency band continued to bombard human-hybrids on Earth with deactivating frequencies to release the Mantis leader's control.

Zach knew it was a checkmate. Kaggen had to realize he was in a Catch 22 situation with no viable means for escape. If he shut down his targeted frequencies, he might lose complete control of his hybrids to do his bidding. On the other hand, if the Mantis leader continued to ramp-up those transmissions to overcome what Zach was transmitting, he would kill even more of his creatures. What would Kaggen do?

It was becoming clear that human purebloods were not being overtly affected by the transmission frequencies aimed at the planet. Some were reporting tiredness and mild headaches, but not much more. Certainly not seizure and death like the hybrid beings. Would Kaggen go after purebloods next? This was Zach's greatest fear. The aliens were unpredictable. Would they destroy it all if they themselves couldn't possess Earth?

Zach was a numbers man. He tried to run a factorial function analysis on the Base's computer system, calculating permutations and probabilities on all the ways Kaggen might respond. He finally gave up. The list of factors became too large to consider.

Caleb had said he would find "his truth" within the 12th portal which was supposedly now open to him. Zach was determined to go there and see for himself. The truth of his life was not open to him in the LOT. It had never been. Satya had seen to that. Had she hidden it to protect him from himself or from something else? He was tired of these truth guessing games. Zach just wanted answers.

Endre insisted on coming with him. His curiosity about the 12th portal was just as strong as his counterpart's. Endre used the code key Satya had given him, moving it counterclockwise in his mind until it made one full rotational stop. The outcome was instantaneous. Like before, their bodies hurtled through the portal at an odd angular momentum, spinning around an axis point faster and faster. Zach now understood this spin factor gave them access to both past and future timelines. The question in his mind was whether they were meant to go back to the past or, as Endre had theorized, to some unknown future.

They spun out into a familiar void of bright light that immediately engulfed them. But this time they easily penetrated the veil that had blocked their path last time. Zach could feel them tear right through the matrix of this intelligent wall of patterned energy comprised of the number one followed by an infinity of zeros.

Zach was not sure what he expected to see, but it certainly was not what he did. Another white void lay beyond the veil, with no visible way out. It resembled a sterile waiting room, only without chairs or reading material.

Endre shrugged. "It's a dead end. Shall we go back?"

Was it some kind of test, Zach wondered? "No," he said. "Let's wait..."

The second they made this decision, visible letters appeared suspended on air. They read:

LIVE ON TIME, EMIT NO EVIL. NAME NOW ONE MAN.

Endre frowned. "What do you think it means?" He looked to his twin who still hadn't said a word. Zach just stared at the letters, with a quizzical look.

He waited, but still no reaction from Zach. "Do you think it wants our names?" he finally asked, for lack of a response.

Zach finally shook his head. He could visually see what Endre couldn't. He went up and with his finger wrote in the air a terse reply that formed into letters:

I DID, DID I. DAMMIT IM MAD.

Endre's eyes grew wide as he read Zach's strange cryptic words. "What's that supposed to mean?" he gestured to the nonsensical message.

Zach grinned. "It's a palindrome, Endre. The words spell the same thing backwards as well as forwards. I just answered with another palindrome."

Something *was* happening. They watched in amazement as the veil of whiteness suddenly lifted, exposing a clear way forward.

Endre was incredulous. "Damn. How did you know it would work?" he asked.

Zach shrugged. "I didn't. I guessed it wanted me to speak its language, like math."

They moved through the passageway wondering what other riddles they might find. But there were none. Instead, they encountered another white room, empty but for two curved metal columns resembling giant parenthesis symbols. A six-foot space separated the standing columns, and some form of radiant energy ran between them. It was subtle, but definitely visible.

Zach took a pen out of his pocket and rolled it across the threshold between the columns. It immediately disappeared, never reaching the other side. Or had it? Zach and Endre exchanged a knowing look.

Endre inclined his head, grinning. "Dare we?" he asked.

There really was no need to ask. They both knew they would. They were like Siamese twins joined at the hip, unable to turn away from an unsolved riddle. Where one went, so did the other. Together they stepped into the unknown energy field and came out on the other side in a swirling vortex that swept them up and propelled them through the immense core of the fiery Sun, penetrating its very heart.

They were both beyond the stage of being surprised. They knew the 12th portal would be like no other, yet they hadn't expected it to feel so familiar—especially for Zach. It reminded him of the time Ishannika had taken him through the Sun to Nordekka to locate the missing *Minerva Files* in that other universe.

Where they were headed now, Zach didn't know. Beyond the Sun was the infinite vacuum of space, a void teeming with possibility and the source of all creation. Out of nowhere Zach felt intense fear flood through him. A part of him wanted to turn back and flee, but he valiantly pushed forward. He remembered reading that when one experiences fear, one is moving closer to the truth--one's own truth. Is this what he now feared?

Endre grabbed his arm, sensing his hesitancy. There was an urgent look in his eyes as if he knew something Zach didn't. "I know what you're feeling, but we have to. There's no turning back. The time is now."

Zach felt sick inside. It was the same sickness he felt when he discovered who his father really was--the mastermind behind Minerva and all its evil. A sense of self-preservation and dread coursed through him warning him to avoid what secrets lay beyond the Sun. How bad could it be? Hadn't Caleb said the way was now open for him to discover his own truth? Dear God, could his own truth be that terrible or painful?

A walled room of mirrors surrounded him, corralling him in and blocking off his exit. At first glance into the mirror, he saw the reflection of his own self staring back at him, scared but very much present. Then the mirror image slowly changed shape and took on another form--the reflection of a Mantis being trapped inside a hologram waiting to be freed. There was no mistaking the creature's intent when he reached out to Zach. He wanted him to release him.

Confused and uncertain, Zach stepped back, bumping up against Endre who was right behind him. Endre turned to him and nodded knowingly, not the least bit shocked at the scene unfolding before them. "It's time, brother," was all he said.

Zach shook his head, not understanding. Time for what? Who was this creature? This was no Kaggen or Ishannika Mantis being, but another who was just as large and imposing. Yet the eyes told an unexpected truth. This creature was suffering. There was no evidence of hate or vengeance to be seen. Those glowing red eyes softened with compassion as they gazed upon Zach. It all felt so strangely familiar, and that's when it hit him.

A cascade of deeply buried memories, ancient in origin, spilled forth into Zach's conscious awareness like a dam bursting open. There was an awakening on all levels of who he was, really was, or had been in the past, hundreds of thousands of years ago at the dawn of man. There was no stopping the flow of information coming through once the gates had been opened.

He, Zachary Eldridge, *was* Nehemiah in his many forms. The revelation hit him like an asteroid striking Earth and blowing away the dirt and landscape to the core beneath. It was he who had once been human and dammed for thousands of years to be Mantis for the deeds he had done. His actions alone had taken on dire consequences for all the races. Because of these transgressions, his past self was trapped in a hologram of his own making.

He suddenly felt a deep affinity for this Mantis being. Where words failed him, a flood of emotions threatened to spill over instead. He finally let go and unchecked tears streamed down his face. He felt instant shame mixed with remorse at all he was learning.

This was the dark aspect of his soul—the path he had never ventured down to question or examine. Buried deep inside him, the karmic wheels of creation were now forcing him to look at his past on all its many levels. It was a disturbing revelation to behold. No wonder a part of him wanted so desperately to flee. How in the world had he fucked up so badly in his early evolutionary process?

The unanswered question still lingered. "How?" was all he could utter, staring at that part of him that was Nehemiah of the past, a being who still seemed very much alive, never having aged, never dying within his holographic solitary prison.

Nehemiah felt and shared Zach's pain of realization. They were linked forever on a soul level. "We were part of the very first human soul movement from energy into matter," Nehemiah explained. "As many souls were getting trapped in the physical creativity of their new world, we thought our soul, along with others, could be of help to free man stuck in his illusion. Instead, we allowed ourselves to get drawn in with other dark forces and alien races, corrupting the path back to Truth. Our fall came about because we wanted to experience the power of our own willful design, our own clever machinations, without considering the risks."

Zach was reliving it all in his head in vivid detail. The truth was indeed more than painful. His soul felt the torture of failure. How could he have done such a thing? How could he have allowed himself to be blinded and led astray from his true intent? His actions had been directly responsible for not only breaking the seals that protected the 12 portals leading into the Library of Truth but opening them to the dark intent of evil forces, both

Minerva and alien, who weaponized it to perpetuate their own human war agenda.

He had sold out his human brethren. The karma reaped from such actions had been enormous. The retribution was becoming one of them, losing his human link, causing parts of his human angelic soul to fracture off until he could, at some point in time, hope to undo the damage he had set in motion in order to retrieve his splintered soul. Zach and Endre had become those fractured human parts of the original soul being of Nehemiah.

"I am so sorry. So very sorry," he confessed, which seemed a lame excuse in comparison to the realization of what his deepest memories had just uncovered. He could see his actions play out like a multi-level life review. This is what his life file in the Library of Truth would have revealed—an ugly truth. He, who had thought he was so noble and true, unlike his father, had a murky history that entailed large-scale inter-dimensional damage borne of arrogance. His actions had led to the very creation of Minerva.

Zach remained silent, saying no more until Nehemiah could finish revealing his or rather their past, as they were all a part of the same wheel cog in this grand cosmic cycle. They shared the same DNA of the hermetic seals that had originally been placed as protection on the Library of Truth portals. Could the truth get any more painful?

Nehemiah continued. "It was decided that the only way we could make amends was to attempt to undo what we had set into motion so long ago with Minerva, the portals, and the Library of Truth. We agreed on a soul level to split off three ways and work together. Endre was our backup should you fail. But you, Zach, were the one we gave most of our soul energy to coming into this lifetime. You were our ball carrier. You were the one we counted on making things right again with the portal system, the Mantis and Minerva."

If Nehemiah knew the entire score, and Zach was certain he did, he wondered if his current actions had made any real progress towards their corrective mission, or was he failing miserably in the eyes of his oversoul?

"Who else knew about what we were attempting to do?" he asked. "Was it Satya?"

Nehemiah nodded. "Yes. Of course, Satya knew. As did Ishannika and a few others. It was why you were not allowed to see your life file. You had to make things right without pre-knowledge of the mission we took on—which is to close up the Library of Truth portals which had been opened to the dark forces of this planetary realm."

The realization of what he had once been a part of was quickly sinking in, and the ramifications were enormous. This is what he had taken on from day one of his birth. His Acquired Savant Syndrome with Synesthesia had been no accident. This, too, had been pre-planned. These abilities would be needed for him to succeed. He wasn't just a part of a planetary rescue--he was both the perpetrator and the star quarterback. However, the game was far from over.

"We need all 12 Minerva statues to close the Library of Truth portals," Zach reminded them, pointing out the obvious. "Endre and I have only found 10 of them. The Antarctica one is still missing."

"No. You now have 12," Nehemiah informed him. "I retrieved the Antarctica statue so Kaggen would not find it there. Had he found it, and he did search for it, it would have made our task even more difficult. He fears he is operating on borrowed time and the timelines might shift, thereby locking him and his race out from their end game. He is not far from the truth, but nothing is finite."

Nehemiah, as a Mantis being--large, greenish blue, with probing eyes, was hard to face knowing this creature was really a part of himself. He seemed to possess so much truth spanning back to the origins of man and souls which entered into this dimension--something Zach was just learning.

"This 12th portal always led to our own past truth," Nehemiah told them. "We saw to that. Only the three of us together could re-enter it again after fighting off the deeds of the invaders. Only the three of us could lay claim to its information, its dynamics and the 12th and last statue. This is because we are the trinity three, in one, which hid every one of these golden statutes in the portals thousands of years ago, setting up this test to save our soul."

Zach heard himself gasp. What??? Yet Nehemiah continued, undeterred in revealing the truth. "This was done as part of a greater retrieval test, initiated by the inter-dimensional Federations of Guardians that oversaw the Earth realm or we would have been doomed to stay in the darkest regions of the multiverse as a Mantis being for our deeds," he admitted.

Nehemiah looked to them both for acknowledgment and understanding, especially Zach, who had consciously known less than Endre about why they had been born in this time. "The Guardians could not undo or intercede in what we had selfishly set in motion for our own gains. The laws of free choice ruling this realm and the Library of Truth forbade it. Only we could undo that harm when the time was right. It became necessary to make a plan—to pave a path in the future where all the right variables could be put in place to set the stage for what we knew had to be done."

Nehemiah was grim-faced. "Even your heritage, your father being Governor of Minerva, and your birth genetics were pre-arranged. It was part of our plan. This is why it was decided to split off and combine our efforts. What you are now recalling is the final download of all our collective memories. The choices we agreed to and made. That future time we prepared for has arrived. Make no mistake. The time *is* now."

Those were the exact words Endre had uttered: "*The time is now*". It was hard to believe that he was one of the "three" individuals who initially hid all the statues. He flashed on Izzie showing him her drawing of the three mysterious persons and telling him she thought he would know who they were. Even the Melchizedeks must have known, which explained their amusement when he questioned them if they were the three unknown persons who hid the statues. Was he the last to remember and know?

And there they were. Nehemiah's hands cradled the last two missing Golden Minerva statues, handing them over to Endre, who turned to him. "It's time to bring forth the others."

It was all happening so fast. His mind was trying to catch up and assimilate the truth about his past. Remnants of past conversations about the nefarious deeds of this Nehemiah person filtered back in. No wonder he knew how to free *The Minerva Files*—he was part of the mind of Nehemiah. No wonder everyone, including Satya, had hid so much from him, yet continued to encourage him to free the Library of Truth and humanity. From the very start, they had all been counting on him to reverse past damage and set things right again—to release the seals he had cast. Yet they were never certain he would succeed. Even now, it was still questionable.

The scattered pieces were quickly coming together, affording Zach a glimpse of the bigger picture. So much more of it now made sense. His thoughts ran to Voltaire's and Emilie's journal in the National Library of Russia. The personal diary had implied that Emilie's scientific knowledge of the universe had come from an alien Mantis being named Nehemiah—a being who had admitted to once being human. Over time and many nighttime visitations, Emilie and Nehemiah had established a close relationship. And then Emilie, a virgin in all respects, had become impregnated shortly after experiencing an unusual exchange of energy between the two of them. In a profound moment of realization, Zach knew who Emilie was and how their paths had once again joined. Emilie of the past was now Meghan of the future, his wife, the mother of their child to be. On his very first day in the Library of Congress, his enamorment of her had been instantaneous. Their coming together again in this lifetime, of minds meeting minds, of physical love finally being realized, had been an act of destiny.

Zach reined in his errant thoughts. There was still a serious job to be done, which he certainly hoped he could successfully pull off. He called on Gizmo to bring forth the other 10 statues hidden away in the stacks of the Library of Congress. Seconds later, they materialized in front of him awaiting instructions.

There came a moment of pause, a profound moment of truth, when the threesome looked at the statues assembled before them, then back to each other knowing what needed to be done. When activated, these 12 statues would shut down all 12 of the Library of Truth portals. That was the plan. If successful, this would activate the 13th Sun portal—the most important primary and stable portal of all. It would immediately seal off the numerous stargates and wormhole entry points into this galaxy which the Mantis, the Greys, the Dracos, the Reptilians and numerous other alien races had been utilizing to manipulate Earth's people for thousands of years. The Sun portal would become the sole gatekeeper portal, barring entrance to all but the most peaceful and highly evolved beings wanting to work within this galaxy.

What Zach, Endre and Nehemiah were about to do would entrap all existing negative life forms within Earth's Milky Way galaxy. As in the past, when Federation Guardian forces tried to drive them away from Earth, they would evade retribution by escaping through the Sun portal, only to return and commit more crimes at a later date. Trapped here they could be dealt with and quarantined against creating further damage.

There were more than 200 billion other galaxies in the multiverse. Thousands of different species existed in all those realms. Some were more highly evolved and open to peaceful exchange. They would always be welcome. All invading life forms of a warring nature would be forever locked out--allowing for a natural evolutionary ascension of human Earth souls of pureblood. Up until present time, these races had intentionally utilized numerous ploys to block this process in order not to lose control of Earth and its people. As a result, enslavement had ensued. Those days were coming to an end.

Nehemiah knew the process. Zach felt his and Endre's mind merge with Nehemiah's to reveal to them what steps were needed. It surprised Zach to realize he already knew the mechanism involved. The information had been there all along, buried within the Mind of the LOT. He inwardly smiled. It was true. The answers to all things did exist within.

The 12th portal was more than a link into Zach's own truth, it was a pathway into the matrix of the entire cosmos. And within that matrix was Nehemiah's hologram prison. Zach and Endre stepped back as the hologram began revolving in a counterclockwise direction, creating a vortex which sucked all 12 golden statues inside it until they were no longer visible. At the same time, it ejected an orb of light which hovered above them.

Within seconds, a chain reaction began in the matrix of the universe. The cosmos yawned wide open, then commenced contracting and expanding with the breath of new life, like a balloon being blown up by some unknown power. Each breath became bigger, creating oscillating energy fields to burst forth that moved across the universe on laser spirals of light. It was like nothing ever seen.

Endre and Zach were afforded a 360-degree view, like a mammoth screen projected into space, where they and others could see the spectacular transmutation and transformation taking place. They bore witness to what was occurring, above them, below them, and to all sides of where they stood in its central core. What was happening was akin to the big bang that brought energy into matter and created the multiverse. Nehemiah's hologram shattered into a million luminescent pieces that wove its way, like spiraling threads of light, throughout the Earth's Milky Way galaxy.

With that shattering, there was no longer any sign of Nehemiah's hologram or Nehemiah himself. Had that part of themselves ceased to exist, Zach wondered? There were no answers, just a cosmos now free to make corrective adjustments.

Zach was spellbound at what the weaving threads of light were attempting to do. They were stitching up the holes, tears, breaks, wormholes, portals, or whatever anomalies man and other species had created which had broken through the matrix of time leading into the Library of Truth.

Each portal closing caused a blow out at the other end, wherein it collapsed upon itself akin to a controlled demolition. It was beyond incredible to watch the universe break down then restore the age-old hermetic protection seals of the Library of Truth back to its original state.

It was evident that the 12th and final portal had yet to close, as they were still accessing it. Zach knew that when this portal went offline, the Sun portal would once again be the only gatekeeper to all interstellar entry into this dimensional galaxy. The Federation and Guardian ships could secure and safeguard the Milky Way's space borders once again like they had hundreds of thousands of years ago before the corruption of the 12 Library of Truth portals. The cycles and epicycles of life would be restored to their true origins. The hermetic seals would be put back in place.

It was time to close the 12th and final LOT portal. The sentient orb of light, which had shot out of the hologram and hovered above them throughout the restoration process, now enveloped Zach and Endre in its protective safety. As one, they bore witness to the last portal's closure and seal. This portal, which revealed the long-held secrets to their own personal truth, their dark past, and was now no longer necessary.

Zach didn't know if Endre felt it as he did, but there was a merging of new energy within him that seemed to come from the orb of light. It felt foreign and yet familiar at the same time. And with it came a flood of knowledge that afforded Zach insight into how Nehemiah had set this whole cosmic drama in motion so many years ago. The orb contained his entire collective memory as well as the remnants of his soul essence.

This human-turned-Mantis being, which was a part of Zach's soul's earliest incarnations in the Earth realm—the same being who bore the infinity symbol upon his head, just as he and Endre possessed, was now finally freed. Nehemiah's memories merged and became his.

There was so much to assimilate. The dark forces who created Minerva had reverently referred to Nehemiah as the all-powerful "portal opener". While his cleverness had become legendary, it had served to feed his ego until there came a time when he realized the catastrophic repercussions of his actions had doomed his soul. Now karmic wheels of creation were allowing him a second chance to undo his deeds and his destiny demanded he take it.

The infinity birthmark he bore upon his scalp took on new significance. It was a reminder of his purpose within the universal timelines. He was a singularity event which opened a new infinite universe or perhaps restored it back to its original timeline.

Now he could see the bigger picture. For him it was about more than just rescuing mankind—it was about rescuing and saving himself. Everything which occurred was because he had set about on a journey to save his soul. All the variables that had to be put in place to accomplish such a mission were staggering. Zach knew the Mind of God had to be a large quantum computer.

With this new realization, Zach and Endre suddenly found themselves back in the Library of Truth. It was now brighter than ever—something Zach had not thought possible. The knowledge of the universe was now safe and secure again from the corruptive and manipulative influence of the dark forces. But the war was not yet over.

Zach watched from the ultimate view inside the Library of Truth as the 13th Sun portal, the gatekeeper to this galaxy became re-fortified and stronger than ever. The energy field that now ran through the Sun portal would repel negative energies, becoming a Portal for Peace. The Federation Guardian ships quickly moved in to see to it.

Human choice, on some supreme level never before exercised, had finally come to a decision that had nothing to do with secret government treatises or pacts. A loudly felt "Enough!" echoed throughout the cosmos for all of humanity to hear and experience. In turn, the entire galaxy felt and responded to this change.

Chapter 23

Kaggen knew immediately, as did others of his kind that something profound had occurred and not necessarily a welcome change from a Mantis perspective. The universal timelines that ran throughout the multiverse were not only moving closer to each other but were practically intersecting. This was a foreboding sign, which the Oracle had alluded to as a high potential outcome.

The reality of such an event taking place was not only unthinkable, but terrifying in scope, for Kaggen knew exactly what it meant. Something of this magnitude could only have happened if an alteration had been made to the 12 universal portals leading to the Library of Truth. This meant Earth' gridlines were shifting and energetic ley lines that had been put in place to stabilize the planet from shifting on its axis and spiraling out of orbit, would soon start spinning again. A distress call went out from the Inter-Planetary Consortium for One Mind to all its rogue members throughout the multiverse.

Many alien species were collectively being told via Federation Guardian decrees to reform or evacuate—immediately. Those who did not would be left behind to meet the consequences. The word had travelled far and fast to all galaxy outposts, intergalactic craft, and space stations, including the one Kaggen now occupied near Saturn's moons. Something had caused the Library of Truth portals to be hermetically sealed and access blocked. And worse, the Sun portal was closing off to all rogue elements coming into this realm. Some had made haste and escaped in time to other galaxies in the multiverse, knowing they might never be able to return. Others, who had been caught off-guard and failed to quickly act, were strategically deciding what to do next as they realized their entrapment.

Law and order had come to planet Earth and the Milky Way Galaxy it inhabited. It would only be a matter of time before such a move emboldened other realms to do the same. Kaggen's kind could and would not allow this unrealistic proposition to move forward. Change begets change and unless they stopped it now, all would be lost.

They were being told their long-time playground on Earth for human experimentation, on all levels DNA and otherwise, was to cease all operations after countless millennia of reign. Did they not know who they were dealing with, making such outrageous rules? Kaggen was having none of their decrees. It was an act of war the humans would regret as well as the Federation Guardian Councils which supported their freedom.

In response to this enforced insanity, Kaggen released a firestorm of destruction setting off warring and physiological elements throughout the Earth. His hybrids, or what remained of them who hadn't glitched out by his directed frequencies, were now weaponized to kill and destroy all obstacles in their path. Governments and their employees which had been infiltrated by hybrids were mobilized. There was no other recourse. If Kaggen couldn't have Earth, then no one else could either.

~~*~~

Speed was of the essence. Zach was prepared for this moment in time and knew exactly what needed to be done. Nehemiah had left him that knowledge. His internal presence and guidance were becoming clearer as the integration progress of soul parts and memories came together. He was now the host personality, the ball carrier that Nehemiah had entrusted to complete the work he had begun lifetimes ago. Within time, would Endre also be soul integrated, or would they work better as two partners in both worlds? This was still undecided and would be Endre's choice.

The two immediately returned to the Antarctica Base, where it was evident Kaggen had swiftly mounted an offensive all around the world in response to this perceived annihilation threat. The Mantis leader no longer cared that his own ramped up frequencies were causing accelerated deaths among his human-hybrids. Everywhere they continued to flail with sudden seizures, collapse, then death—their hearts giving out as they fatally freed themselves from Kaggen's grasp and control.

Kaggen knew all too well what he was doing. However, his new goal was to inflict the most crippling damage possible before the final demise of his experimental species. He was confident he could always resurrect his work and make more human-hybrids when needed. Right now, they were expendable to him, no more than livestock. But since they were all linked to the Mantis hive mind, he knew his own kind would be furious at the carnage he had wreaked on those containing some, if not all, Mantis DNA. Shades of past errors committed back on his home planet of Arjun crept in, reminding him that his primary objective was and had always been to save his race from ultimate annihilation. The humans and their planet had only been a means to meeting that end.

Experiencing similar concerns, Zach feared for the survival of his own human pureblood race. The use of Mantis high frequency tectonic technology was unleashed into the stratosphere where the people of Earth could not detect it. It caused the Earth to rumble and move, horizontally, vertically, and with rolling land waves. He watched in horror as earthquakes were triggered, causing massive walls of water to roll across the land, flooding cities and communities. Millions were dying in the wake of such destructive forces being unleashed. Nature gone awry was an easy scapegoat.

He had to stop it now. The satellites in space had been programmed that in such an event, activation codes aimed at human purebloods would be transmitted. Only he and Endre knew what those transmissions contained and what they were meant to accomplish. The answer had been there all along, hidden within the Sakya Monastery genome scrolls. The question was whether what they had deciphered would ultimately work. There was no time for testing what was only theory.

The order was given to start the designated satellite feed and then connect it to the network of hundreds of other Minerva space satellites transiting Earth. Transmission required it be everywhere at once, reaching the very farthest corners of their world. It was a bold, risky move, but Zach felt the power of Nehemiah within him telling him it must be done.

It was not an easy task bringing every satellite online, including those which had been unused for years. What was to be transmitted only the Anunnaki would have scientifically understood. This race of highly advanced beings had seeded the first humans on Earth in their DNA likeness. However, they were smart enough to make sure their creations never rose above them prematurely by possessing all of their genetic coding. A slow evolution was supposed to see to that.

The Sakya Monastery map had specifically shown which human DNA strands had been deactivated and their unique sequencing. There were several of them. What their purpose was, the map did not specify. Nehemiah's memories showed Zach that these strands had been shut down until a future date and time when they would be re-activated. Whether this would come about by natural or unnatural means Nehemiah was not saying. He was being left to trust the process, wherever that took him.

Zach was a person who liked data and facts, not conjecture. This "process" was tearing him up. The genome map made no reference to the specific future event that would re-activate these dormant strands. Zach worried his plan might be forcing them to prematurely open before their time and evolutionary process. Then what would happen? No one knew. He silently prayed he had not been sent on a fool's mission.

Endre was leaving the final decision to him but believed what they were to do was inevitable. Zach's decision could mean saving humanity or bringing about more destruction. The Library of Truth would not weigh in on what was the right thing to do. It had to be a judgment call of his own accord. Was this the end of times, biblical scholars talked about, Zach wondered? Would it all come down to only one man's ultimate decision?

After being plagued with such rare apprehension, Zach felt his thoughts suddenly turn crystal clear, sharp and razor focused. The fog of indecision had lifted leaving only one way forward. The dormant human stands would have to be activated. The satellites were ready, but was he?

"Do it," he said quietly, giving the final order to his remaining team of loyal scientists and technicians. They had been patiently standing by knowing something momentous was about to happen and they would be part of it.

Nothing happened at first. It seemed like any other transmission feeding information to all communication centers on Earth. But this information feed contained algorithms which spoke to man's DNA and cellular body in a language it understood--math. The internal biological program of man recognized the instructional coding sequence and accepted it.

Everyone waited, knowing the Anunnaki legacy might affect all human purebloods as well as those still inhabiting the Antarctica Base. What would it do? It was gradual at first, like a heavy weight finally lifting and feelings akin to joy flooded in. As emotional and cognitive genetic blocks dissolved, memory slowly returned containing knowledge and understanding of man's origins and the universe at large that most never knew. Dormant areas of the brain came back online and cerebral cortexes lit up, making new neuronal pathways. Zach felt it, as did those around him. They were developing new access pathways to identify and know truth—their own as well as others. They were becoming 5th Dimensional beings.

On televised feeds coming from all over the world, people were waking up. The Age of Discernment had finally arrived. What they had been blinded to before was now clear and evident, as well as the lies and deceit that had been perpetrated against them for many millennia.

As this mass awakening accelerated and spread to millions, then billions, the vibrations of Earth began to change to a higher frequency which hybrid beings could no longer sustain. It weakened them, revealed to all who they really were—aliens who walked among them sowing discord. Because they didn't contain the original Anunnaki genetic coding to affect this transformation, they turned confused and perplexed at the changes occurring around them, which only served to paralyze their actions even more.

That's when things took an unexpected turn. The Earth began to spin with the growing light of truth and understanding being opened around the world. It stopped Kaggen's tectonic earthquake technology, the massive flooding from oceans and lakes, and the resulting destruction of the Earth's infrastructure.

As Earth humans embraced this expansion of growth and accepted the evolutionary change taking place, it was celebrated as if they had finally reached a long-awaited milestone. The Earth's Schumann Resonance frequency accelerated in response. Night turned into day and day into night in rapid succession. As humans claimed their advanced DNA abilities, the heavens expanded with the immense influx of light human purebloods were now emitting. This light grew exponentially, causing an energetic wave to move quickly throughout the water and landmasses, cleansing it from all invading negative forces. When it was finished a profound silence was heard around the world.

Chapter 24

Kaggen found himself on a dark forbidding planet. He scanned the desolate rocky landscape wondering where his space craft was, or his people, even Mapu his trusted right-hand. Terror overcame him as he realized he was alone, without allies. This place felt like a sealed coffin devoid of biological life. Perhaps over that mountain ridge he would find his people.

He delved into the deep pockets of his long purple robes and found, much to his relief, that he had somehow managed to bring his reliable Oracle cube with him. It had served him well throughout his extensive lifetime. Perhaps he could count it as his only true friend.

In this place he didn't need his protective black eye lenses against which Earth's environment warranted wearing. It felt good to remove them, reminding him of Arjun, his home planet, where such things were unnecessary.

"What is this place?" he asked the Oracle, only to receive the terse reply: "You do not recognize it, sire? You are back home on Arjun."

Kaggen laughed. Very funny. Arjun, a star planet in the constellation Lyra, had died out thousands of years ago. He ought to know. His actions had led to its destruction when he accidentally ripped a hole in its time matrix causing his people to abandon their home and necessitating him fleeing into the future to escape punishment. Earth had been his target until he could return to his planet and possibly reverse the damage he had once rendered. Ishannika had never forgiven him for his scientific "tinkering" and banished him in the process. Their once close and trusting relationship had forever suffered. But Kaggen had thought his hybrid program could someday restore all that, as well as her confidence in his abilities to save their species.

His long tentacles tensely locked together, as they often did when he thought of her. She was an unpredictable yet also very predictable Mantis matriarch—an enigma at times. Perhaps she would never forgive him for what he had caused to happen on Arjun. Clicking and hissing signs of disapproval were directed at the Oracle. It was not a time for levity. Kaggen wanted facts.

"Tell me where we are!" he demanded once again.

The Oracle flashed brighter, as if to emphasize that the information being given a second time *was* the truth. It did not lie.

"You have been sent back to the past. You are back on Arjun after its light died out," the Oracle informed. "The timelines have been altered. The future is no longer accessible to you. You are doomed."

Kaggen's outraged and defeated hissing screams echoed throughout the dead planet.

~~*~~

The energy gridlines of Earth all responded to the influx of light pools of higher vibration streaming into the planet, with the dormant human DNA strands being activated. A cascade of change began taking place. It caused closely intersecting timelines to momentarily merge, then bifurcate. As a new timeline was born. It propelled those with higher frequency DNA to move to a 5th Dimensional version of Earth called Terra. There they would join those who had already ascended to this level during past evolutionary juncture points. Death was unnecessary on this 5th Dimensional level. Here their lives would be devoid of the manipulation and untruths that pervaded the lower dimensional realms, where death was inevitable. Many were finally freed from the endless cycles of reincarnation, which trapped souls from moving forward.

This accelerated timeline jump affected all the higher infinite dimensions as well, causing some to move to the next level as a massive influx of new human angelics came to 5th Dimensional Terra. Some would require acclimation to their new home as they realized a profound evolutionary and transformative event had taken place.

~~*~~

Zach also moved to a higher level. With the timeline jump he surprisingly found himself onboard the largest craft of the Federation Guardian space fleet that monitored the multiverse and the galaxies. This vehicle was now parked outside the 13th Sun portal. He glanced around the large UCHPG Council room where he was met by sea of faces comprised of all galactic species, including the Mantis Matriarch Ishannika. Had he gone too far? Would they be angry with him for what he had caused to occur in the timelines and dimensions? Never in his wildest dreams had he expected what had happened to have actually happened. Like Nehemiah, he had changed the world in a major way that might not be appreciated. Zach nervously gulped, waiting to hear what they would proclaim his sentence to be. Would it be karmic isolation and retribution like Nehemiah had endured? If so, he might never see Meghan or Izzie again. The feeling filled him with sorrow and dread.

Ishannika finally stepped forward. "Well done," she declared with an appreciative smile.

Zach brightened. "You mean I didn't make things worse?"

There was a chorus of amused looks and chatter heard around the Council room. "No," Ishannika replied. "You did exactly as you set out to do." She looked around the room, nodding to RoyDol and Mikchris, both High Council members. "We have been waiting for this moment in time for thousands of years—256,000 to be exact."

Zach was speechless. "And Kaggen?"

Satya appeared and waved a hologram into view where they could see Kaggen alone in an underground cave scavenging for food. "He has been banished to his home planet of Arjun, trapped in a past of his own making. You need no longer concern yourself with him."

RoyDol nodded in approval. "He will have many millennia to contemplate his deeds. The human race is finally free of him."

Zach's head was reeling. Kaggen had jumped to a past timeline where hopefully he would stay, never to return to Earth to continue his human-hybrid experimentation. This alone, was monumental. "What will then become of 3rd Dimensional Earth?" he finally asked.

Satya's words were chilling. "That dimension will eventually die out in time. There are those evolved souls who chose to stay behind and help bring light and understanding to the lower density human lifeforms that thrived on hate and discord. Some of those less evolved souls will have difficulty letting go of the delusions and divisions of their world. They will be given every chance, but should they continue in these ways, they will perish as well. The rest will move on to Terra."

Zach realized now what had been at stake all along. "Did you all know how this would turn out?" he asked, looking round the room for answers. Had all this been pre-destined?

Ishannika shook her head. "We could only hope for your success. Nothing was certain. Even your Library of Truth life file would not reveal the final outcome. It was being written in real time without probable futures. We had never seen this before."

They were back to discussing his mysterious life file that everyone seemed to know something about but him. "Why me?" he asked, still confused. He deserved to know that final truth, now more than ever.

Ishannika moved towards Satya. "Shall we tell him?"

Zachary caught their quickly exchanged looks. There was an underlying hint of uncertainty. He could sense it. Was there more bad news coming his way? What more could they want from him?

"I think Zachary and I need a private moment alone," Satya replied, whisking them both away from the High Council Guardian ship.

~~*~~

Satya returned with him to the Library of Truth where together she suggested they walk amongst the endless paths to knowledge and information. She could feel his restlessness, his pressing need to understand all that had transpired. But there was still that last unanswered question. Would he accept the final step?

She started at the beginning, revealing to him the unshared knowledge of her own life file that she had never divulged to anyone. Satya knew he deserved to at least know this much.

"I have been the recordkeeper in the Library of Truth for the last 26,000 Earth years," she began, shocking him to his very core. "That may seem like a very long time to you, but in this dimensional realm, it's not long at all. As you have already surmised, time moves differently here. Much quicker."

She paused, deciding how to best to proceed. "I have free access to move between all the dimensional realms, as an earned right of all recordkeepers—past, present and future."

Zach stopped her. "Wait a minute. Back up. How did you come to 'earn' such a right? What did you have to do?" He waited, knowing how important her words were, had always been. He suspected there was a hidden purpose to her admission.

Satya chuckled. "Well, yes. I *was* getting to that part," she replied, recognizing his eagerness to learn about her, a subject she had never openly discussed with anyone. "I was tested, Zach. The details of that are not important right now because, in time, you will know all that anyway."

"Really? How?" Zach asked, curious as to why that would be.

"I have been informed that my job as recordkeeper of the Library of Truth has come to completion," she revealed, taking him by complete surprise. He had never anticipated such an announcement. Satya always was and, he assumed, always would be the keeper of truth.

Outrage at the absurdity of her leaving filled him with indignation. "That's crazy. Whose stupid idea was that?"

The Higher Council members were no longer there for him to question such an irrational decision. "Was it the Council?' he demanded to know.

"No, Zach. Every recordkeeper knows when it is their time to move on," Satya explained.

"You can't go," he tried again to convince her otherwise. "The Library of Truth needs you. You have to stay. Who could ever take your place?!"

Satya put her hand on his shoulder. It was the first time she had ever touched him. It was electrifying and conveyed an immediate calm. "*You* will take my place, Zach," she said looking him in the eye. "*You* have passed all the tests."

Zach stared at her blankly not knowing what to say. She let him work it out in his mind, until finally he turned to her and finally asked, "You're serious?"

Satya nodded, very serious. "Should you decide to take the job, you will have unlimited access to all knowledge and truth. The decision, of course, is yours."

Zach was totally stunned. She was asking him if he wanted the master keys to the candy store of all truth and wisdom. Who wouldn't want such a thing? The importance of the job was beyond enormous. Could he ever fill such big shoes? His thoughts strayed to all his Library of Truth visits and time spent here. He had never thought to ask why Satya allowed him so much freedom within the LOT to explore, discover, and find his own way to merge with the information stored so he could retrieve it at any time. Had it all been just a test from day one?

Even now, she knew his most innermost thoughts. "Yes, it was a test," she admitted. "However, you demonstrated honor and integrity. You never violated any of the rules or misused the information. This is of primary importance to anyone who keeps the records. I could not protect the records from Minerva's misuse because of the open portals to the Library of Truth."

Yes, he knew all too well who had been responsible for that. He, who had made such a mess for the Library of Truth thousands of years ago as Nehemiah, was being asked to be its protector now? The world was indeed a strange place.

"And if I decline," he tentatively asked.

Satya was prepared for his hesitancy. She knew he understood the magnitude of what he was being asked to take on. "Then the testing process will begin anew with another entity, who may or may not be successful. It is the way of this position each time the dimensions ascend. No one has ever turned down such a position."

Oh, great. That made him seem like he was being ungrateful, which was the furthest thing from the truth. This was indeed an honor and his soul wanted to shout, "Yes. Absolutely, yes!" But this was not something he alone could decide. Meghan had to be part of that final decision. What would it mean for his new family? Or even Endre?

~~*~~

Endre found himself all alone inside the protective white orb as he witnessed the transformation of the old world. There had been great beauty there, but great evil as well. The Antarctica Base had vanished along with Zach--to where he did not know. The activation of the dormant human DNA strands had caused a massive chain reaction in the universe that no one could have anticipated. As a result, this primary Minerva stronghold ceased to exist, along with their other bases when the timelines collapsed, and a new timeline sprang forth. What was once the frigid icy continent of Antarctica was now lush and green, with a tropical climate as it once was many millennia ago. This new timeline, or altered reality, had a lightness of being. The heavy dark evil of man and alien was no longer present.

Endre still didn't know how or what all had happened. However, a strange feeling came over him, which he found himself struggling with. He missed his brother, Zach, and did not want to be separated. With him he felt a part of something greater. He had been needed like he had never been needed before. That they had once been whole with Nehemiah rang so true with him. He had suspected as much yet had remained silent about his mounting suspicions. While Zach had been the so-called "ball carrier" of this rescue mission, Endre held many more of the fractured threesome's memories. This is how he knew to tell Zach that the time was now.

There was one thing he could not deny which was stronger than ever. When one confronts truth, one feels it in every fiber of their being. It was what he felt in the 12th portal when they had encountered their brother, Nehemiah, and learned what had fractured them and what had now brought them together again to become whole. The truth was he had always known this was to be a temporary assignment and the extent of his involvement would be limited. The circumstances of his early years, or lack thereof, which amounted to a virtual blank slate, spoke volumes. The "time was now" for him as well. Integration was calling to him as it had this day to Nehemiah. Zach would need all his parts in his new role moving forward. It was a bittersweet realization.

The orb of light that encased him in its protective sphere seemed to agree and began to move away from the transformed lush lands of Antarctica. The "time was now" he heard over and over in his head like a mantra. It filled him with new resolve.

While Endre did not know the exact mechanics of integration, he trusted that their higher self knew and would facilitate what needed to be done. The orb moved into the Library of Truth where he spotted Zach and Satya walking amidst the halls of knowledge.

The integration process turned out to be rather quick and simple. The white orb ball released him straight into Zach's solar plexus area, causing an internal implosion of energy which coursed up his spine to his mind, as matter and memories became one. Endre's last thought was one of love and gratitude as he realized Nehemiah had already made the transition and all three parts of their fractured soul were re-united. Zachary Eldridge now contained the power of all three—the power of the trinity.

Zach staggered backward in surprise, yet instantly knew what had occurred. He could feel the traits, knowledge, and memories of Endre and Nehemiah merge and become his own. There was no need to say goodbye. They would always be within him.

Chapter 25

Izzie was with Caleb in the astronomy dome when they both witnessed the heavens open up and the change ripple through all the dimensions. It was beyond magnificent—a rare event as Caleb had informed her. Here she was, seeing up close two timelines merge to spin off a new one. The immense light that streamed through the universe was like the birth of a new star.

She had been spending a lot of time with Caleb with Zach away and her mother finding her women's "tribe" as she termed it. This new world was a non-ending adventure of discovery. Caleb had become her very own personal tour guide to everything going on within this dimension. And the marvels of science and advanced technology all around her filled her with a craving to know and experience more.

Izzie was in total awe of Caleb's ability to anticipate her questions. He would then easily explain to her in minute detail, and in terms she understood, the very workings behind many things she was seeing for the first time. Like a sponge, she sopped up every morsel of knowledge he was willing to impart.

Caleb had become her very favorite person in the entire universe. She loved that he didn't treat her like a seven-year-old child either. He was the best brother-to-be she could have asked for. Undoubtedly the day would come when their roles would be reversed and she would take the upper hand as his older big sister, teaching him, but she knew she would always just love him for the person he was and always would be.

Izzie wanted to share with Caleb what she had learned about Satya, but she didn't dare. Would he already know? He did seem to know everything, didn't he?

"What happens if Satya is no longer here to guard over the Library of Truth?" she asked, innocently, fishing to hear what Caleb had to say on such matters. There was no doubt in her mind he knew more about Satya than he was willing to share. He had been studying texts in her office that day she had unknowingly popped in and invaded her personal space. Satya had to have known he was there and allowed such a visit.

Caleb looked at her sternly with that grown-up look she had seen too many times before in her life which signaled that she had overstepped some adult boundary. It was evident that he was not pleased with her question. Perhaps, she had gone too far in revealing what she had discovered. Now he knew she knew. Would he stop liking her?

As if in answer to her doubts, he affectionately tousled her hair. "Izzie, Izzie, Izzie," he said rolling his eyes. "That's not a matter for you to concern yourself with. Trust me. Everything has a plan."

Well that certainly sounded like a non-answer to her, but she got the message. He hugged her and gave her a little scoot. "Now let me get back to work."

Izzie had spent so much of her life with grownups, that she naturally gravitated to adults versus children her own age, unless of course, they were as adventurous as she was. What she did notice was that the children in this dimension seemed so much better informed, perhaps even smarter. There was no bullying or I'm prettier or smarter or have more money than you do kind of thinking. They, too, were more interested in how things worked.

She started tagging along to see what they did for fun when Caleb was not around to guide her.

That day she followed along with a group only to discover space platforms built on concentric rings on the edge of an expansive body of water. Children her own age were piloting orb-like craft and whizzing through the air before blinking out and vanishing to parts unknown.

Izzie was totally entranced. *I want to do that, too,* she fervently wished. Often forgetting that thoughts became reality in this new world, an orb scooped her up and encased her inside it. To her unending delight she quickly realized that she could steer it with her mind as it soared over the vast landscape of mountains and valleys, cities and towns, both far and wide. Never had she felt this level of excitement before. The feeling of flying intoxicated her with possibilities. In that moment she felt what her father, Lieutenant Brett March, must have experienced. She had become her father's daughter--a flight pilot in the making.

Down below she saw crowds of people, who looked up to see her. Like a stunt pilot, she made her orb spin and dive bomb, laughing with total abandon. It was so easy. The mind was her control panel. *I'm in an air show*, she told herself, proudly, coming in for a landing to see what that might also feel like. She was not the only one in the air who wanted to find out what was going on down below. Welcoming holograms of information filled the sky.

The orb released her gently as she came to a rest on a soft grassy surface. "Stay here," she told it moving towards what looked like thousands of new incoming arrivals, both adult and children, being oriented to this their new home. Curiosity got the best of her. She moved through the people, hoping to help if she could. She loved volunteering.

"Well if it isn't Little Betsy Ross," she heard a loud voice from somewhere behind her. She spun around and her eyes grew big as saucers. Oh my God. She had not expected to see Cali Cavaleri ever again, but here she was on Terra, dragging some guy behind her and so excited to see her. All Zach had told her was that Cali was safe back in Maui in some far-off place called "Hana".

Izzie ran up to her and threw her little arms around her waist and hugged her tightly. "I'm so glad you're alive!" she whispered gratefully.

Cali turned to Eric. "This is the kid I told you about who saved my life."

Izzie beamed all over. This was turning out to be an incredible new day. "Come with me," she said beckoning them towards her parked flying orb. "You are not going to believe this place. Wait until Mommy sees you!"

~~*~~

Meghan knew Zach was coming home. Everyone in her dimension, and she suspected, other dimensions as well, knew instantly what he had accomplished. The evolutionary gates were open, while closed to malevolent interference. Her heart swelled with pride for him. While he claimed to be nobody's hero, he was hers. That would never change. The man she had married, her husband, the father of her child-to-be, was indeed an extraordinary being. She knew this more than anyone.

She could barely contain her excitement at seeing him again. Even though time moved quickly in this realm, and it felt like only a few days had passed since he left, to her it felt like an eternity. And then he was there in the flesh. Popping in out of nowhere and surprising her from behind as his arms came around her. She spun around in his grasp and couldn't stop kissing this man she loved.

Without another word, he picked her up and headed for the bedroom.

"Where's Izzie?" he thought to ask at the last moment. "I want you all to myself."

She wrapped her hands around his neck and laughed with sheer happiness. "She's out, which could be anywhere or everywhere. Oh, Zach, she loves it here and they love her." Meghan could read his thoughts. "I'm just going to send her a mental message and tell her not to come home for a while just yet."

Zach laid her out on the bed and started removing his shirt. "The problem with that is she will want to come home immediately to see what you're hiding." He got up from the bed and went to close and lock the bedroom door, before turning and grinning from ear to ear.

Meghan threw off her clothes and dived under the comforter. Zach dived in right after her, kissing every inch of her body. "I have so much to tell you." She sighed, reveling in bare flesh to bare flesh. The feel of his body against hers was heavenly. Could it get any better?

"Me, too," he whispered in her ear. "Love, you're not going to believe this, but I got offered a new job today." He was unable to keep the silly grin off his face, at her look of surprise. "Let's just say it's an out-of-this-world opportunity."

The End

A Note from the Author

The STACKS Library of Truth trilogy series has been a thrilling ride for me to write. I have truly enjoyed every minute of living the adventures of each of my characters. And now many are asking if the saga is truly over, or will there be future tales to tell? I hate to give away secrets, but it's quite possible someday you will all learn what is to become of little Izzie all grown up.

Until then I want to thank so many people for their continued help and support. Chana Messer for her cover designs, Cheryl Salerno for her editing expertise, my brother Mike, a writer/researcher himself, who is my biggest cheerleader. Then there is my Maui Girls Group, and fellow pickleball players, who are like soul sisters of encouragement. Not to leave anyone out--thank you to all my dear friends who gave me their supportive feedback throughout this literary process. You know who you are. I love each and every one of you.

If you purchased this book from Amazon, please leave a review, even if it's only a few short words. I read them all and deeply appreciate what you say as well as the time spent sharing your thoughts. Many of my media interviews about my life, both the weird, wacky, and unbelievable, can be found on the StacksLibraryofTruth.com website and blog. Please join my mailing list for updates.

Love to all and Mahalo from the Valley Isle.

Made in the USA
Columbia, SC
27 April 2023